QUEEN OF THE DAMNED

DEBRA DUNBAR

debra dunbar

FIENDISHLY FUN FICTION

CHAPTER 1

"*I* would like to request a favor of you," Raphael announced. We were standing in my kitchen drinking shots of Fireball. It was far too sweet and really had no more than a passing nod to whisky, but I'd been on a cinnamon kick lately and bought a gigantic bottle of the stuff when I was at the liquor store last week—a gigantic bottle that was now half empty.

"Ask away," I slurred. I liked being drunk. It was fun. And I'd been told by my human business partner, Michelle, that I couldn't be legally held responsible for any contract I signed while drunk, so I was seriously thinking of making it my default state. I was a demon-sorta-angel. If I really needed to be sober, I could do so with the snap of my fingers. But who wanted to be sober when there was sticky-sweet cinnamon whisky liquor to imbibe?

"I want your support for my Ruling Council candidate."

And now I was sober. Which totally sucked. With all the angels kicked out of Aaru and wandering around among the humans like a bunch of whiny homeless winged dudes, we'd needed to have weekly Ruling Council meetings. Since no one beyond me and the archangels knew that we were indefinitely-possibly-permanently locked out of Aaru, we'd reduced the Ruling Council to those with a need-to-know. But angels were weird motherfuckers, and four on the Ruling Council was making everyone but me break out in hives. Everyone was divided on whether to hold Uriel's spot until she got back from her pilgrimage thingie or bring someone on to temporarily fill her spot, but besides that opening, we needed two more members. And no one knew who to trust right now.

"Sure, as long as you support *my* candidate."

Rafi rolled his eyes. "We've all rejected the last three Lows you've put forward."

Which had totally pissed me off. Snobby fuckers. "You'll rue the day you didn't vote Snip in. He's pretty awesome."

"Yes. He showed us just how awesome he could be. Even *I* wasn't impressed with how he could play Yankee Doodle Dandy on a penny whistle shoved up his butt."

"That takes some real talent," I informed the angel. "I've got a different candidate this time. I'll vote for yours if you vote for mine."

Which sounded an awful lot like "Show me yours and I'll show you mine." I would have totally been on board with that. Rafi was smoking hot, and I'll bet he was incredible in the sack. Unlike the other angels, he was pretty close to the edge of chaos, and I got the feeling he didn't skimp when it came to the sexual organs of his corporeal form.

"Sam, I love you like a sister, but we can't approve a demon as a member of the Ruling Council."

Loved me like a sister. Spoil sport.

"I was a demon when I was first on the Ruling Council," I countered. "Leathery wings and all. So don't give me the 'no demons' routine."

"You had the sword of the Iblis." He picked up the giant bottle of Fireball and poured two more shots. Actually they were more like tumblers than shot glasses. No wonder I was drunk. "Anyone who is the Iblis has a position on the Ruling Council."

"So I could have been a donkey with the sword in my mouth, and I would have been on the Council?"

"Yep." He handed me the "shot glass" of Fireball. "And I'm thinking it would be really funny for you to show up at the next Council meeting as a donkey with the sword clenched in your teeth."

We clinked glasses and downed the liquor. "I'll take it under advisement."

That was a Gabe-ism. And my dour imitation of his brother nearly had Rafi blowing cinnamon whisky out of his nose.

"So who is this angel you're putting forward for a Ruling Council spot?" I asked once we'd downed a few more shots. "Which choir is she or he in?"

I assumed the angel was in his own, but Rafi was almost as tricky as I was when it came to these things.

"She's unaffiliated with any choir at this time, which I think makes her an ideal, impartial candidate." He gave me one of those knowing, inscrutable looks that suddenly reminded me of his eldest brother. "She'll be more willing to vote with you than any of the others aside from me. I'm not saying she'll be in lockstep with your crazy ideas, but she won't be as rigid as Gabe."

"Eight tons of hardened steel aren't as rigid as Gabe," I told him. I got a weird feeling from Rafi, that maybe he was personally involved with this angel. He was trying to hide it, trying to be all nonchalant and blasé, but either he and this angel had a past, or they had a present. Which was a bummer since Rafi was my most-eligible-bachelor right now at Infernal

Mates. I'd taken to texting pictures of him along with a list of his attributes to demons I thought might be suitable matches, and had been compiling a list of possible matches. Guess I'd need to put that on hold and set Gabe up with someone instead. They'd have to be really strong, and not take no for an answer though, because that angel wasn't gonna go down easy.

"Can I count on your vote?" Rafi asked.

"Maybe. Can I count on yours?"

"Yep. I'm down for some quid-pro-quo action here. Although we're both going to fail. Gabe will vote against us. Michael will be the swing vote, and he doesn't always agree with you, no matter how big of a tantrum you throw."

My beloved was less likely to agree with me since I'd gotten the entire angelic host banished from Aaru. He was also grumpy because the Elf Island thing was more work than he'd originally expected. Elves kept escaping, and the job placement contractor had been taking kickbacks and bribes. I smiled at the thought. Humans. It was almost like they were my very own children.

He would most definitely vote no on my choice. So I needed additional votes on my side. This candidate of Rafi's was hopefully a step in the right direction, but I needed one more vote to be positive of getting my agenda, and my candidate, approved.

"We need to have someone temporarily take Uriel's spot," I told Rafi. "That last guy, whatever the fuck his name was, sucked. We need someone who will be on our side."

Rafael pushed his tumbler aside and just took a swig from the bottle. "Yeah. Good luck with that. You really are crazy if you think we're going to get three of our candidates onboard."

Suddenly I had an idea. There *was* someone who I thought I could get past Gabe and Gregory. If I could get her in one of the two openings, then vote Rafi's candidate in for the other, I could slip my own special candidate in as a temporary placeholder for Uri. It was perfect.

"I've got a plan." I told Rafi. "The best plan ever. Brilliant. Yuge. Bigly. This plan is a winner."

Rafi eyed me and took another drink of the Fireball. "Yeah?"

"Yeah. If this works, we'll be able to fill all three spots, and you guys won't be spending half the meetings with your wings in a knot over how many are on the Council."

And I'd have five, possibly six if Gregory was in a good mood, voting my way.

Rafi waved the bottle at me. "Go on. I'll just drink more of this stuff while you tell me this brilliant bigly plan. Hopefully I'll be drunk enough that it will actually sound brilliant. And bigly."

"You suggest that we vote in a new member on the Council, but express concerns because we can't have just anyone being exposed to all this confidential shit we discuss. Suggest someone from Gabriel's choir, and flatter the heck out of him. Say his choir is the most reasoned, balanced, enlightened, almost-divine, of all the angels, that of all the rebels, very few were from his choir, because it was so well organized and managed, and that you had no doubt that Gabe's influence would ensure secrecy if we chose someone from his choir."

"He's not stupid, you know," Rafi interrupted. "He'll never believe all that blatant flattery, especially from me."

"Well, then tone it down a bit. You know him better than I do. You've been his brother for billions of years. Just make it convincing."

"He'll pick someone horrible," Rafi said. "We won't be any better off. In fact, we'll be worse off because there'd be three of them to vote against us. We'll never get our candidates on the Council."

"Very few of Gabe's choir have been down here among the humans at all. I'll guide the conversation to suggest that we need someone who truly understands humans as well as angels. Someone who has proven themselves as being able to weigh human interests in any proposed rulings. Someone who has had experience with angels, humans, and demons."

"Someone who has served as part of the Grigori," Raphael interjected. He wasn't slow, that angel. No, not one bit.

"Exactly."

Rafi's eyes narrowed in thought. "Asta. She's the only one from the first choir who has been a member of the Grigori in the last few hundred years."

"Exactly."

"She's an Angel of Order. Gabe adores her like she was his own child. She's strict and stern, but also is known to be fair and compassionate."

"Exactly."

"And, although it is a pretty well-kept secret, she's in love with your foster brother. Door? Something like that."

"Dar. They live together. They're fucking like dogs in heat." I did the index-finger-in-the-finger-circle-hole as a visual illustration.

Raphael smirked. "Naughty girl."

"Oh, more naughty than you'd ever imagine. They're not just exchanging bodily fluids; they're exchanging other things as well."

"Like their hearts and souls," Rafi teased. "Human-style wedding rings? Collections of velvet kitten paintings?"

"Let's just say there *has* been angelic offspring since the banishment."

Raphael froze, Fireball bottle halfway to his mouth. Then he slowly lowered it. "What do you mean?"

"Angel and demon and baby makes three." I did the finger-in-the-hole thing again.

He relaxed. "You mean Asta and Door have created?"

"Well yeah. Duh. Who the heck did you think I meant?"

He tensed again. "No one. No one at all. Wow. That's cool. A baby. Is it of Order or Chaos?"

I've been accused of being a bit slow sometimes, but this wasn't one of those occasions. "Order," I said, watching him carefully."

He smiled. "Cute. Do we get to meet the little bugger?"

"Asta may have to bring her to Ruling Council meetings if Dar's busy and they can't get a sitter. I've got a dwarf lined up for them, but he doesn't get here for a few months yet. Until then, they're kinda pulling their hair out. Do you have any idea how hard it is to get a sitter nowadays? And this angel baby is just as much of a pain in the ass as a demon child. She melted a babysitter's cell phone, and Asta and Dar came home one night to find that she'd locked one in the oven. The sitter nearly suffocated."

Raphael snorted. "Angel-young aren't easy. Although it would go smoother if they were able to raise her up in Aaru. Poor little thing. The humans must be driving her nuts with all of their rule-breaking and immoral behavior."

Actually I was pretty sure Dar was driving his daughter nuts with all of *his* rule-breaking and immoral behavior. Oh well, not my problem.

"Here's the deal," I told him. "Step one: we get Asta on board. As of now only Dar, Asta, you, me, your eldest brother, a dwarf, and a succubus know about the baby, so Gabe will be clueless. The baby is key, though. Asta isn't going to want to be tossed into Hel, or deemed Fallen for breaking the rules, so we can blackmail her into voting our way."

Raphael's eyebrows shot up. "And how long have you

known us? You seriously think you're going to be able to blackmail an Angel of Order?"

"Uhhh, yeah. Have you ever had a kid? Do you have any idea what human parents do to protect their children? Angels are going to be ten times as susceptible to blackmail. Asta's totally gonna be my bitch."

Rafi had gotten this dreamy, faraway look when I'd asked, quite rhetorically, if he'd ever had a kid. A tiny smile curled up one corner of his mouth. "Have you ever created? I mean, I know demons do with other demons, so I'm sure you have."

My mind immediately went back to Ahriman's dungeon. The pain. The fear. The desperation. My kitchen vanished and suddenly I was shivering in terror, waiting for the moment when he'd come back. I'd had to give him my personal energy, a portion of my spirit-self. He'd formed an offspring with me, only to kill it because it wasn't what he wanted. And he'd taken it out on me.

He'd murdered my child, before it had a chance to take its first breath. I'd never really thought of it before, had locked all of that down deep inside me with the rest of the experience, but now it came roaring back with the pain and the fear.

Rafi was giving me a concerned stare. "You okay? I didn't mean to pry. If you—"

"No. I mean yes, but no. I've never created, and I never will." I scrambled for a reasonable explanation. "I'm a devouring spirit. It would be dangerous for anyone to sire, or create, with me."

The expression on Rafi's face was bringing me really close to tears. And I hated tears.

"You wouldn't devour Michael. I mean, I'm pretty sure you couldn't even if you tried, but I don't think you would even try. I see how you look at him, how you are with him.

8

You love him as much as he loves you. And I think you guys would create an amazing angel together."

The fear threatened to overwhelm me. "No. I don't want to create. I don't even like babies, or demon young, or probably even angel young. That baby of Dar and Asta's is a little terror. It's not my thing."

He stared at me for a long moment. "Well I do. I want to create. I can't wait for the chance to contribute a portion of my spirit-self, and help a young angel grow to its potential."

"Well, you'll need to hook up with a demon for that because this angel you're smooching with right now, whoever it is, isn't gonna be able to give you babies."

He froze again. "I…I mean in the future. Not right now."

"I've got a list of eligible demons," I told him. "I think they're very compatible, and they're interested."

"No!" He jerked as he said it, nearly sloshing his Fireball out of the glass. "No, I'm fine. I don't need you to set me up with any demons. I'm not…available."

Ah, a jealous angel lover. I totally understood. Even we demons occasionally wanted an exclusive contract with another. Still, if he truly wanted to create, he'd need to either reconsider, or speak to his angel lover about a breeding incident outside of their relationship.

"Okay, okay," I reassured him. "It's all good. No problem. Let me know when, or if, you're ever interested."

"Never." Rafi poured us another two shots as I contemplated the definitive nature of his statement. "So step one: I orchestrate the suggestion of Asta as a member of the Council. Then once she's confirmed, we'll add my candidate. That's step two."

"Step three: vote my candidate in as a placeholder for Uri." I picked up the glass and threw down the cinnamon whisky. "And bam! Between the two of use, we'll have locked down five of seven votes on the Ruling Council."

Rafi laughed. "Yeah. I'm warning you now that Asta may not always vote your way, regardless of your blackmail. Even I don't always vote your way."

"Still better odds than I had before." I clinked his glass with mine. "And right now, I'm all about improving my odds."

CHAPTER 2

*A*sta was a shoe-in, as I knew she'd be. Even though Gregory pointed out that her relationship with my foster brother, Dar, might pose a conflict, Gabe waved the argument off saying if his eldest brother could claim impartiality with his imp lover a member of the Ruling Council, then Asta's choice of partner shouldn't be held against her. Besides, her vibration pattern, integrity, and all that other shit were beyond reproach.

So here we sat, in a newly rebuilt Marriott conference room, with one additional angel at the table. Asta was practically glowing with excitement. She was wearing a smart 40s era navy suit with matching hat and shoes that made me wonder if her ideas of humanity were from the same decade. Didn't matter because Raphael was about to put forth his mysterious candidate, then it would be my turn.

"As Asta will be serving as the representative of the seventh choir, my candidate would serve the sixth. She is currently unaffiliated—"

"How can she be unaffiliated? No one is unaffiliated." Gregory scowled. As I mentioned, he'd been particularly grumpy after the whole me-locking-everyone-out-of-Aaru incident.

"Unaffiliated," Rafi repeated without further explanation. "She has considerable experience both with humans and with the werewolf population and would bring much-needed insights and knowledge in those areas."

Hey. I had insights and knowledge about humans and werewolves, and no one seemed to think that mattered when it came to me. I narrowed my eyes at Rafi, wondering what he had up his sleeve and if I could get out of voting his way. Probably not. Not if I wanted his support for my candidate.

"I have worked closely with her on some projects recently, and have found her to be loyal and discreet. She can be trusted to keep what goes on in these meetings confidential." He waved a hand and an angel appeared.

And all hell broke loose.

Gregory jumped to his feet, his face more pale than usual, the irises of his eyes bleeding out to solid black. Asta gasped and clutched a gloved hand to her chest. Gabe snarled.

"What is that?"

"How in all of creation...?"

"Well, fuck me up the ass with a two-by-four."

The last was me. Rafi's angel had a very convincing human form—a short curvy native girl with long dark hair and brown eyes, skin a light shade of mahogany brown, and a nervous tic at the edge of her frozen smile. She was wearing torn jeans and a Powerpuff Girls T-shirt. She was clearly an angel, but the energy signature she exuded wasn't like any other angel I'd ever met.

Correction, it *was* like an angel I'd met. It was like mine.

"Hi." She cleared her throat, forcing her smile up higher. "I appreciate the opportunity to be of service. I don't know much about angels, but I'm a fast learner. I...uh," she shot Raphael an uncertain glance. "I'm young, but very dedicated to fairness and protecting humans, werewolves, and the other life here. I've willingly put my life on the line to save others. I can sense rifts and help to close them. I've assisted in killing and/or relocating manticores, drop bears, and other creatures."

"And a hydra," Raphael prompted. He had a silly expression on his face, a mixture of pride and adoration that I'm sure no one was missing.

The angel's smile softened. "Well, you helped with the hydra."

Raphael made a "pfft" noise. "I merely assisted. You could have taken care of it solo."

Oh for fuck's sake. And they said Gregory and I were mushy. Sheesh.

"She's younger than *I* am," Asta announced. "How can that be? I was born shortly before the war, but she's not even a million years old."

The angel's dark eyes latched onto Asta, a tentative spark of hope in them. "I never knew my parents, but evidently they were an angel and a demon. I'm around five thousand years old."

Damn it all. Why was I always the youngest? Couldn't Rafi have found an angel under nine hundred years old? Was that too much to ask?

"She's an Angel of Chaos," Gregory said, as if we hadn't all realized that. "There is only room for one Iblis on the Ruling Council."

At his words something odd happened to Raphael. The silly, irreverent clown of an angel vanished, and a stern powerful archangel took his place.

"And that needs to change. It was ridiculous to have only one Angel of Chaos on the Board before the war, and it's just as ridiculous now. They're angels. They deserve equal representation of their interests. It's unfair to have that all fall on the shoulders of the Iblis. Ahia is the only other Angel of Chaos that we are aware of. She has skills and knowledge that we sorely need, and she has enough Order in her that you don't need to worry about her spiking the coffee with hallucinogenic mushrooms, or putting whoopee cushions on all of our seats."

Oh, like he hadn't laughed when I'd done that!

The angel in question bit her lip hard and shot me a quick glance, her dark eyes dancing. I got the feeling that in spite of what Raphael said, she was likely to be onboard with whoopee cushions and shrooms in the coffee.

"All those in favor?" Gabe asked.

Raphael's hand went up. Mine went up. Gregory sat down with a glare that looked like he was burning holes through his brother. Gabe's hands remained unsurprisingly down.

Asta's hand went up. Everyone turned to look at her in surprise.

"Her choice of clothing is atrocious, but she seems earnest. And Raphael is right, we do need broader representation on the Ruling Council. I was too young during the war to know what was really going on, but maybe if those angels had been given additional voices to be heard, the disagreement wouldn't have turned violent and Aaru wouldn't have been torn apart the way it was."

That very fine and unexpected speech was greeted with a significant moment of silence.

"She's brand new. Does she even get a vote?" Gabe asked his eldest brother.

"Yes, she does. And you're the one who enthusiastically approved her addition to the Ruling Council," Gregory added sardonically, "so now you have to deal with the fact that your young protégé just voted against you."

Gabe's shoulders slumped. "Fine. This new angel, Ahia, is voted in. And now on to our agenda items."

"Wait. I've got a candidate as well." I stood up. "As you've told me repeatedly, six is a very bad number, so we need someone as a placeholder until Uriel gets back from wherever the fuck she is. I have someone I want to put forth to temporarily take her spot."

"Cockroach, we are not going to approve a demon on the Ruling Council," Gregory told me with a growl of frustration. We'd argued about this one a lot. Even promising him sexual favors hadn't swayed my angel.

"Please tell me you're not going to spring another Angel of Chaos on us." Gabe rubbed his face. "Two of you is enough. I don't think I can tolerate any more than two right now."

"No, but Raphael was right when he said we needed members on the Ruling Council who understood the humans and their world. We've...well, I've just dumped a bunch of angels down into their midst. Humans are going to be living side-by-side with angels and elves. There are rifts opening up with monsters and mermaids and unicorns roaming around."

"We've got three of you that have experience and knowledge of the human world," Gabriel interrupted. "We don't need any more. Whatever candidate you propose will be completely unacceptable. I'll *never* vote for whoever you're about to haul in front of us, so just forget about it."

He was such an asshole. "But who among us has deep knowledge of the elves? We need someone who knows demons, and humans, *and* elves. So to fill in for Uriel while she's wearing a hair shirt and beating herself with nettles, I present to you my candidate."

I waved my hand, but instead of an angel appearing from

the ether, the conference room door opened and a human woman walked in. She was young with sun kissed, dark blonde hair that hung down past her hips and deep blue eyes that held flecks of stormy gray and ocean green. She skipped up to the table with a bright smile. "Did they vote yet? Am I in?"

My sort-of adopted daughter, Nyalla.

"She's a human. This is the Ruling Council of *Angels*, in case you've forgotten," Gregory snapped. Grumpy ass.

"Well, we're all stuck down here among the humans, in case *you've* forgotten," I snapped back.

"I'm hardly likely to forget that. Angels. Not humans. Not demon Lows. Angels. I was overruled about adding a second Angel of Chaos, I'm not about to start adding humans."

What the fuck was wrong with him? He loved Nyalla. I didn't expect him to embrace the idea with open arms, or even to vote my way on this, but I also didn't expect him to be a complete dick about it. He was so not going to get laid tonight. So. Not. Happening.

"I love your shoes," Asta commented, pointing at Nyalla's footwear. I blinked at the completely random nature of her observation.

"Thanks. My sister bought them for me in Italy." Nyalla wiggled a foot clad in leather, lace-up boots.

"Oh, I'm dying to go to Italy," Ahia said. "Actually I'm dying to go anywhere outside of Alaska. Can we have the next Ruling Council meeting in Italy?"

"I'm all in favor of our next meeting being in Italy," Rafi chimed in. "And a shopping expedition to follow."

"I think I saw a pair just like that in a store down on State Street," Asta said, still fixated on the shoes. "Although if we're in Italy for the next meeting, I could pick up some while I'm there. Where did your sister purchase them?"

"We're *not* having a Ruling Council meeting in Italy so two, or three, of you can buy shoes. And we're *not* having a human on the Ruling Council." Gregory was reminding me quite a lot of his brother Gabe at the moment. I'd expected these sorts of snippy barbs from that uptight stick-in-the-ass, not my beloved. Speaking of which…I looked over at Gabriel, anticipating all kinds of angry on his face. Instead he looked…stunned. Actually he bore a striking resemblance to a cornered animal.

"We need to vote," Raphael chimed in. "Regardless of how unsuitable you feel the candidate to be, a member of the Council has put her forward and we must vote."

There was a staring contest going on between Gregory and Raphael. "Yeah, we need to vote," I repeated.

"Vote, vote, vote," Ahia chanted, pounding her fist on the table in time with the word. I was beginning to like this angel a whole lot.

"All those in favor?" Gregory asked between clenched teeth.

It was gonna be four against two if Asta liked Nyalla's shoes enough to vote for her. If not, then a tie. I shot my hand up and looked around noting that Ahia, Asta, and Rafi were all in favor.

Slowly, Gabriel's hand eased upward. He actually cringed as he did it.

"You've got to be kidding." Gregory glared at his brother.

Gabriel took a deep breath and straightened his shoulders. "I think she has valuable insights that will contribute favorably to our meetings."

Nyalla squealed and bounced, clapping her hands together. "I'm *so* excited to get started! What's the first item on our agenda?" She dragged a chair over and squeezed it between Gabriel and me, plopping down in it.

"I…uh…I…" Gabe shuffled the papers in front of him, then looked helplessly around the room. "I think maybe we should adjourn and reconvene in two days to give our new members time to review the agenda and bring themselves up to speed, and for the rest of us to...come to terms with...everything."

He was being so weird. I knew Gabe was awkward around humans, but if I'd known that putting him in close proximity to one would result in this level of confusion and distress I would have done it a long time ago. Why had he voted for Nyalla if humans flustered him so? Maybe he was so thrown off his game that he thought he was voting no?

Gregory regarded his brother with narrowed eyes. "Two days, then."

"In Italy?" Asta asked hopefully.

"No. Here. Same time. Same place." Then Gregory stood, turning a glare toward each of us in turn. "Meeting adjourned."

Without another word he vanished, leaving me behind. We might not always arrive at the meetings together, but we always left together. And we always went back to my house to discuss the events, plan, scheme—well, I schemed—and drink coffee. I knew he was stressed. I knew he had a lot on his mind. But just leaving like this, without a word, without even a loving glance...it hurt.

CHAPTER 3

"He didn't mean anything," I told Nyalla. "Gregory adores you. I hope you're not upset by his no vote."

I'd teleported her back home and we were out on the back patio next to my closed, covered-up pool, enjoying a few beers in the warm September sunshine.

"Oh, I know," Nyalla took a swig from her bottle. "I can see inside his heart. He loves me, and he didn't want to hurt my feelings. He's just upset about the Aaru thing. He's homesick. It's making him short-tempered and less thoughtful than he'd usually be."

That made me feel like shit. It was my fault the love of my life was locked out of his home possibly forever. "I don't know what to do, Nyalla. I tried to get us back in. I even went to Sharpsburg and jabbed my sword into the wild gate that used to lead to the fourth circle. Nothing happened."

She shot me a sympathetic glance. "The other angels will eventually find out. What are we going to do when that happens?"

There was no "we" about that one. As much as I wanted

Nyalla's swing vote on the Ruling Council, I didn't want her involved in any continuation of the angelic civil war. If the winged started throwing energy around and blowing shit up, Nyalla was going somewhere safe. Probably Hel.

Oh the irony, that Hel would be a safe place for a human compared to the human's own world.

"Right now they're trying to cope with the shock and challenges of dealing with a corporeal form. That will buy us some time to figure out what to do."

And we *needed* to figure out what to do. If I couldn't manage to reopen Aaru soon, it would be bound to leak out. Then Gregory and his brothers would have more than the rebels to deal with. Even the angels who'd supported them would quickly turn to the other side once they realized there was no going home for any of them. It would be non-stop battles right here. The humans would be crushed in the middle, and I was very much afraid this would be a war that the archangels would lose. It was another irony. Gregory had always said I would be the one to bring the apocalypse. I always figured that would be through my devouring, not by shutting down Aaru and causing the angels to destroy the world.

"There's got to be a way back in," Nyalla assured me. "I refuse to believe that a sword, no matter how powerful, can banish every being from Aaru without some kind of over-ride. Maybe if you say the banishment backward and jab your sword into the sky, like the half-naked cartoon guy does? You know, the one with the terrible blond pageboy haircut and the wimpy tiger?"

"I already tried that." I stared gloomily down into my beer bottle. "I even paid Gareth to put me in a salt circle and try to send me there. No dice. I've got all my Lows looking for Samael in hopes that he can tell me how to reverse this. If he's still alive, that is. I know Gregory said no one has ever fucked up like this before, but I'm sure Samael probably came close. He's got to know what to do."

"Gregory never said that you 'fucked up'." Nyalla's tone was scolding. She even waved her bottle at me like a glass, reprimanding index finger.

I sighed. "No, but that's what he meant. He's really pissed at me, Nyalla. I'm worried that if I can't somehow manage to fix this, it's going to be that thing that rots away at our relationship, that kills everything good between us."

"Sam, he loves you. You all were losing. They were going to kill him. You did what you needed to do to save him. He'd do the same if it were you, and he knows it. If he had to choose between Aaru and you, he'd pick you. He's just having a hard time with it right now, and all the other problems here with the human world, including having his brothers suddenly all up in his business, aren't helping."

All up in his business. Nyalla couldn't speak anything beyond Elvish and some Demon up until three years ago and now she was throwing slang around like she'd been born here. My clever girl.

"Do you think the party is a good idea?" I asked, my thoughts turning back to my angel. I never used to doubt myself like this, but I hated seeing Gregory so grumpy and depressed. I'd do anything for him. I'd do anything to give him his beloved homeland back.

"I think the party is a brilliant idea. We need something to reinforce that we're all in this together. We need things like parties to bond as a family." She shifted on the lounge chair to face me. "And have some faith in yourself. You'll make things right. You're more than just an imp, Sam."

"Yeah, yeah. I'm the Iblis. I'm probably the one who brings the apocalypse to this world, if not to the entirety of creation."

"I think you're fate's right hand," she told me. "I think

there's a reason for everything. And I think that sometimes, when people are too darned stubborn to learn a lesson, fate whacks them over the head with it a few times, then shoves it down their throat."

I was beginning to worry about where Nyalla was getting these violent ideas. Oh yeah. Probably me.

"So I should hit Gregory over the head with something at the birthday party I'm throwing for him? Then shove it down his throat?" I didn't want to talk about this anymore. I'd fucked up, no matter what Nyalla said, and couldn't fix it. End of story. I'd rather we talk about whether to have strippers at the birthday party or not.

"You're not changing the subject, Sam," Nyalla scolded. "I know you're getting beat up over it, but I think this temporary banishment is a good thing. Angels have been locking themselves up in Aaru for millions of years, isolating themselves to work on their vibration and all that. Even the ones who came here for a short stint on the Grigori team held themselves apart from human lives and society. They *need* to open their hearts and minds. How do they expect to assist humans in attaining positive evolution if they only view them through a telescope? They need to experience life among the humans, not only to better help us, but to help themselves."

I stared at her. "Sooooo…I *should* have hookers and tequila and blackjack at the party? To better help my angelic guests understand the human experience?"

Nyalla looked for a second as if she were going to throw her beer bottle at me. "No. Just a normal party. Cake. Presents. Balloons. Streamers. People singing the happy birthday song. Angels and humans and werewolves and Nephilim all hanging out together, talking about their lives and laughing over funny stories. Sam, you've been here over forty years. You know that human life is about more than booze, sex, and gambling."

I blinked at her.

"Okay, you can have tequila at the party if you really want. But no prostitutes or gambling. If you want to have sex, do it with Gregory after the party is over, in your bedroom. And be romantic about it."

"Romantic. So swallow after the blow job?" I teased.

She rolled her eyes. "Use your body, or your spirit-self, to show him how you feel about him. And yes, swallow after the blow job."

"I *knew* it." I did a fist-pump and settled back in my lounge chair. Little did Nyalla know, but I bared myself to Gregory every time we were intimate. I bared myself to him every time we were not intimate. I couldn't help it. No matter how much I tried to pretend, or put on a bold front, he could see right through it. It's one of the reasons I loved him. He truly saw me for what I was, and loved me because of it.

Okay, maybe Nyalla did know that. She was far too smart and world-wise for a human woman her age, even without her gift.

"What did you get him as a present?" Nyalla asked. "I picked up something in Aruba for him. It's kind of funny, but I think he'll like it."

"I got him…" Crap. I couldn't tell Nyalla because I don't think she'd understand. There were things between Gregory and me that were a part of our history together—a history I didn't want to get into too much detail with my sort-of adoptive daughter. "I got him something really personal that no one but he will understand."

I know what I *wanted* to give him. I wasn't just looking for Samael to figure out how to get back into Aaru. I wanted a family reconciliation. And if I couldn't have that, I at least wanted Gregory to know that his brother was still alive. If he was, that is.

It was a completely unrealistic idea, but I wanted the pair of them to be brothers again, like they were so long ago. It had only been two-and-a-half-million years since the end of the war. That might be too soon to expect a forgiveness of all wrongs, but I hoped that eventually, maybe in another million years or so, all these old wounds might finally be healed.

Nyalla gave me a warm smile. There was something odd in her eyes, something about the gray and the green flecks that made me realize she was seeing into my heart. It didn't bother me. Of all the beings in the universe, Nyalla was one of the few that was welcome to whatever my heart could tell her. I'd bought her from the elves as a present to Wyatt, to bring back his long-lost sister that had been stolen from her crib and replaced with a half-elf changeling. When she'd asked to live in my house instead of his, I'd reluctantly agreed. And within days she was a part of me, someone I'd give my life for, someone I loved with every inch of my spirit-self. I was terrified of producing offspring, but Nyalla was every bit my daughter. She was the child of my heart.

And wasn't that a weird thing for a demon to have?

She smiled, a hint of a dimple at the corner of her lips, her eyes warm. "I love you too, Sam."

"Should I come back another time?"

I turned at the unfamiliar deep voice and saw a demon walk around the side of my house, escorted by Boomer. My hellhound looked like a regular dog with his tongue hanging out and normal brown eyes, so I knew this guy wasn't a threat. Still, my visitor was a powerful demon, with energy rolling off him in waves, in spite of his casual, friendly demeanor.

Wait. I knew this guy. It was the warmonger that was

infatuated with Amber. I'd never seen him in a human form before, but I recognized his energy.

"Harkel." I jumped to my feet, putting myself between the demon and Nyalla. Warmongers didn't tend to bother with individual humans, but it didn't hurt to be safe. He was an Ancient, so I didn't think I could do much more than hold him off while Nyalla got away, but Boomer would help. He adored Nyalla and I knew he'd protect her with his life.

"Iblis." Harkel bowed. He was kind of cute in this form. All he needed to do was break into some Asian-style martial arts, and I'd be all over him. Yeah. No wonder Amber was boinking him, although as a half-succubus, she boinked pretty much everyone.

"What can I do for you?" Might as well get to the point. I had a beer to finish, and a birthday party to plan.

"It's what I can do for you that has brought me here." The demon pulled a lounge chair over, wincing at the screech the metal legs made on the concrete.

I narrowed my eyes, waiting, because demons didn't do anything for free. There would be a price. I just needed to keep my mouth shut and not commit myself until I knew what that price was.

"I'm very fond of your Amber. I'm fond of her Irix as well, but he's not in your household, so there is no need to discuss my dealings with him to you."

Harkel sat down. I did the same, shooting a quick glance behind to me make sure Nyalla was safe. She tilted her head and regarded the warmonger, then with a quiet chuckle, leaned back in her lounge chair. If she'd read anything alarming in the demon's heart, I would have seen it on her face. Even so, I jerked my head at Boomer, sending him over to stand next to the girl. He'd drool slobber all over her jeans, but he'd also turn into a monstrous hellhound and protect her if needed.

25

"I want Amber in my household." Harkel got right to the point.

"That's up to her. If she asks me, I'll release her. I have to say that she probably won't ask, though. There are some advantages to her being in the household of the Iblis that you wouldn't be able to provide."

The warmonger scowled. "Such as?"

"Immunity from the angels for both her and Irix."

I could practically hear him grinding his teeth. "I see. Yes, that is one benefit that I cannot provide, but in Hel, an association with my household would be far more advantageous than an association with yours."

It was a sad state of affairs that being connected with the Iblis carried so little weight in Hel. "True, but she's not in Hel and I don't believe she has any intention of returning there, at least not in the next ten thousand years or so. She likes it here. And Irix likes it wherever she is."

I got the feeling this was the issue Harkel was struggling with. He wanted both of them, and as he didn't have immunity, there was considerable risk to his being here on this side of the gates—especially for any length of time.

"You could always bring yourself and your household under mine," I proposed. "That way you'd have immunity as well and could remain here with the two of them, although you'd need to curtail some of your more unsavory activities."

His eyes blinked wide, then he laughed. "You cannot be serious! As tempting as immunity is, I doubt the terms of it would allow me any leeway to perform my hobbies unfettered. Outside of visiting with Irix and Amber, that sort of immunity would be useless to me. It certainly wouldn't be worth the humiliation of subjugating myself to an imp barely out of the nursery."

"I'm the Iblis," I reminded him.

"Are you?" He arched an eyebrow. "You are nothing. You

are a cockroach with a sword that does not obey you. Only the Lows in Hel follow you. You haven't managed to command the respect of the Ancients, to bring the demons under your control. In Hel, you are unknown to most, and a laughingstock to others. Here, the only power you wield is due to the protection of your archangel lover. Without his support, you wouldn't be given either immunity or granted a seat among their ranks. You're not the Iblis, you're an imp playing dress-up games."

I heard Nyalla suck in a breath and saw her shoot me a concerned look.

But it was true. Every word was true. I had luck. I sometimes had a powerful sword, if the damned thing felt like helping me out. I was difficult to kill, I devoured, I could store huge amounts of energy. But power? He was right. I *was* an imp playing dress-up games.

For a second I envisioned myself storming into Hel, taking charge, enforcing my will at the point of a cooperative sentient sword. Did I even want that? Most of the time I just wanted to crawl back under a rock and enjoy my life without these endless meetings, and werewolves, and humans, and demons, and elves. And angels.

But then I thought about how much fun it was to outwit them, to throw a big wrench into their stupid rules and endless procedures. I'd battled angels, battled elves, battled all sorts of weird shit. I'd negotiated with a huge powerful dragon. With my sneaky, back-door, imp antics, I'd changed the course of the world. And whether for good or for bad, I'd shaken all the stagnation up and gotten things moving again. Life under a rock seemed boring in comparison. But to take control of Hel? To become the ruler of the demons in more than title? That was a job that called for a commander, a leader, an organizer of beings, not an imp. I knew my shortcomings, but it still stung to have an Ancient, a powerful warmonger, point them out to me.

"Such flattery," I drawled, taking a sip of my beer. "I wasn't going to give you Amber before, and I'm definitely not going to give her to you now. I don't want whatever you have to offer. Now get lost before I call that powerful angel I'm fucking and ask him to pretty-please turn you into a pile of sand."

"Oh you won't do that, because you really want to hear what I have to tell you. And if you don't, that angel of yours definitely will. The Ancients are awake. All of them. They have been awake for a while now, but you're not in Hel often enough to notice."

I lifted my eyebrows and shook my head. "So what? What do I care if the Ancients are awake or not?"

"You're too young to understand, and even with those wings, you're still a demon. Two-and-a-half-million years in Hel, banished from our homeland and forced to live in corporeal form or die is torture for us. Some have adapted, but even those who have still feel the pain of our exile every moment of our lives."

Oh, for fuck's sake. "I've been in Aaru. It sucks. Hel is so much better. Here is so much better. You Ancients need to get over yourselves, quit whining about the past and all you lost and live a little."

"All you have ever known is Hel. Aaru was our home. And a great many of those Ancients who have survived since the war want to take it back. All of them are awake, and they are searching for a leader to put together an army to take back our homeland."

A leader. My heart beat double-time at the thought that I might finally be able to locate Samael, to reunite him with his siblings, to get him to tell me how to get all the angels back into Aaru. I wondered if he would want his sword back?

Hopefully not. As useless as the thing was sometimes, I kinda liked it. And I kinda liked being the Iblis as well.

"Who?" I demanded. "Who is their leader?"

"They don't have one yet. There are six Ancients who are front-runners, but none of them has yet proven himself qualified to head an invasion into Aaru."

"Is one of those six Ancients Samael?"

Harkel laughed. "Samael hasn't been seen for over two million years. He's dead, or you wouldn't be carting around that sword and these six wouldn't be the arguing over who will lead the demons."

I didn't want to believe that, but something inside me worried that Harkel was right. If Samael had survived exile this long, slumbering as so many of the most powerful Ancients had done, then he would have awakened with the rest of them and taken his rightful place. But I'd heard nothing of him, these other Ancients were jockeying for position over who would take charge of the forces of Hel, and I still had the damned sword.

There was one bright spot in all of this. "They'll never get into Aaru. These Ancients are gonna look like idiots in front of tens of thousands of demons when after all their efforts, they're still in Hel."

"Oh, they'll get in." Harkel smirked. "If they have to force their way in, they'll do it."

"Banished. They can't get in, they're banished. Do you seriously think the archangels would have ejected the Angels of Chaos without putting some safeguards in place to ensure they didn't get up, dust themselves off, and head right back into battle?"

"You got in. And you took a demon army with you."

Huh. He knew that? Although, even with the spread of that story, I still didn't get any respect.

"Yes, I have entered Aaru. I'm the Iblis, I'm allowed in.

And I'm not folding a few hundred powerful Ancients and their demons into my household and heading the charge into Aaru."

Not that I could get into Aaru anyway. Not anymore. That was one bright spot in all of this. Even if the Ancients tried to pressure me into helping them, I couldn't.

Harkel shrugged. "I'm just warning you that you should take this seriously. I've heard rumors, and if they're true, then as the Iblis, you should get involved."

I waited for Harkel to expand upon that, but he clearly wasn't going to let me in on what this secret was.

Rumors. Now I was feeling mildly paranoid, wondering if there was some workaround for the original banishment, and if that workaround would also get them past whatever I'd done to kick the angels out of Aaru. No. There couldn't be. If there was some way around the original banishment, then the Ancients wouldn't have waited over two million years to attempt a return. Harkel was just blowing smoke up my ass, pissed off that I wouldn't hand Amber over to him.

Besides, none of the Ancients or demons knew about Aaru being locked down, about *all* the angels being banished from it. If Harkel was going to remain silent about his little secret, then I fully intended to continue remaining silent about mine. Let the Ancients bash their heads against the door. I'd just sit back and laugh at them.

"Oh, and one more thing," Harkel spread his hands wide. "All this? It's about to be inundated with demons. We know the angels are preoccupied with their own squabbles, and that the human world has decreased in terms of importance to them. Get ready for thousands of high-level demons crossing the gates in groups and doing whatever they want to do. It's party-time here in the human world, and we intend on taking advantage of it. So if you have humans or territory you consider your own, make sure to mark it, or you'll find someone has snatched your riches out from under your nose."

Little did he know that the world was inundated with angels right now as well. And once they got their feet under them, I'm sure Gregory would be able to marshal their forces to fight the rag-tag demons who decided this was a perfect time for a vacation. No biggie. I shrugged and took a drink of my beer.

Harkel frowned at me, snatching the beer from my hand and tossing it into the azaleas. "You want to be the Iblis? Well, you need to get off of your ass, draw up your plan of attack, and engage. If you won't lead, someone else will, and I don't think you or your angel lover will be happy with who that 'someone' is. Take control of your sword. Take control of Hel. Take control of the demons. Then deliver an ultimatum to the Ancients: either they kneel before you, or you will crush them. And do it now before it's too late."

He spun around and left. Boomer's eyes glowed, his fur upright in a ridge down his back as he took a protective step that practically put him on top of Nyalla. I watched the warmonger leave.

Take control. Was that a shit-or-get-off-the-pot speech he'd just delivered unto me? Asshole. Like he knew anything. I was an imp. I was young. There was no way I was going to be able to take control of anything at all, let alone rule Hel and force the Ancients to their knees. Maybe in a couple million years if I lived that long, but not now.

"He's right you know." Nyalla sat up, pushing Boomer gently to the side to rummage in the cooler.

"Right about what? Me being a weak, useless imp play-acting at the whole Iblis thing?" I held out my hand for another beer.

"He said that to get you angry and make you do something, so you would be proactive, and throw the first blow."

She popped the cap off a bottle and handed it to me. "I don't know what he's got against these other Ancients, but he wants you to take them down."

"He wants me to start a fight, a war. Because he's a warmonger, and that's what warmongers do. If I storm into Hel and try to take charge, all that will happen is me ending up dead and the sword going back to hang out with the vampires for a few hundred thousand years or so. I've argued this before. Like, over and over and over before. I can't be what they want me to be. I'm not a leader. I'm not the sort of demon, or angel, who can get tens of thousands of demons and Ancients to obey her and follow her. I'm not the sort to lead the battle charge."

"Then don't do it Harkel's way, or Gregory's way, or even how you're envisioning Samael's way to be. Do it your way. But do it."

Yeah, yeah. Be the imp. "So trickster all of Hel into following my lead? With what, whoopee cushions and hallucinogens in their coffee?"

She shrugged. "Yeah, if it works. When you play to your strengths, you're downright terrifying, Sam. You're unpredictable. You somehow manage to prevail even in ridiculously unbalanced fights. There's something crazy about you that's scary, even to demons. I don't want to see you hurt, and I sure don't want to see you get killed, but you can't keep dancing around this decision. Grab that sword of yours, even if it manifests as a pool noodle, and become the Queen of Hel."

"That's a battle I'm going to lose." That's what I was really afraid of. I'd been lucky, really lucky, and there had been a time in my life when I didn't care whether I won or lost. But that time was past. I cared. I cared a lot. I couldn't lose, and the scared young imp in me somehow thought if I didn't fight, I wouldn't run the risk of losing at all.

I knew that was a lie. Inaction was a choice. Halting, half-assed action was a choice. And if I was going to lose, I wanted to do it with every bit of my effort and crazy-self in play. Harkel was right. Nyalla was right. I glanced over at Boomer and he gave me a toothy grin, his ears flat against his head. Damn. Even Boomer wanted me to go for it.

"You won't lose, Sam." Nyalla reached out and ran her hand over my hellhound's head. "I know in my heart that you won't lose. The world needs your chaos and your crazy far too much for you to lose."

CHAPTER 4

I wasn't ready to go storming into Hel with my pool noodle sword raised before me, so I took a baby step in my "I'm the Iblis, hear me roar" campaign. Step one would be to let the Ruling Council know to expect an influx of demon visitors across the gates. Step two would be to figure out what the Ancients were really up to, and if this whole "take over Aaru" thing was a viable threat or not.

Snip had been my go-to Low for quite a while now, so I dragged him out of the guest house where he was throwing darts at a Taylor Swift poster and sent him to Hel with an errand. Then I got to work.

Beatrix had called while I was talking with Snip and let me know a demon had gotten past her at the Columbia Mall gate. Normally she'd call in an enforcer to chase the dude down, but that would make her look weak, like she couldn't manage to do her job. Beatrix had been on a leave-of-absence for months following the battle with a souped-up demon that had destroyed the mall, killed two enforcers, and left her with her wings pinned to the ground. Gregory had put her back on the job, telling me that she'd never gain the respect of the other angels if she let this horrible experience keep her from her duties. Still, the angels looked at her funny, like she was a weakling.

Beatrix didn't want to reinforce that opinion, so when a demon snuck through she called me. Sometimes I told her to get bent, because I was busy with a gazillion other things. Sometimes I actually chased down the demon, and if I found them, I dragged them back to apologize to Beatrix before I tossed them through the gate to Hel. Technically the demons fell under my purview, and those that were violating the treaty by crossing into the human area were mine to punish and return to Hel.

Baby steps.

Beatrix usually couldn't leave the gate unattended, so other than giving me a description and a general direction, there wasn't much she could do in helping me locate these demons. I wasn't a Bloodhound, and Boomer didn't take to teleporting, so if I couldn't find them in the first fifteen minutes, I usually gave up.

Luckily this time I didn't have to look far before finding my target. It helped that Beatrix had told me exactly where to find him, and that she was standing outside the Bobby's Burger Palace at the Arundel Mills Mall, staring at the demon with her lips twisted into a snarl.

"What are you doing here?" I demanded. "Aren't you supposed to be guarding the gate? What if a dozen warmongers come through while you're tailing this guy?"

"I have a helper," she told me, her gaze never straying from her target.

A helper? It actually was a good idea to have a team on the gates for this very reason, but I didn't think Gregory had the resources to double up like this. "An enforcer? Why isn't the enforcer taking out this guy and saving me the effort while you stay at the gate?"

She shot me a scathing glance. "No, I don't want to call in an enforcer. That would make me look weak, like I couldn't handle trespassers on my own. I've got unofficial backup. It's none of your business who he is."

Unofficial? "Is this helper able to handle demon trespassers?"

A hint of a smile quivered at the corner of her mouth. "Yes. He's very handy with a backhoe. And I bought him a rifle. He can only stay for a few hours, because he's got something he needs to do, so we need to hustle up here."

Okaaaay. I'd never known an angel who was handy with a backhoe and knew how to fire human weaponry, but there was always a first.

I leaned past her to look for my target. I'll admit it was kind of weird that he'd left the rubble of a mall to head up Route 100 to one still standing. I actually kind of dug this mall. It was right next to a casino, had some cool shops and restaurants, and the police were here several times a week breaking up a massive fight in the parking lot. This place was totally cool.

"I've been meaning to come and eat here," I told Beatrix, scanning the crowd for the demon and noticing the food.

"Me too." She eyed the menu posted next to the entrance.

"I doubt Bobby Flay has a burger with sweet and sour sauce," I teased.

She shrugged. "Yeah, but beer battered onion rings are on my top ten list of foods."

Mine too. I suddenly spotted the demon, at a table by himself with a huge milkshake in front of him. I'd pretty much recognized this demon as Mestal from the gate guardian's description. I'd known him for over four hundred years, and he tended to use the exact same human form every time he crossed the gates. The greed demon was predictable. And the past three decades he'd proven himself to be very tech-savvy. A few decades back we'd partnered on a pyramid scheme that had added considerably to my bank account. Then there'd been those short sales he'd tipped me off on three years ago. Mestal was a useful demon to know. Well, he used to be a useful demon to know. All he was now was more work. Every time he showed up, I ended up with Gabriel breathing down my neck about the rapid nosedive in human FICO scores. Greed demons tended to wreak havoc on human finances.

I'd already booted Mestal's ass back across the gate last month with a stern warning, but here he was again. And in the exact same sort of place he'd been last time—a restaurant with free Wi-Fi. He was bent over a stolen laptop, the huge milkshake in one hand as he one-finger typed with lightning speed on the keyboard. I motioned to Beatrix to stay back then tip-toed over behind him. Glancing over his shoulder, I moved to sit down across from him and reached out a hand to shut the lid of his laptop.

"You don't belong here, Mestal."

He yelped and jumped to his feet, smashing me in the face with his laptop. The force of it knocked me backward in my chair and I crashed to the ground in a heap. I heard Beatrix shout, a rush of footsteps, and a bunch of angry humans yelling. By the time I'd gotten up off the floor, Mestal was halfway to the exit, trying to shove his way by a burly man who was winding up to punch him in the face. A burger sailed across the room, bouncing off the back of the greed demon's head. He spun with a curse, and shot a bolt of lightning toward Beatrix just as she launched a plate of fries.

No way was I going to let this guy set a gourmet burger joint on fire. I reached out and pulled, yanking the bolt toward me where I absorbed it as best as I could. Unfortunately, there was still enough live electricity cause a painful jolt to my heart and frizzle my hair into a smoking, twisted afro.

Beatrix took the opportunity to launch six more plates at the demon at the same time the burly guy punched Mestal in the face. The plates missed their mark, and Mestal slid across the floor into a table full of bearded hipsters. They shouted. One picked Mestal up and slugged him. Two seconds later, the whole lot of them were beating him to a pulp while the manager screamed and two security guards ran through the door.

I grabbed Beatrix by the shoulder and yanked her backward. I'd been arrested more times than I could count and knew exactly what was going to go down here. Sure enough, one of the guards yanked a box from his utility belt and fired. Two darts, still connected to the box with wires, shot out and sank into Mestal's shoulder. He danced around a bit then fell facedown onto the ground as the hipsters jumped out of the way.

"She was throwing plates and food." The manager pointed at Beatrix.

"If they tase me, someone's getting more than a plate thrown at them," she growled.

"She was attempting a citizen's arrest," I told the manager. "The guy hit me with a laptop and was trying to run out on his check. You should be thanking her."

"He had an eight-dollar milkshake, while she broke about fifty dollar's worth of plates," the manager protested.

The security guard not holding the Taser dragged Mestal to his feet. "You want us to call the police and file charges or take him back with us for a little discussion?"

Whoa. These mall cops were hard-core.

The manager scowled at Mestal. "You gonna pay for all this? Broken plates too?"

The demon shot me a quick glance. I knew if he was here

solo, he would have flipped the manager the finger and taken off, but between the Taser, Beatrix, and me, he knew he wasn't going to get far.

"Yeah. I'll pay."

The security guard disengaged the Taserdarts while the demon dug in his pocket and pulled out a wallet. He carefully peeled off sixty dollars and handed it to the manager. Then muttering a few choice words under his breath, he picked his laptop up off the floor and reluctantly followed me out into the mall. Beatrix stayed behind the pair of us, just in case Mestal decided to try to make a break for it.

He didn't. And because he was being subdued and cooperative, I bought him one of those giant twisty lollypops and sat him down on a bench in the middle of the mall.

"You don't belong here," I told him once more.

The greed demon gave the sucker a few licks as he narrowed his eyes at me. "Neither do you. None of us belong here according to that stupid treaty that none of us signed."

He had a point. "Look, if you were just here playing the slots for a few days or trying to pick up hookers, I'd be fine. You're a pain in the ass, Mestal. You're a pain in *my* ass."

"Wasn't always a pain in your ass, Az," he countered. "As I recall, I made you quite a lot of money over the years. Don't go getting all holy on me now after you raked it in on that vacation property scam I put together."

Yeah, he had a point there too. Most demons reveling in the sin of avarice tended toward the acquisition of gems, or museum-quality art, or Beanie Babies, but Mestal liked playing the market—particularly the junk bond market, and fleecing people to fund his acquisitions. If he'd slipped through my fingers, I would have noticed the sudden influx of humans in the area with shitty FICO scores. I knew his game, because I'd once happily played that game with him. He spun his magic, and the humans raided their retirement plans, took out second mortgages, and borrowed from every subprime lender who would write them a loan to invest in this demon's incomprehensible get-rich-quick investment plans. He was good—really good. And I felt kinda guilty busting him when years ago I'd gleefully profited from his schemes.

Sadly, humans who defaulted on their loans were mine, so tossing Mestal back into Hel wasn't just a favor for Beatrix, it was self-preservation. Everyone thought the Ha-Satan would be in charge of punishing the murderers and the rapists, but angels had their own view of sin, and somehow FICO scores had, in their eyes, become an indicator of low vibration patterns. Being a credit risk was now one of the seven deadly sins.

Yeah, that was sort of my fault. I might have had something to do with that whole mess. And now it was *my* mess.

"I know, I know. Personally I don't think the treaty applies to us, and you should be able to come over here and do as you wish, but that isn't possible. If I don't take care of you, the angels will, and their idea of 'take care of' isn't sending you back to Hel. I belong here as the Iblis. You don't. Hope you enjoyed your five minutes of freedom, because it's back to Hel with you, buddy."

He pulled the laptop closer and opened the lid, wedging the lollipop between the slats of the bench. "Fuck off, Az. You might have wings and a sword, but you're still a demon inside, aren't you?"

Was I? There were days when I wondered if I was more angel than demon anymore.

"Yes, and I'm a lazy demon. Your being here is causing me grief, Mestal. You sneak through. I get a phone call. And if I ignore the phone call, then I have to deal with all the mess you leave in your wake. It's in my best interests if you go back to Hel, so back you go. Please."

He typed something on the laptop, watching the screen intently for a moment. "I'll go if you finish this mutual fund scam for me."

I rolled my eyes. "Who is it targeting? Because if people are gonna be losing their houses and defaulting on their credit cards over it, then the answer is no."

He held up a hand, his face solemn. "Half a dozen billionaires. I swear on all the souls I Own, Az, it's get in and get out. Two weeks and then you can shut it down."

I sighed. "Okay. But if I find out so much as one investor ends up on a skip trace list, I'm going to wrap you in duct tape and stick you in the swamp for the bitey fish to eat. Got it?"

He grinned. "Got it. Can I stay if I promise not to do anything beyond this one mutual fund scheme? And maybe rig a blackjack game and score with some hookers?"

"No." I liked this demon, but I really couldn't trust him.

"Oh, come on! Do you have any idea how many demons are sneaking through from Hel every day? None of the gate guardians want to admit it so they're covering it up."

I looked over at Beatrix. She grimaced then nodded.

"I'm the least of your worries", Mestal continued. "Go hunt down the demons who are blowing up shopping malls, killing babies, and beheading kittens. I'm not harming anyone."

I sighed. "Yes, you are, Mestal. Two weeks after you arrive I'll be seeing shit on the news about scams, and increased bankruptcy rates, and a sharp decline in the housing market. And FICO scores. Dude, you're killing me. Go behead some kittens but don't screw up people's FICO scores, for fuck's sake."

"I'm not doing anything wrong," he protested. "I buy some stocks here and there, open up a company, do some marketing. What's the harm in that? Humans do that shit all the time. I don't see you throwing *them* through the gate into Hel."

I'd been sorely tempted to do just that. And I might in the future if there was a stock market crash or the dollar took a nosedive.

"Yeah, that's a problem too, but I'm not talking about humans running Ponzi schemes right now, I'm talking about you. If I let you stay, you'll fuck up my humans, Mestal. Short sales, Ponzi schemes, internet scams? I can't let you stay here. No pyramid marketing, no Nigerian princes, no 'we're in the neighborhood with steaks and/or extra blacktop', no convincing humans to empty their retirement fund to buy a vacation timeshare in Antarctica."

Mestal snorted. "Why do you give a fuck about humans? A fool and his money...how does that go? A fool and his money are soon taken to the dry cleaners?"

Yeah, something like that.

"You're making me work, Mestal. You wouldn't like me when I'm working." The Hulk reference slid right over him. "I'm the Iblis, the Ha-Satan. And I'm in charge of humans that default on their debts. It's considered breaking a contract, a vow, and I need to rehabilitate them. I need to shepherd them toward the light. Or beat them until they see the light. Or some shit like that."

His eyes narrowed. "What's the lowest FICO score before you have to get involved?"

Mestal was clever. He was a pain, but I liked him, so I told him the magic number.

"So if I cut people off before they reach that point, I'm good?"

I hesitated. There was so fucking much that I had to do right now. I needed to let some stuff slide. "First off, you're not part of my household so you don't have immunity. Any angel that catches you, you're dead. Secondly, this is no 'three strikes' thing. You fuck up once, and I mean once, and I won't be tossing your sorry ass back into Hel, I'll be slicing and dicing with my sword. One human, and I mean one mother-fucking human, drops below four-ninety because of you, and you're toast."

I remembered I was suffering with an image problem, so I summoned my sword and jabbed it point down into the bench. Luckily this time it actually appeared as a sword and not as a pool noodle, or a banana.

The humans in the mall screamed, diving into stores and racing toward the entrances. I figured I probably had ten minutes before the security dudes were back with their Taser, so I glared at Mestal, urging him to make a decision. At least we were in Maryland and not in Texas or I probably would have had four bearded guys shoving pistols in my face.

Mestal eyed the sword. "I just want to explore all of my options here. What exactly are the benefits of joining your household?"

I looked around to make sure the security guards weren't racing toward me. "With certain restrictions, you are allowed to come and go from Hel as you please and live among the humans unharassed by angels. As in other household agreements, I'd protect you and yours and defend you as well as demand a blood-price on your behalf if any of your minions were killed. And as a special bonus, you'll get moved up on the eligibility lists for Infernal Mates. Which means that you too can meet, date, and possibly present a breeding contract to an eligible and eager angel."

Mestal turned to the angel beside me.

"Not me," Beatrix announced. "I'm already in a relation-ship. Look elsewhere, buddy."

He looked horrified. "I'm not... Is what she said true? I can come and go as I please through the gates?"

"Yes, that's one of the benefits of being in the household of the Iblis," Beatrix told him.

The negatives were that he'd be surrounded by a bunch of annoying Lows, his activities here would be severely restricted, there was a good chance if I needed to call upon my household to battle he'd be killed, and, like the late Rodney Dangerfield, he'd suddenly find that he got no respect when it came to the other demons.

He wrinkled his nose. "Although the idea of fucking an angel *is* certainly appealing, I don't think I want to get that close to one. What sort of duties would you demand of me? Do you have a project in mind, or would I be 'on-call'? And what is the minimum length of your household affiliation contract?"

I needed to dismiss the sword soon, or risk having an up close and personal discussion with the mall cops. "I'd be willing to do a six-month contract so we can both evaluate the fit, then discuss something longer at that point. You'd need to carry a cell phone and answer immediately when I call. Right now I just need information on anything that's going on that you think the Iblis should know about—such as a stock market crash, or the Ancients in Hel awakening and trying to amass an army. That sort of thing."

His eyes grew so big that I could see the whites clear around the blue irises. "The Ancients are awake? All of them? Fuck! I'll take it. Anything to stay here and out of Hel. No fucking way I'm going home to get conscripted into service under some asshole who wants me to fight a bunch of angels."

I winced. Little did he know that I just got done fighting a bunch of angels with my household and some conscripts of my own. Either way this guy was screwed. Might as well be screwed on my side, though. Standing up, I yanked my sword out of the bench and jabbed the flat of the blade against the back of Mestal's hand. It sizzled and he jumped, nearly knocking his laptop off the bench. Before he could protest I dismissed the sword and turned to leave.

"Welcome to the household, Mestal. You're mine now."

Beatrix and I walked out of the mall before teleporting—me back home and her back to the gateway in Columbia. One tiny bit of progress in my "take charge" project was complete, and I had an additional greed demon in my household, one who owed fealty to me. Now I only had the rest of Hel to worry about.

CHAPTER 5

*G*abriel banged the gavel on the table. I hadn't told him that instead of an official gavel, he was using one of my crab mallets. It still had stains on the end of it from the Old Bay seasoning. Nyalla was once again wedged between the two of us on Gabe's right, Gregory on my other side. Asta was to the left of Gabe with Rafi beside her, and Ahia between Gregory and Raphael. It was a round table, and I was seriously tempted to start making King Arthur references. If I had known, I would have brought a big boulder to shove my sword into, just as an appropriate decoration.

"Post-lockout Ruling Council meeting number eight now called to order," Gabe announced. He never missed an opportunity to remind us all that they were unable to enter Aaru. And insinuate, if not outright say, that it was my fault.

"Don't you mean post-*fall*?" I corrected. The whole thing with Mestal had put me in a good mood. Yeah, I was somewhat worried about the Ancients and their plans, but I loved teasing Gabe. And I loved reminding these guys that technically they were all considered Fallen angels. Not that I really wanted the entire heavenly host in my choir. Not that I really wanted Gabe in my choir.

"We haven't Fallen," Rafael reminded me. "We were simply ejected from Aaru and can't get back in."

"Fallen," I insisted. I did appreciate that Rafi wasn't rubbing the fact that it was my fault into my face at every moment.

"Banished by an idiot who is so inept she can't reverse it." And then there was Gabe, who *did* rub it in my face at every moment.

"Oh, stop. Sam had good reasons for what she did, and she'll find a way to reverse it." Nyalla's reproof was gentle, but I was impressed that she was scolding the archangel, especially Gabe who intimidated and frightened most humans. She'd come a long way, my girl.

Gabe tensed. "I certainly hope she finds a way to reverse it because having the entire heavenly host here among the humans isn't beneficial for anyone. Vibration levels will fall. Angels will struggle with the temptations of being in corporeal form. And humans will be caught in the middle. This isn't a good situation, and I doubt our ability to keep it a secret for long."

"*I* think it's a good situation," Nyalla countered. "Angels need to understand the human condition. They'll gain empathy and a breadth of experience that will only help them on their path to divinity."

I stared at her in amazement. Where had she learned all this stuff? It was the perfect thing to say to that stick-in-the-ass angel. Clever girl.

Gabe visibly relaxed at her words. "Perhaps, but I fear what may happen in the meantime. Who will protect the humans from angels who do not understand the role they must play here? We're powerful beings, and not all of us feel this experiment with the humans is a successful one. Many may think, as I once did, that it would be best to end all human lives and begin again with another species."

"I'm working on it." I glared at the angel, exasperated. "In the meantime, I'd expect the angelic host to behave themselves. And if they can't, well you archangels need to get off your asses and take care of those who stray. I seem to be in charge of everything else, the least you guys could do is make sure the angels don't go around committing genocide, or conjuring up a global tsunami."

"Speaking of duties that belong to the Iblis that she is not taking care of, several angels have brought to my attention that there are growing concerns about the werewolves—also known as Nephilim and their descendants," Gabriel drawled in response.

Before I could say a word in rebuttal I saw Ahia stiffen. Her reaction was understandable given that she'd considered herself a Nephilim until recently and had been living for the last few centuries in a wolf pack. Whatever slight Gabe was building toward wasn't directed at her, though. I was the one in the archangel's crosshairs with this topic.

"What concerns?" I snapped before Ahia had a chance. "Did they mistake one of the angels for a chew toy? Did some angel spout off racist bullshit in a bar and is now crying to you because a big bad wolf smashed his face in?"

Gabe looked down his nose at me. "They're undisciplined, unregulated, and running wild without any supervision. Ever since you've assumed control of that population, they've been flouting the rules of their existence contract. They're forming mate relationships with humans. They're changing packs, even becoming unaffiliated lone-wolves without angelic permission. They're holding hunts without following procedures. There are even YouTube videos of them changing and attacking people."

"Those were staged," Ahia sputtered. "Those videos were

edited. The werewolves were shot with magically tainted bullets to force them to shift and go rogue. The videos were meant to turn the human public against us...them. They're propaganda. Fake news. It's not our...the werewolves' fault."

I didn't give a damn about YouTube videos of werewolves or any of Gabe's complaints. These were the least of our problems right now. Leave it to him to focus on the inane minutiae while Rome burned to the ground around him.

"Yeah, well no surprise there. I tore up the existence contract." The room fell oddly silent at my announcement. "I tore it up, burned it, then took a big five-pound shit on it."

Gregory took an audible inhalation. "So you've left a group of powerful individuals with superhuman powers and shapeshifting ability to run about without any regulation. Anarchy is what we are heading toward if you continue down this path, Cockroach. I cannot support you in this. Unrestrained chaos such as this will herald in the end-times."

As if he didn't see the apocalypse right in front of our faces. "Herald? Babe, that trumpet blew a long time ago. Did you sleep through it or something?"

Gabe scowled. "I most certainly did not blow the trumpet."

I waved his comment away. "Doesn't matter. The were-wolves aren't running amuck like monsters in some big-budget dystopian movie. I put Candy in charge of them."

"Candy?" Raphael's lips twitched. "Isn't that putting a fox in charge of the henhouse?"

"No, it's putting a fox in charge of the fox-house. Or den. Or whatever the fuck they call it. She's a werewolf. She's one of the most dedicated Alphas I know. She's fair and orga-nized, and all those things I'm not. Let the werewolves govern themselves. I've got enough shit to do without approving Phil's transfer from the Atlanta pack to Van

Buren, or whether the Austin pack should hold their annual hunt in the fall or the spring."

"Which you wouldn't have to approve anyway, since you tore up the existence contract," Asta reminded me.

"Werewolves still have rules," I told her. "They're just self-imposed rules instead of draconian ones handed down from on high and made up by a bunch of angels who never even met a werewolf or Nephilim and haven't been out of Aaru more than a handful of times in the last five million years."

"What happens when their interests conflict with those of the humans?" Gregory had one eyebrow up, as if he doubted the sanity of my decision. Imagine that. "Are you planning on stepping in then, or just letting humans try to battle it out with beings that could kill them with a swipe of a paw?"

"Well, let's see…there's seven billion humans in this world and I'm guessing about fifty thousand shifters at most. And given that most of them are clustered in the U.S. where every man, woman, and child owns at least twenty firearms with or without the magic bullets that pretty much kill shifters on contact…. Hmm, I'm thinking we need to worry less about the humans and more about those poor wolf shifters. And bear shifters. And cougar shifters and other shit."

"Yeah!" Ahia sputtered, raising slightly out of her chair. I think the only thing keeping her from jumping up and leaping onto the table was Raphael's somewhat panicked attempts to restrain her. "Magic users, and elves, and hydras, and manticores are coming through ever-increasing rifts. Why are you focusing the problem on us…I mean, the were-wolves? Nephilim and their descendants? They're not invulnerable, as recent events in Alaska have illustrated. They're the least of your problems."

Gregory stared at Ahia in surprise. Gabe glared at her, then shot a quick look at his younger brother. I thought for a second he was going to make the fatal mistake of telling

Raphael to "control his woman" or some shit like that. Instead he just shook his head and leaned back in his chair.

"We're not focusing on Nephilim and their descendants," Gregory said. "It's one of many situations we're juggling right now, all of them of equal importance. We're in the middle of dealing with the elven integration and the challenges that proposes, a recent war in Aaru that is *not* over by any stretch of the imagination, those interdimensional rifts you mentioned that are spitting out all sorts of monsters and creatures *some of whom are being allowed to remain here...*" he shot a stern glance at Asta with that one, "...and more. Keeping control of a group that was formerly well organized and regulated seems to be what the humans would call 'low-hanging-fruit' as far as items on our agenda."

Ahia muttered something under her breath about how the angels needed to meet a guy named Jake if they wanted to see an organized group of shifters, then spoke up. "The wolf packs in Alaska have been fairly unregulated for centuries, living in peace beside the humans who know who and what they are. Werewolves are beings who like a structured, well-ordered existence, some more than others. I don't think you need to worry about wolves running around harassing and killing humans. We police our own. And although many of us didn't know Candy before a few months ago, she seems to be someone the angels can trust to set the rules and procedures that Nephilim and their descendants live by."

I looked at her in surprise, wondering if she was really an Angel of Chaos, or not. That speech sounded rather conciliatory for someone of my ilk.

"Let's keep a close eye on the situation and we'll revisit the topic if problems arise." Gregory turned to me. "Please tell your proxy, Candy, that we expect regular detailed reports regarding their rules, regulations, infractions, and punishments, as well as a list of exemplary individuals that we may wish to bring forward to the public in order to counter this negative publicity Ahia alluded to."

I liked Gregory so much better when he was not taking control and running things among the angels. Clearly Gabe being in charge as his puppet dictator had been a short-lived situation. I should have known my beloved could never hold back from being the boss for long.

"Aye-aye captain." I saluted. Candy would love this shit. She'd have enough reports and charts and Venn diagrams to make even Gabe happy.

"Moving on." Gabe shuffled a stack of papers that I was pretty sure were there just for show. "Elf Island. Progress?"

"Progress," Gregory replied. "We had an incident involving corruption with our employment placement contact, but that's been resolved. We now have over two hundred elves that have cleared our program and are currently suitably employed. Our concern is monitoring their assimilation. We've put in place a program similar to the human parole system where the elves need to check in with a local Grigori enforcer who also will occasionally make a surprise visit to their home or workplace, but we don't have enough angels to monitor all the elves once they are released from the island. It would be more than a full-time job for the existing numbers of Grigori to manage. So the issue we need to address is how long do the elves require this level of monitoring, and should we put together a special task force to do this under Grigori supervision or add to the ranks of Grigori?"

"I think this is an ideal opportunity to put idle angelic hands to use," Raphael spoke up. "The entirety of Aaru is now here among the humans. We can claim that this situation is one of the reasons we're delaying their return to our home-land, and hopefully keep them busy enough that they don't decide to start up the rebellion again."

"I know I would welcome the assistance," Asta said. "I've got four elves working in Chicago right now, and have been told I'm slated to get another twenty to thirty before all this is over. There's no way I can manage their progress and continue to ensure order and peace within my area of responsibility."

"I guess not, with all those sirens and mermaids running around," I snarked. It had come up before that Asta was selectively allowing certain "creatures" who came through the rifts to remain in her territory. I thought it was hysterical, especially given that she was an Angel of Order, and couldn't help mentioning it.

"One siren." She eyed me serenely. "Five mermaids, three selkies, and four-to-six nymphs because they come and go."

"What, no mermen?" Nyalla asked. "*Are* there even mermen? Is that a real thing?"

Asta blinked and tilted her head. "I really don't know. I'll have to ask them. I'm assuming there must be mermen as they appear to be gendered. I mean, of course they are or they wouldn't be called mermaids, they'd be called merbeings, or merthings, or something."

"Someone told me that they eat people," Ahia said. "Is that true?"

"Not on my watch, they don't eat people," Asta retorted. "If a drunk human falls off a sailboat and drowns, they're welcome to him, but I draw the line at grabbing people off ships or luring in joggers along the lakefront."

Oh sheesh, we really were about to go down the rabbit hole on this one. As interested as I might be in the specific dining and sexual practices of mer-people, I wanted to get this meeting over with before my one-thousandth birthday.

"I'm voting for a wait-and-see on the timeline for elven supervision," I announced. "We can readdress the topic in five or so years. In the meantime, let's assign an angel for every ten to fifteen elves in the workplace, and that angel will report to their local Grigori. Deal? Vote? I'm saying yes."

I stuck my hand in the air, ignoring all the surprised expressions around me. Yeah, yeah. I might be an imp, but I could do angel-speak when I had to.

We voted. And for once something was actually unanimous.

Gabe shuffled his papers again. "Next agenda item: increased demon activity at the gateways."

Hey, that was my topic and as far as I knew I hadn't added it to the agenda, preferring instead to spring these things on the Council mid-meeting. Had Beatrix ratted me out? No, it had to have been some other gate guardian spilling the beans on this one.

"My guardians have reported a significant increase in attempted crossings," Gregory said. "And they are not the usual Lows and imps either. Many high-level demons have been coming through. Successfully. I've had to shift enforcers to act as back-up ever since the gate guardian in Seattle was overrun by a dozen well-organized warmongers and nearly killed."

Everyone turned to look at me.

"What? Oh, that is not my job." It was, but I wasn't going to admit to it easily. "I'm not responsible for gateways and that stupid fucking treaty you and some long-dead angels signed millions of years ago. In my opinion, they're allowed to cross. The treaty doesn't apply to them. And they're not my problem."

"Yes, we know. The Grigori will continue to handle trespassers, but as the Iblis, we are looking to you for guidance on any plot that may exist in Hel to mount a large-scale attack, or perhaps some sort of organized effort to relocate among the demons," Gregory explained.

I remembered Harkel's comments. There probably *were*

more demons sneaking through now than a year ago, but that was to be expected. The angels had been busy with their own matters. The elves had been a distraction. If anyone wanted to vacation here among the humans, now was the time to do it. But large-scale attack? The only large-scale attack planned was the Ancients' plans to move on Aaru. Allegedly planned, because although Harkel had seemed to be telling the truth, he was still a warmonger who might have his own reasons for lying about such a thing.

"What, organized like the Elven exodus?" I snorted. "Hardly. We're not relocating. Demons like it in Hel. We come here to vacation. Of course there's an increase in activity. We're not stupid. We know the angels are somewhat inattentive at the moment. Someone got wind that you angels were a bit busy with your own shit and decided now was a good time to promote tourism. It's probably nothing. Don't worry about it. It'll all be okay."

I should have realized that by my saying that, I was pretty much assuring that no one would ever think this was "nothing" or that "all would be okay".

Asta shook her head. "I turned back a warmonger a few months ago who tried to bargain information for his release. He said that an Ancient was going to cross over with over four hundred legions of demons. I'd thought he was lying, but now I wonder...are the banished planning on mounting an attack?"

Great. This was all I needed right now.

"No, he was lying. Demons lie, if you haven't realized that yet," I scoffed. "If an Ancient, or a group of Ancients ever got off their lazy asses to do anything, it wouldn't be to come here," I scoffed. "The only thing that would get them moving would be if they had a chance to take Aaru back. It's Aaru they want, not some place overrun with humans and elves where they still have to be in a corporeal form. Trust me, they're not going anywhere."

"They can't get into Aaru," Gregory reminded me. "I'm not worried about an attack on heaven."

"Yeah, yeah. Because everyone is locked out and it's all my fault." I was getting tired of having my nose constantly rubbed in this one.

"It's not that, Cockroach. They were banished. You were allowed in Aaru as the Iblis, and I had to use some creative interpretation of the treaty to allow you to bring your demon forces in for the battle, but an army led by an Ancient won't be able to get in even if we weren't all locked out. The banishment is ironclad."

It probably was, Gregory's smug insistence that he'd properly done this banishment made me think once more about how I'd fucked everything up.

"I've heard they found a loophole." I shrugged. "Maybe you didn't do such a great job as you think. Maybe you should be grateful that I locked everyone out and you don't have to deal with a few hundred legions of Ancients and demons busting in the back door."

Gregory glared at me. "I did not allow any 'loopholes'."

"Even for Samael?" He flinched at the name. "You admitted that you built the gates in the hope that he'd return here to neutral ground to attempt a reconciliation."

"We built the gates nearly five hundred thousand years after the war," he snapped back. "At the time of the banishment, I was not interested in any future reconciliation."

He'd been seriously injured fighting his brother. He'd nearly sliced the other angel in half with his sword. I'd seen Gregory lose his temper before, knew that he could do things he'd regret later. Maybe he *had* meant the banishment as a finality, but there was always a loophole. There was always a little spot somewhere that could be worried away and made to unravel the whole thing.

Well, always except it seems for the banishment I'd done.

"Banishments are never forever." Gabe's voice didn't have the usual arrogant, judgmental tones as he spoke this time to Gregory. "There was always a chance for redemption, for forgiveness and a reinstatement that would allow penitent Angels of Chaos back into Aaru. As ridiculous as the idea is, it is possible."

Gregory's eyebrows shot up. "Ridiculous is the appropriate word, brother. A Fallen, an Angel of Chaos, who repents? And then is granted forgiveness? It would never happen."

"So it would have to be an Ancient, right?" I pressed, trying to figure this out. If I could see the loopholes for reentry in the banishment Gregory had done, maybe I could find the ones in my own. "Not a demon? So, like, if Dar wanted to get into Aaru, and Asta forgave him, the banishment for him would be lifted and he could get in?"

There were a whole lot of significant glances that I didn't understand. For once I wasn't alone, because Ahia and Nyalla clearly didn't know what the heck was going on either.

"Dar could enter as part of your household if you brought him," Gregory explained. "Although now Dar would be denied entry because you included yourself in your own banishment, and that rolls onto him as well. The banishment I put in place was similar. Under that banishment, an Ancient, as you call them, would need to repent and be granted forgiveness, then that would apply to all the demons in his household."

That was the loophole. "So Samael repents, because it's been almost three fucking million years, and an Angel of Order forgives him, and he gets in?"

"Samael's dead." Gregory's voice was rough, raw with

pain and anger. "He's dead. And even if he wasn't, he'd never repent. And without repentance, there would be no forgiveness."

"Okay, then some other angel. Like.... Stupid-Ancient-el angel."

Ahia snorted, then clapped a hand over her mouth.

"Hypothetically," I added. I knew I was probably going to have to deal with these Ancients, but I didn't want to do it now. Or in the next century or two. And there would be no need for me to deal with them if there was no way for them to get into Aaru at the moment.

"Hypothetically, yes," Raphael told me. "But they wouldn't repent. And there's no Angel of Order in existence that would forgive them. Plus, just in case it's slipped your mind, you banished everyone. As far as I know, a banished Angel of Order can't override your edict. So even if one of us snuggles up to a repentant Ancient and grants forgiveness, I doubt he'd be able to get in."

Whew that was a relief.

"Good. Then we don't have to worry about the Ancients and a few thousand demons storming into an empty Aaru and taking up residence." I was so thrilled. And now I could truly sit back and enjoy watching powerful, arrogant Ancient demons bashing their fists against a door that wouldn't open. "And, just for the record, there is no proof at all that tens of thousands of demons eager for vacation are descending upon the human world."

Crap. Maybe I shouldn't have said that last part. Gabe's eyes widened. Asta sucked in a breath. Raphael and Ahia exchanged concerned glances.

"We need to immediately move to defend the gateways," Gregory demanded. "Each of you is to pledge five of the most trustworthy, the strongest angels of your choir to ensure these demons do not bring their armies into this realm."

"What if the Ancients still have retained the ability to form their own gateways?" Gabe asked. "If they assist these demons, or even decide to lead them, then they could appear anywhere, at any time. We need to be ready to defend this world at a moment's notice."

"The timing of this is terrible." Raphael shook his head. "We're weakened just coming off the recent battles, and many of our choir are not skilled in fighting in corporeal form. Actually, they're not skilled at *anything* in corporeal form. Did I tell you that I had to rescue a member of my choir who wandered into a dwelling and was unable to leave? I had to teleport in to teach him how to turn a doorknob."

"He couldn't teleport himself out?" Asta asked, her eyes big. "Was the building lined in lead and surrounded by a salt circle with runes? I'll admit I still have great difficulty in managing to navigate revolving doors."

Great. I'd now just inadvertently convinced the entirety of the Ruling Council that the Ancients and demons in Hel were mounting an attack. As in right now, grab your swords, kind of attack.

"No, I didn't mean—"

"Cockroach, you employ your household in Hel to collect intelligence on this matter. We need names, current rank, as well as the number of legions they command, plus where and when they plan to attack and any strategies they might employ. I'll put two guardians at each gate. We will meet again in five days for a status update."

"That's not necessary. I—"

"Excellent idea," Raphael interrupted. "Five days? Here? Same rodent time, same rodent channel?"

"It's bat time and bat channel," Ahia corrected him.

I shut up because it wasn't like anyone was listening to me anyway.

"Actually, I propose that we vary the location of our meetings to increase visibility among the humans," Gabriel announced. "We should also take human transportation to arrive there whenever possible, and spend time before and after the meetings walking about among the humans in our full glory."

There was a long shocked silence following his pronouncement.

"Excellent," Gabe continued. "Since there is no objection, I propose our next meeting to take place in Reykjavik. It will serve a dual purpose of reassuring the humans there of our presence as well as warning the elves they've elected to public office that we're closely watching their actions."

Nyalla shot him an approving glance. No, it was more than approving. Damn it, I'd told her what a complete dick this angel was, and here she was eyeing him like she admired and supported him. Although, come to think of it, the suggestion *was* absolutely in line with what I wanted to see happen. Gabe and I never agreed on anything. What the fuck was going on here?

"Who are you and what have you done with Gabriel?" I demanded.

"I'm not flying on an airplane," Raphael announced.

"Iceland? I'm so excited." Ahia squealed. Then she punched Raphael in the arm. "And you are too flying on an airplane. I've never been on a commercial jet before, and you're coming with me. Maybe we can join the human-style mile-high club. Won't it be fun to fuck in an airplane?"

I liked this angel. "It's really not that much fun to fuck in an airplane," I told her. "Cut his arms and legs off and it won't be so crowded. Or better yet, just cut his dick off and take it in there without the body."

"No one is cutting my dick off." Raphael scowled at the idea.

"Why are you suddenly so concerned about making our presence known among the humans?" Gregory asked his brother, getting to the heart of the matter.

"They already know about us. When the entire angelic host drops down from Aaru among them, they're hardly going to look the other way. It's been all over the news and the internet and the papers." Gabe looked around at all of us. "What? You don't keep abreast of top stories and world politics? For shame! How are we to be good stewards of this world if we don't stay aware of current events? I do apologize, brother, for not having realized the extent of the situation down here," he told Gregory. "Clearly we tasked you with something far beyond the ability of one archangel and a handful of Grigori to manage."

"Are you saying I haven't been performing to your satisfaction?" Normally such an accusation would have resulted in a glowing, pissed-off Gregory, but instead the archangel looked shocked.

"No, of course not." Gabriel's tone was both soothing and condescending. "So many of our brethren are wandering around the human world, lost and confused. It doesn't inspire confidence. And those who were rebels in Aaru will most likely work against our interests here as well, once they get used to being in corporeal form. It's important for us to establish order and rule of law now, before that happens. We're clearly going to be here for a long time…" he cast me a glowering look, "…if not forever. Let's make a refreshing tart drink from the sour fruit we have been given, and use this as an opportunity to finally put humanity on the path to positive evolution."

"His body has been taken over by a motivational speaker." I pointed at Gabe. "Dr. Phil? Steven Covey? No, Zig Ziglar."

I was a bit worried that Gabe's speech hovered on the edge of benevolent dictator. So maybe it *was* Gabe in there after all and not some alien imposter pod-person.

"I think that's a wonderful idea," Asta chimed in. "I suggest we begin to think of a framework of how to manage the situation."

Fuck me, I'd created a monster. How did I ever think it was a good idea to suggest Asta for the Ruling Council?

"We've already begun by establishing rules concerning the elven integration," Asta continued, "including a registry and punishments regarding inappropriate use of elven magic and failure to be an asset to society. It seems that Sam is doing the same with her werewolves and Nephilim."

No, I was not.

"I've made strict guidelines for the mermaids, selkies, nymphs, and the siren living in Chicago."

"You were supposed to gather them together, send them through the gateway and lock it down." Gregory scowled.

Asta's golden brown skin took on a pink tone. "Well, I have found them to be useful. And it seems they've been coming through naturally occurring rifts for thousands of years, unbeknownst to us, although usually into the oceans, not the freshwater lakes. I felt I had the need to grandfather in their presence somewhat."

"I've been thinking that the angels need to be open about their presence here," Nyalla chimed in. "With monsters coming through the rifts, werewolves outed, elves working next to humans, and a potential army of demons descending upon us, it's vital for humans to know they have someone to turn to—beings with the supernatural clout to protect them and assure them that their way of life will not be destroyed with all this change."

I was so glad I'd managed to get Nyalla on the Ruling Council.

"Yeah," Ahia did a fist-pump. "We'll all fly commercial, rack up some bonus miles, then spend a few hours roaming the shopping district with our wings out, healing the sick, kissing babies, and buying shoes. I'm totally on board with this."

"All in favor?" Gabe asked with a smug smile.

My hand shot up, as did Nyalla's and Ahia's and Rafi's. With a soft, whispered "shopping", Asta raised her hand.

Gregory sighed. Then his hand also went up. "Fine. Reykjavik it is. And may the Creator help the poor humans who happen to be in the shopping district."

CHAPTER 6

*H*el felt...different. I wasn't sure what it was, but something about the place sent a wave of sorrow through me. It used to be nostalgia I felt each time I journeyed home. I'd walk the broken streets of Dis and think about the time when I had been newly released from my dwarven caretakers and school, when it seemed like my only worries were to keep from getting killed, to not devour anyone, to claw my way through the hierarchy and Own as many souls as possible.

All my Owned souls were gone, given up in a sentimental gesture when I thought I was dying, a last act of love, something Gregory had been pressing me to do. And as for my status...well, I had no fucking idea where I stood in the demon hierarchy. I was the Iblis. I held the sword. Technically I was the ruler of Hel, but the title hadn't brought me any additional respect. I could stand on top of the rubble of Pamersiel's house and wave the damned thing around and nobody would look twice at me, or give a shit. The few things that seemed to garner any attention among the other demons were my unsavory propensity for devouring, and the fact that I'd somehow managed to steal and integrate Gregory's archangel essence into my being. It had given me my wings, changed me into an Angel of Chaos, and given me some additional skills, but it wasn't those that intrigued the Ancients. All they wanted to know is how I'd done it, and if they could do the same.

I had a bad feeling that it was tied up with my devouring. And I didn't really want to let that secret out into the open. Ahriman had wanted to breed a powerful demon with my capacity to hold energy and my devouring skill, but he'd wanted to create a weapon capable of bringing Aaru to its knees, someone who could walk right through the door of heaven and start shredding angels, chewing up their spirit-selves and growing more powerful with every one. Normally that would be a self-limiting exercise—a demon could only hold so much energy, after all. A devouring spirit might top out after six or seven angels, then they'd be vulnerable, their most-feared weapon dull and unusable. But me...I seemed to have an unlimited storage capacity. Like some kind of weird black hole, I could devour until there was nothing left to consume.

I'm not sure what would happen after that point, but I had a feeling it would probably result in a Big Bang, that would both take me out and restart creation.

I'd always wondered if *that* was the apocalypse that Gregory had referred to. Was I truly fated to do that very thing? If so, I hoped it was a long, long way off. I hoped that the ancient archangel was wrong, and that the sort of chaos, the apocalypse I was foretold to bring, was something very different.

"Mistress!" I turned around to see Rutter and Snip. "I hoped to find you here, Mistress," Snip told me. "I made the appointment you requested. Criam says to come tonight if you can, and you will be granted an audience."

I was surprised Criam remembered me, let alone actually arranged a meeting with the head of his household. As demons go, Criam was pretty fucking old. He was one of the first few generations of demons created after the banishment from Aaru, and had served the Ancient who formed him since the day he'd left his dwarven nannies. I'd come across him during an issue in Eresh with half a dozen trolls and a fire serpent, and we'd parted on good terms. It wasn't often I parted with someone on good terms, so when Harkel told me about the Ancients awakening, Criam was the first demon I thought of.

Still, it shocked the fuck out of me that my request for an audience had been granted. I couldn't believe a chance association from three hundred years ago would buy me a meeting with one of the most powerful Ancients in Hel.

"Thanks Snip. And while I'm here, I've got a few other tasks I need you and the household to handle for me."

Both Lows squealed and hopped up and down, excitedly slapping tentacles and claws. "New work? Are we having a party? Every time you come to Hel with work for us, we have a party."

I wasn't sure when me returning to Hel and assigning work started equating to have-a-party.

"Uh, sure. Actually, I need to have a household meeting for this one. Is everyone here in Dis, or at the Patchine house?"

Ahriman had owned dwellings in both Dis and Patchine, as well as one up in Eresh that seemed to be vacant most of the time. When I'd killed him, I'd inherited all his shit including these houses-of-horror. Demon law was weird that way. My inheritance rights had been partly because I'd been the one who murdered the Ancient, partly due to the rights afforded me under our breeding contract, and partly because no one had bothered to challenge me for all this shit. Yet.

Probably in a thousand years or so, some asshole would come out of nowhere and insist that I had no right to it. Then I'd need to decide whether to let him, or her, have it all or fight to the death for it. I'd most likely just let him have it.

Which was probably one of the reasons why no one in Hel took me seriously as the Iblis.

"Most of our household is in Patchine," Rutter told me.

"How many are here in Dis?" This was important as I didn't want to have to teleport a few hundred Lows. First off, they tended to puke when I teleported them. Secondly, they'd learned how unpleasant the experience was and ran away if they knew what was about to happen. This resulted in me running all over my house, trying to catch Lows. The process reminded me a lot of what happened when I needed to give Boomer a bath.

"Us is it," Snip said. "And nobody is in Eresh except for a few of Ahriman's old household. They can stay there. We don't like them anyway."

Relief over only having to grab and teleport two Lows warred with a niggling feeling of concern. "Why are you the only two in Dis? Did something happen to the house that rendered it unlivable? Did Snot vomit all over the place again?"

Rutter laughed. "No, although that was pretty funny. I knew that was gonna happen when Fatty dared him to eat a barrel full of pickled bitey fish."

"Lows aren't safe in Dis right now," Snip said, answering my question. Out of all my Lows, he was the one most likely to keep focused.

"And why aren't Lows safe in Dis?" I prodded.

Lows really weren't safe anywhere. Other demons liked to catch them and play with them, and that play usually resulted in their deaths. No one cared. There was no blood price for killing a Low. They didn't have friends or family that would avenge them, so they were fair game. But that had always been the way things were with Lows. Their short life expectancy and usual violent death didn't keep them from living where they wanted to live and doing what they wanted to do. If you knew you'd probably be slowly dismembered tomorrow, you might as well live it up today.

"There's a demon who's taken up a new hobby." Snip grimaced, telling me exactly the nature of this "hobby." "He's snatching Lows left and right, off the streets, out of their beds. He even is taking them out of their homes."

I would have liked to say this was a surprise, but it wasn't. Eventually this demon would get bored and get a new hobby. Until then everyone would just need to stay out of his way.

"You guys don't need to leave Dis," I told the Lows, thinking that I'd need to add this to my announcements at the meeting. "You're affiliated with my household. I've made sure to mark every one of you. You're safe here."

Household members were under the protection of their head demon. Mess with them, and you would find yourself on the pointy end of a powerful demon's claw. Outside of my weird, quirky group, Lows were not technically considered members of a household. Stealing one wasn't a big deal unless they were marked. Even then it wasn't a capital offense. Retribution might happen, but no one would lose a head over a broken Low. It was the same type of punishment allowed if a demon were to swipe a bowl of roasted beaks, or an ugly piece of artwork. They weren't even considered as valuable as toys—those humans and other creatures we called our own for the purposes of whatever enjoyment they might bring to us.

"We're not safe here," Rutter whispered. "That's why we were so glad to see you. Not that we're not always glad to see you, Mistress. You are the best thing ever. Better than a steaming pile of entrails, or a quart of eyeballs, or shredded brains."

Nice to know how I ranked in terms of "cool and desirable stuff".

"You're safe here," I repeated. "I marked you." There were a zillion Lows to grab and play with. No one would bother grabbing one that had been marked. It wasn't worth the annoyance of a slightly irritated master or mistress when five feet away an unmarked Low was there for the taking.

Snip shook his head, his yellow eyes big and sad. "No, Mistress. Not after they took Sinew, and then Booty, and then Lash. We figured it would be best to leave Dis and hide in the Patchine house instead. Rutter and I were just here to grab a few bowls because all those ones in the Patchine house got broken last night."

I was mildly interested in why all my bowls at the Patchine house were broken, but that curiosity was completely overridden by the first part of Snip's statement.

"They took Sinew, Booty, and Lash? Who took them? And did they get taken all at once, or over a period of time?"

I knew the risks of asking three questions of creatures that generally struggled to answer with a one-at-a-time approach, but I was starting to get pissed. Was I so disrespected that someone would take a household member that I'd marked? Even if that household member was a Low?

"Yes, Mistress," Rutter replied. "They was taken one at a time. When Sinew went missing, we didn't think much about it. Figured maybe he'd fallen down a well, or got eaten by a sand wyrm or something, but the Lows on the street said they saw him being snatched. Even then, we thought maybe someone didn't see his mark, or didn't care, but then when Booty went missing, we knews something was going on. Then Lash…well they dragged him right off our front porch a few days ago. That's when everyone decided to leave Dis. I mean, next time they might even come inside and take us! At least if they tried that in Patchine, we could hide in the dungeon."

That house was like a labyrinth, and the dungeon was pretty inaccessible. It was a good place to hide if someone was coming after you. If they really wanted to get my Lows, they could always just fireball the place into debris. Although, there wouldn't be much left alive to play with after repeated fireball attacks.

Still, my brain furiously chewed over the situation. Were these demons targeting my Lows in particular? Was this a personal slight to me? I was the only one who afforded Lows an actual rank within my household, so I could be wrong. Maybe these demons were just grabbing whatever Lows caught their fancy, not realizing the offense in snatching mine.

"Did they follow you to Patchine? Are you all under any sort of attack there? Have any of my Lows gone missing since you moved?"

Again I doubted I'd get all these questions answered, but couldn't seem to summon the patience for one-at-a-time line of questioning.

"I don't know, Mistress." Rutter wrung his tentacles together. "Poo-poo went missing last night, but he's probably just lost on the third floor again."

Okay. Now I'd need to mount a search for Poo-poo on the third floor, just to be sure. Now for the big question that neither one had answered.

"Who is doing this? I thought you said it was just one demon, but then you mentioned 'they'?"

Snip and Rutter exchanged a wary glance. "Rumor has it that they are nabbing these Lows for a higher level demon, maybe even an Ancient. The ones who took Sinew, Booty, and Lash are Cheros and Oor."

"They live in Dis?" I asked.

Rutter nodded.

As if I didn't have enough to do, now I needed to look for Poo-poo on the third floor. Come back to Dis and make Cheros and Oor regret the moment of their birth, then go attend this meeting I'd set up with Criam and his Ancient mistress. So much for a quick trip to gather intel and send out some spies, then getting the hell out of Hel. It seemed like every time I stepped foot in this place, I had more shit to do. Hopefully this shit wouldn't take very long because I had birthday party planning and a Ruling Council meeting on my schedule, and neither of those two things could be put off while I searched my house for a lost Low and beat up some bullies.

Before they had a chance to realize what I was doing and run away, I shot out my arms and grabbed Rutter and Snip by the ear and horn. Then as they screamed in protest, I teleported the three of us to my house in Patchine.

CHAPTER 7

*P*oo-poo was indeed lost on the third floor and not kidnapped like the others had been. We found him locked in a closet, gnawing on an old coat that must have belonged to one of Ahriman's former servants. He'd obviously been there for a while to be attempting to eat a coat. Or not. With Lows, there weren't usually a high degree of gourmet sensibilities.

After gathering them all together and promising them a party, then waiting for the cheering and body-slamming joy to quiet down, I got to business.

"Groups of demons are planning to sneak through the gates into the human world," I told them. "I need you guys to find out who the leaders are, how many are in the groups, and what they plan on doing once they're on the human side of the gateways."

Half a dozen arms, legs, claws, tentacles, and other limbs shot into the air. I sighed, wishing I hadn't taught them this, but waving appendages was better than a bunch of Lows trying to talk all at once.

I randomly pointed to one, figuring they all had the same question anyway.

"We're gonna need a lot of parchment and stuff, because there's a lot of demons wanting to go vacation with the humans and I won't be able to remember them all," the Low whined.

"Yeah," another spoke up. "And how big of a group is a group. If there's two demons wanting to cross, do we write that down?"

I thought for a second. "No. Five or more. And I'm especially interested in groups of a hundred or more. And don't just stand by the gateway and make a log of who is crossing. I need to know about those who are *planning* to cross. I need enough time to get out a warning before they actually go through the gateway."

"How the fuck are we supposed to do that?" another Low complained. "I can stand by one of the gates and take notes, but I can't read demons' minds to figure out if they're thinking of crossing or not."

"Might as well put every demon in Hel on that list," Rutter spoke up. "Everyone wants to vacation sometime or another."

"No, no, no." This was one of the major drawbacks of having a household full of Lows. They were idiots. "Groups of five or more, and especially groups of a hundred or more, who are planning on crossing sometime in the next few weeks to six months."

I figured anything longer than six months out would pretty much net me every demon in Hel as well. Almost every Ancient and high-level demon had fantasies about storming the gateways and running unhindered around the human world for a glorious century or two. It was kind of a bucket list item for demons, but I only wanted those who were actually laying down concrete plans to do something in the near future.

"When should we check in, Mistress?" Snip asked.

"If you find out that something is going down in the next week or two, then I want to know right away either by mirror or sending someone across the gateway to tell me. Otherwise, compile a report and get it to me weekly."

All the Lows looked at each other, then down at the floor where their various lower limbs shuffled.

Ah yes. Asking for a report was like telling them to sprout feathered wings and fly. I'd been hanging around with angels for too long. These were Lows. They weren't going to do a report if their lives depended on it. Lucky bastards.

"Okay, not a report, then. Get me a list. I want a list weekly of any groups of demons planning to cross the gates. Get me names, if you know them, level and specialty, number of demons in the group, their leader's name and level, and when they plan to cross as well as their intentions once they're on the other side of the gateways."

That got a me a lot of confused expressions. Ugh. How the fuck was I going to get this information? It was just too much for these little guys to remember.

"Okay, work in teams of three. One in your team remembers to get information on the leader, the second one on the group members, the third the timing and intentions. Is that easier?"

There was a chorus of "Yes, Mistress."

"Snip, you're in charge of compiling the information on one sheet of paper and getting it to me every week. Can you do that?"

He saluted. "Do you want me to continue working on our extra-special, secret project as well?"

At his words, the other Lows erupted into loud complaints of favoritism and demands to know what this special secret project was. I couldn't remember what the fuck it was, so I just gave Snip a blank look.

"Amael-say," he prompted. "Ancient emon-day who led the ebellion-ray in aru-aay?"

I winced, but thankfully none of the other Lows was smart enough to figure out pig Latin.

"Yes. Continue with that project."

I was immediately subject to an onslaught of whining that had me making up special project designations for what I'd just instructed them to do. It was time to get the party show on the road, but first, I needed to figure out what the fuck was going on with my missing Lows. Then meet with Criam and his Ancient.

"So what's up with these demons who took Sinew, Booty, and Lash?" I demanded.

"Cheros is just an asshole," Snot spoke up. "She likes to play with Lows, although she's pretty good about letting us go before she kills us. She's fast and sneaky. Got me once." Snot wiggled a stump of a bony tail at me. "She doesn't usually work with another demon, though. And neither Sinew, Booty, or Lash have turned up. None of the Lows they took are turning up. Word has it she's grabbing them for someone else."

That was what Rutter had alluded to. "Why? And who?"

About half of my Lows shrugged.

"Sometimes demons like to kill us," Snip told me. "Happens every couple years or so. Usually it's a frustrated warmonger, but could be any type of demon. They'll kill a few thousand of us, and either get bored and stop, or get bored and start trying to kill higher-level demons. If they do the latter one, then usually they work their way up the hierarchy, killing more and more challenging demons until someone kills them first."

"How often does this happen?" I asked. "I know you said

every couple of years or so, but how often do they kill a few thousand then get bored, as opposed to the other, self-destructive, type of activity?"

Rot wrinkled his snout. "Every year or two this sort of thing happens. About ninety percent are the demons who kill a few thousand of us, then get bored eventually and stop. Most aren't stupid enough to kill anything higher than Lows."

I was appalled. "So what happens when one of those demon serial killers starts up? Do you all run and hide or something?"

They all stared at me.

"Uh, no, Mistress," Snip replied. "Ain't no sense in that. We all know we're gonna die sooner than most. When the killings start, we just try to be smart, and hope they'll take other Lows. Figuring it's like that Darwin human wrote about. Only the smartest and strongest Lows survive. We just all hope we're one of the strong and the smart."

That was gut-wrenchingly pitiful. They were so resigned to their fate. Like a bunch of fucking lemmings, hoping a few thousand others were ahead of them on the cliff edge.

"But this is different," Rutter added. "This isn't a Low-killer like usual, and it's not Cheros just wanting to play. She's partnering up with Oor, and he's not usually a demon who pays any special attention to Lows unless they're in his way or something. They're both collecting Lows for another demon, and none of us know who that demon is or if he's killing the Lows or just torturing us somewhere long-term."

"So maybe this is the serial-type Low killer, only this guy doesn't like to do his own shopping?" I conjectured. "He likes the Lows delivered to his door so he can torture and kill them in the privacy of his own home?"

"Maybe." Snip chewed one of his tentacles. "I don't know why we haven't found bodies, though. They're not coming back injured and broken, and we're not finding bodies. They're just snatched up and taken away, and never seen again."

It bothered me. And it really shouldn't bother me beyond the fact that these two assholes were taking my Lows, ones I'd marked as part of my household. I needed to stop being a sentimental fool and just ensure that my own Lows were safe. Not because they needed to be safe or anything. No, it was because this was a slap in the face to my authority. These demons were showing me great disrespect, taking what was mine. That was it. That's what was pissing me off, not that my Lows were scared, or that they were sadly resigned to the fact they were going to be murdered or anything.

And not the rest of the Lows, not the hundreds and thousands who weren't in my household. What happened to them wasn't my problem. I needed to confront these two asshole demons, teach them a lesson, and make sure that they were snatching Lows who weren't mine. That was the extent of my problem here. Whatever happened to the non-household Lows wasn't my concern. I had enough on my plate without becoming their savior. Nope. Not happening.

"How many other Lows have been taken?" I asked, unable to help myself. Damn it.

"We don't really keep track," Snot explained. "Lots of Lows are out on their own, all solitary like. They're usually the first to go. It's safer when we group together. From what I heard, I'm thinking maybe twenty or so Lows from Dis. Not too many."

A few others agreed with his assessment. Not too many. Twenty Lows snatched off the streets of Dis in the last few weeks was "not too many." I guess not when they were used to losing a few thousand to killers every few years.

"This should have come to my attention the moment it

started happening," I scolded. "You guys need to let me know when Lows go missing like this."

Snip tilted his head as he stared at me. "You mean in the household, Mistress? Or do you really want to know when other Lows go missing as well?"

There were a collective inhalation, a sense of electricity as all eyes turned to me, their grotesque faces raised up to mine with…hope. No one had ever given a flying fuck about them before. No one.

Well, that needed to change. I was a stupid idiot for adding one more thing to my list—and an impossible one at that. There was no way I could safeguard all the Lows in Hel, not when for millions of years demons had been allowed to kill them, to do whatever they wanted to them, without any penalty. If I was going to do this, I needed to be able to enforce it. I needed to have the status and strength to rule. Every demon in Hel needed to know that what I said went, and they needed to fear for their lives if they crossed me.

I didn't have that kind of power. I didn't have that kind of mojo. All I had was some black feathered wings, an apparently bottomless energy storage capacity, the unsavory inclination to devour, and an unreliable ceremonial sword that could kill just about any demon in Hel if it bothered to show up and act as a lethal weapon instead of a petunia or hairbrush.

"I want to know if Lows are being killed. Any Lows. Because this bullshit needs to stop right now."

I'd expected cheers, not this wide-eyed silence.

"Welp, it's been nice knowing you, Mistress," Snot told me. "Can I have your chicken wand when you die?"

Hopefully I wasn't going to die. "No. Now everybody party. I've got a few things I need to do in Dis, and I want you all out and working on my extra-special top-secret project at first light tomorrow. Got it?"

That resulted in cheers. My Lows ran off to pull together food and drink as they loudly discussed which party games they should play. I think pin-the-durft-on-the-Low was getting top votes. It was a shame I was going to miss it because there were few things in life quite as amusing as one Low trying to impale a furry, ferocious durft onto the ass of another Low.

It sucked. Me and my big mouth. I was going to miss all the fun, as usual. With a reluctant glance at the bowls of beaks, beakers of blood-wine, and the durft someone had pulled from a cage, I turned to go and felt a tug on my arm.

"Mistress, I have someone I want you to meet." Snip looked at me nervously, as if he wasn't sure I was going to like this person-of-interest.

"Can it wait?" I really needed to get to Dis and put the stop on this poaching of my household members, meet with Criam, then go back to the other side of the gates.

"You said it was important, Mistress. I know you're busy, but I think I found Samael."

CHAPTER 8

*E*verything else slid to the bottom of my to-do list. I hadn't had a lead on Gregory's youngest brother since I'd sent my Lows to searching for him. Like Harkel and everyone else, I'd begun to think he was dead.

"Where is he?" If I could find Samael…all these visions of happy family reunions ran through my head.

"Outside." Snip darted through the crowd of partying Lows and out the front door, while I followed at a slower pace, thinking how I should introduce myself to Gregory's brother. *Hi, I've got your Iblis sword and I'm banging your eldest brother, the one who nearly killed you and banished you.* No, that wouldn't work. *Hi, I'm an imp and things have changed a lot in two-and-a-half-million years and I want to smooth things over between you and your brothers.*

Ugh. I'd dreamed of this day, but now my hands were sweaty with worry that things weren't going to go the way I'd been envisioning.

Just outside the front door, Snip stood with another Low. He was ugly. Well, both of them were ugly, but I'd gotten used to Snip's kind of ugly. This guy had bulging eyes that looked like he was perpetually astonished. He was short, fat, balding with a comb-over of greasy brown hair, and was staring as he picked at his cuticles.

"This is Gimlet," Snip announced.

Who the fuck was Gimlet? Was Snip introducing me to his date, a prospective household member, or a new playtoy? I was never really sure when it came to the Lows in my household. And where was Samael? I thought Snip had said he'd found the former Iblis and that he was outside my house.

"I know where he is," Gimlet told me. "Well, maybe I know where he is. Sort of. Because I kinda maybe saw him once. Or twice. Maybe."

I turned to Snip, because of all the Lows I'd met in my nine hundred some years, he was the most coherent.

"He says he knows that Samael Ancient you're looking for," Snip said. "And if Gimlet knows something, he knows something. He's that kinda Low."

So Samael wasn't on my front porch, but I was one step from finding him. I jerked my face around to Gimlet so fast that I nearly gave myself whiplash. His bulbous eyes widened, and he took a precautionary step backward.

"You know him?" It was more a demand than a question. "*The* Samael? Not just some idiot who included that in one of his dozen names? He's an Ancient. He led the war against Aaru two-and-a-half-million years ago. He used to carry the sword. This sword."

I summoned it from the ether, and for once the damned thing appeared obediently, although it was a knitting needle instead of a sword this time—one of those big-ass knitting needles that can whip up a scarf in two seconds. If it hadn't been aluminum, it could have doubled as a fencing foil.

Gimlet squealed and shielded his eyes. "Put it away! Put it away!"

DEBRA DUNBAR

I put it away. It wasn't like I needed a knitting needle right now anyway.

"Yes!" the Low continued. "This guy is an Ancient. Samael. He's a mighty and powerful being, the Ancient who lead the Angels of Chaos during the war. He can tell the good and bad deeds of every human in the world."

That last part kinda made sense. I wouldn't have expected that Gregory's younger brother would be a lightweight. I'll admit to being a bit jealous about the good and bad detection skill. It would make my job of ridding the world...I mean *reforming* humans with crappy credit scores a whole lot easier if I didn't have to turn to Equifax fifty times a day. Sounded like the guy I was looking for, but all the Ancients were mighty and powerful beings, and there might be one or two that had these superskills.

"Are you sure? *The* Samael, not just some general or prince or something? He was the Iblis before me."

Gimlet nodded enthusiastically. "That's him. He has enslaved a group of elves to work night and day for him in a cold dungeon where they cannot escape. It's always winter there, and the ones who try freeze to death."

How the fuck had Samael gotten away with that? The elves would have gone on the warpath if there was a demon snatching them up and enslaving them. It's not like that sort of activity could be done all sneaky-like. Elves were gonna notice if Uncle Hank went missing one day. That was pretty fucking impressive, but even more remarkable was the skill Samael must have in environmental manipulation to create an endless winter in the middle of Hel. Even up in the mountains there wasn't more than a patch of snow here or there, and those spots were in Dwarven territories. Dwarves were not going to put up with an ancient demon running a sweatshop full of elves on top of one of their mountains. And I don't care how powerful Samael

82

was, he wouldn't prevail against thousands of pissed-off dwarves.

"Are you *sure*?" I asked Gimlet. "How cold are we talking here? Subzero? Or like maybe fifty degrees with a brisk wind? And how many elves? Five? Two?"

"Hundreds. And the snow never melts, so it's really cold."

Huh. "So where is he? Can you lead me to him?"

"He's very fat, but can shrink his belly to wedge himself into small spaces," Gimlet told me. From the look of rapture on his face, I could tell I wasn't going to get my questions answered until he finished his description.

"Eyes like glowing coals?" I asked. "Black feathery wings?" The fat thing kinda threw me. These archangels liked to manifest into a worshipfully beautiful physical form, but Samael was the contrary one. Could be that he decided to truly rebel and be a fat dude.

"No." Gimlet scowled at me for interrupting his spiel. "In spite of his girth, he's lively and quick. His eyes twinkle, and he has dimples."

Weird. He actually sounded cute aside from the fat part. Maybe if I could get Samael to get on the treadmill a few times per week...

"His cheeks are like roses, and his nose is like a cherry, and his mouth turns up like a bow, and his beard is white as snow."

Wait. What the fuck?

"He has a broad face and a round belly that shakes when he laughs like a bowl full of jelly."

"That's fucking Santa Claus, you moron," I shouted. I was going to kill this Low. And then I was going to kill Snip for bringing me this Low.

"That's one of his many names." Gimlet waved his hands in front of his face as if he were trying to conjure something. "Santa is an anagram for Satan, after all."

"So I'm assuming you want to join my household?" Of course he did. That's probably why he made up this crazy Samael-as-Santa scheme. Lows tended to gravitate toward my household, and with a kidnapper on the loose, this Gimlet probably wanted to be somewhere safe.

"No," he scoffed. "I don't need to be in anyone's household. And I certainly don't want to be in yours. An imp. Yuck. I'd rather jump into an active volcano."

The little jerk didn't have to disparage me like that, but his loss. I secretly hoped that this kidnapper took him next. But just in case there was a thread of truth in his improbable story...

"So where is this Santa Samael?"

"Told you. North. Where all the snow is, cracking a whip over those elves so they get all the toys made in time. Say what you will about the guy, Samael always keeps his word. If he vows to deliver toys on a certain day, it's gonna happen."

This was ridiculous. "Well, thank you very much, Gimlet. I'm sure I'll see you around. Feel free to join in the festivities going on inside. Eat some roast beaks. Throw some poisoned darts at Poo-poo. Have a ball."

He skipped inside eagerly. I grabbed Snip as he made to follow his friend. "Walk with me a bit, would you?"

He grinned and happily fell in beside me. "Did I do well, Mistress? You have been looking for this Samael for a long time. I'm glad I finally found him for you. I should have known to ask Gimlet, because he knows everyone and everything in Hel. Of course, sometimes he's not easy to find. He told me that he fell into a hole one time and couldn't get out for three months until someone came along with a rope. That's a problem when you're short. He had to eat a lot of worms to survive."

"Snip, he's an idiot. You can't just bring me any random

demon who claims to know Samael without doing a bit of checking first. I mean, Santa? Really?"

The Low shrugged. "Gimlet does lie a lot, but I got the feeling he really does know Samael. Why don't you go see Santa just to be sure? You'd recognize this Samael if you saw him, right? I wouldn't, so I figured you'd be wanting to check it out yourself."

I opened my mouth to argue only to snap it shut again. *Would* I recognize Samael? I'd assumed he'd either be like the other Ancients, sort of decayed and rotted looking in his demon form with an oppressively huge energy signature, or he'd be a gorgeous hunk, just like the other archangels. Charming. Suave. A powerful demon whose very presence drew others irresistibly toward him. He'd be like the Pied Piper of demons. And his spirit-self would be horribly scarred from the battle with his eldest brother, but then again, who among us *wasn't* horribly scarred? My spirit-self was a mess. Even Snip looked like he'd had a few trips through a chipper shredder.

"How about you tell Gimlet to convince Santa Samael to come visit me instead?" I compromised, unwilling to go haring all over Hel with an ugly, crazy Low looking for a fat guy in a red suit.

"Gimlet says he's never where you expect him to be, but he's always listening," Snip replied. "So maybe you can just shout that you want him to come visit you?"

This was ridiculous. "Snip, who the fuck is this Gimlet? I've never seen him before, but you act like he's some kind of Low celebrity."

"Well, he kind of is. He's very lucky, although not always lucky because he's just as scarred as I am, so clearly he's been a play toy for a lot of demons in his life. Sometimes he stays in the abandoned buildings in Dis with the other unaffiliated Lows, but he travels a lot."

So, he was pretty much just like any other Low. "How old is he?" I asked, figuring that he probably grew up with Snip.

"Two."

I waited, but Snip didn't elaborate. "Two what? Years? Decades? Centuries?" He couldn't be two thousand years old, because Lows didn't usually live that long. Besides I couldn't imagine Gimlet being older than me. Although if he was as lucky as Snip claimed, maybe he had managed to avoid death for that long.

"No idea. He always just says he's two. He's older than me, so maybe he means two thousand."

"Or maybe he's not very good at numbers," I added drily.

"Could be. I think he can only count to two."

Great. And this was my only lead on Samael. Well, an idiot Low who could only count to two and thought Santa Claus was a banished archangel was better than nothing. "Keep him around, will you? Bribe him with some beaks or the promise of a chicken wand or something. Just don't let him slip away. I don't want him to go a-traveling just in case the guy actually does know where Samael is and suddenly remembers in the next week or so."

Snip saluted me and turned to jog back to my house, where I was sure he would keep a tight watch on my newest Low, the only one who didn't seem to want to join my household. I watched him for a seconds, then teleported away.

To Dis. To see a couple of demons about my missing Lows then to see an Ancient about a plot to take Aaru.

CHAPTER 9

I made sure to stroll down the main street of Dis as I headed to my empty house, past the blocks that were lined with the homes of the Ancients. Past the more modest homes, and the run-down flop houses that the Lows tended to live in. Reaching the edge of town, I turned around and walked back down another street, through the merchant area, past Gareth's shop with its layers upon layers of wards. I made sure everyone saw me with my big-ass wings out. I even summoned my sword and carried it prominently, whirling it around my head as if I were part of a high school color guard team.

I was trying to make a statement, a show of power, but from the attitudes of the demons who were watching me, I think the statement I was making was that I was a complete idiot, an imp who had gotten lucky, or unlucky depending on how one looked at it, and managed to attach herself to a powerful sentient object that no one else wanted.

I went through my home, quickly making sure that no one had robbed it while it had been left unattended, then I stood on the front porch where Lash had been taken and felt for the Low's energy. It was faint, but still there. I quickly sorted out the traces of energy from the rest of my household and through the process of elimination, identified Oor's and Cheros's energy signatures. It wasn't all that difficult. My household consisted almost entirely of Lows, so the two mid-level demons were easy to detect. It wouldn't have been easier if they'd taken pictures of themselves and stapled them to the floorboards.

Flipping my sword around in a circle, I jumped off the porch and strode down the street toward Oor's house. I figured I'd confront him first, since at least I knew where he lived. There were a few demons milling around outside, one of them burning holes into the bushes that dotted the sand-and-rock lawn.

"Hey," I shouted. "Looking for Oor."

It would have been more badass to just mow these demons down and plow through the front door like a steam-roller, but I didn't want to waste my energy fighting these guys if I didn't have to.

"Fuck off," the pyro shouted back.

Guess I was going to have to force my way in after all. I pushed open the gate with my sword, the electrical shock muted by my magical weapon to a merely unpleasant tingle. Then I walked up to the pyro and punched him in the face.

The other demons hooted and lined up to watch. It was telling that none of them came to their buddy's defense. Either they didn't care if he got his ass kicked, or they didn't think I was enough of a threat to actually be delivering an ass kicking.

The punch that he returned told me it was most likely the latter. I went back on my ass, the dust cloud from my fall extinguishing the sparks in my hair. Asshole had not only hit me, but set me on fire as well. I stood and swung my sword, not hesitating to use lethal force.

My sword had other ideas. Yes, it knocked the guy's head to the side, cracking one of the six horns on his head. Yes, I saw a nice amount of blood coming from said horn and from his snout. No, it didn't kill him, or even knock him out.

He recovered quickly and went to grab my sword, only to find his fingers passing right through the blade. I swung it again, and it became solid with just enough time to break that cracked horn right off the top of the guy's head. He let out a howl and dropped to his knees, one hand coming up to feel the stump where the horn had once been. Taking advantage of his distress, I walloped him twice more with my sword. Then once more for good measure once he was face-down in the sand at my feet, not moving.

"Next!" I shouted.

One of the guys on the porch pointed to the door. "You made it past Chin, you can enter," He laughed. "Oor is in the third room on the right. You a friend of his?"

"Not in this lifetime," I replied, climbing the steps and pushing through the door.

The door made a loud creak noise, hanging crooked on its hinges as it swung open. The foyer area had a grayish rug with some questionable-looking stain on it. The stone walls were pockmarked and had lewd stick-figure drawings all over them. The doorway leading down the hall had clearly been regularly used for gnawing and sharpening tusks and claws. I felt something cold drip onto my head and looked up to see blobs of spit on the ceiling. This house was a dump. Still, it was better than Ahrimans' had been when I'd acquired them. I'd yet to see any dead bodies or furniture made from bones and demon-skins.

I counted three doorways and stood in the opening, looking at the demon inside. Oor was bipedal with short tree-trunk thick legs that ended in stubby feet with long yellowed claws that clacked as he tapped them. He had four arms, longer than the legs and thinner, also ending in those long yellowed claws. He turned to face me, his hair like Medusa snakes swaying with a life of their own. He had tiny little eyes, nostril slits for a nose, and a mouth that pointed outward like a broad beak.

"Who the fuck are you?" he snarled.

"I'm the Iblis, and I'm here to discuss some missing members of my household."

He looked up and spat, making me realize where the ceiling decorations in the foyer had come from. "Do I look like someone you hire to investigate missing household members? Because that's not something I do. Now get the fuck out of my house."

"Three Lows were taken from my household." I stepped into the room. "Now some people might not give a shit about Lows, but I'm rather possessive when it comes to mine."

"Ain't got em'."

"I know you don't 'got em'." I rolled my eyes. "You were there during the kidnapping—you and this Cheros demon. I just want to know where you took them so I can go and retrieve my Lows."

"Kidnapping?" He snorted. "Who the fuck kidnaps Lows? There's nobody to ransom them. Lows are fair game. Just grab them off the street, and go have some fun. It's like a smorgasbord."

"Well the smorgasbord doesn't include Lows that I've marked as part of my household, you sack of dicks. Take mine, and feel my wrath."

He nearly fell over laughing at that, so I summoned my sword. Evidently he couldn't see my impressive weaponry through the haze of hilarity, so I poked him in the belly. His skin puckered and blistered, but the blade didn't penetrate the skin.

"Hey! What the fuck? You're cruising for some serious smackdown, assaulting me in my own home, imp."

I'd had it. There were zero fucks left for me to give. Outside of Doriel and her household, no one in Hel took me seriously. There was a time when being discounted and underestimated was very useful, but that time had passed. I was done wasting time trying to prove I was someone who should be, if not feared, at least respected.

"I'm the Iblis, you motherfucker! You took three members of my household," I yelled. "You took what is mine, and when I muster up the considerable patience to stand here and calmly demand information, you laugh at me. Tell me right fucking now where my fucking Lows are, or I will skin you, slice the guts from your belly, and dump your weighted body in the Maugan Swamp for the bitey fish to feast on."

Just to illustrate how very serious I was, I jammed my sword into the floor. The sound of thunder rumbled through the house and an eight-inch crack shot where the blade impacted the stone. I stumbled as my sword sank through the hole, quickly gaining my balance and trying to regain some semblance of badassery.

"Okay, okay." Oor held his hands palms-out toward me. "Just don't fucking destroy my house. I don't have your Lows. I didn't even take them. Some dude named Birch hired me to watch Cheros, just to make sure she wasn't skimming off the top—you know?"

No, I didn't know. "Why does this Birch care about Cheros skimming, and what does that have to do with my Lows?"

He eyed my sword. Deciding that I'd made my point, I dismissed it.

"Cheros takes Lows. She likes them, so she takes them, plays with them, and lets them go when she's done."

"Yeah, I already know that." I made a rolling motion with my hand to hustle the story along.

"Evidently she has a reputation for Low-catching, so someone hired her to catch him or her some Lows. I don't know who, but seems she was claiming she was delivering more than she did and keeping a few. Skimming, you know."

That sort of thing got a demon killed. Cheros must be of more value alive than dead for someone to overlook this sort of betrayal and violation of a contractual agreement. Either that, or whoever hired Cheros didn't feel confident that they'd win in a fight with her, and graciously forgave the behavior with a stern warning.

"So I'm assuming that Birch is the one who hired Cheros to get him some Lows? Then this Birch hired you to make sure she actually delivers as promised?"

Oor scratched the spot of skin between the spikes jutting from his forehead. "Don't think so. Birch isn't very powerful, and he seems to think Lows are kind of yucky. Maybe he's the Low-collector's steward? Or in his household? I got the feeling that whoever wants them doesn't like to deal with any of us directly."

Ugh. That worried me. That sort of behavior sounded like something an Ancient or high-level demon would do, and as much as I wanted my Lows back, I really didn't want to have to get into a life-or-death fight for them.

"So Birch pays you, and he pays Cheros when she delivers the Lows?"

"Yeah."

"Well, she's got to deliver them somewhere, doesn't she? Where does she take them? Does she do the hand off with Birch in the middle of the street?"

"No idea. Ask her."

I thought about stabbing more holes in his floor to help jog his memory. As if he read my mind, Oor backed up a few steps. "I swear I don't know. I just go with her when she grabs the Lows, then she takes it from there. Her house is three streets down, turn left, first house on your right. Go ask her 'cause I don't know anything else."

I summoned my sword once more, just for effect. "If I find out that you're lying, I'm coming back, and your floor won't be the only thing with a six-inch crack running down the length of it. Understand?"

He nodded frantically. "Yes, Iblis. I understand."

I headed out past his buddies on the porch who eyed me warily, then followed Oor's directions to Cheros's house. The sword stayed out because it had been very cooperative lately and I didn't want to push it. I never knew what it would appear as, and I'd discovered that repeated summoning in a short time period tended to piss it off. I was trying to build some street cred here, and having my sword fail to appear, or show up as a butter knife wouldn't help my cause at all.

I climbed the steps of the first house on my right and banged on the door with the pommel of my sword, noting that Cheros didn't have any physical or magical barriers in place to prevent entry. She was either really confident in her ability to take care of intruders, or she didn't give a shit if anyone snuck in and trashed the place or stole her furnishings.

A tall, thin demon with rough leathery skin and compound eyes answered the door. "Yeah?"

"You Cheros?"

Her eyes zeroed in on my sword. "Who wants to know?"

"The Iblis. I'm looking for some Lows."

She grinned. "Well, you've come to the right place, then! If you want a Low for the evening's entertainment, Cheros is the demon you want to hire. She can get any Low to suit your needs, and deliver promptly."

"That's not what I heard." I wasn't about to correct this

woman regarding the purpose of my visit, but I couldn't help the dig about Cheros's habit of skimming.

Her narrowed bug-eyes jerked to my face, then back to my sword. "Well, you heard wrong. Cheros is out right now on business, but she'll be back soon if you'd like to wait...and keep your sword outside."

The sword in question was glowing and sizzling, so I understood her reluctance to allow it past the doorway. "Business? For that Birch guy?"

"Uh, he's a client." Bug-eyes was clearly not sure whether Birch was a reference she should leverage on behalf of her mistress or not.

"Is Cheros out getting Lows?" I demanded. Mine were all safely in Patchine. I thought. Hopefully they were safely in Patchine, but I got the weird feeling I should accost Cheros in the middle of her business, just in case.

"She'll be back soon, if you want to wait inside—without your sword. She's just picking up some product a few streets over—"

I spun around and headed back down the street, forgetting to ask her what Cheros looked like, or exactly which street she was picking up her "product" on. Product. It pissed me off that she was referring to Lows as product. All my life I'd been one step above a Low, degraded and mocked, spat upon and kicked around. I'd turned that around to my advantage. I'd learned that power and energy signature weren't always the best indicators of a demon's—or angel's—ability. And I hated that the Lows I'd found to be loyal, gutsy, and brave were treated as "product".

I was going to find this Cheros. And when I did, I was going to make her return Sinew, Booty, and Lash, or I was going to make sure every demon in Dis knew the folly of fucking around with those the Iblis called her own.

CHAPTER 10

$\mathscr{I}$ wasn't a block away when I saw her dragging a screaming and thrashing Low by the tail as she strode down the street. Cheros was small with shiny green scales on an upright-lizard body. Her eagle's head had scales instead of feathers, and a whip of a tail curled up from her ass. Since she wasn't with Oor, I figured this Low she was hauling along must be for herself or a different client.

I walked up and stopped about fifteen feet in front of the demon. "Drop the Low," I commanded.

She ignored me so I waved my sword in her general direction and repeated myself. Then I slammed it into the ground with both hands. I'd expected that the ground would quake, my voice would echo menacingly, bushes would burn and fire would rain from the sky. Instead all that happened was the tip of my sword broke off, clattering across the uneven pavement.

Guess I'd pushed my sentient weapon too far.

"I hate you," I told the sword. Stupid fucking thing wasn't really broken. I wasn't sure if it was protesting my treatment with this lame-ass display of weakness, or if it didn't really give a shit about my mission here. Probably a combination of both.

"Out of my way, imp," Cheros commanded. Her voice didn't echo either, so I felt a bit better about the whole thing.

"Let the Low go." The rhyming wasn't making me seem any tougher, so I waved my broken sword at her. It was still glowing and sizzling, and I hoped that the jagged edge still looked dangerous.

She stopped, eyeing the weapon. "Fine. I'll share him with you, but only because I like imps. You guys are pretty creative. Could be fun to share a Low with an imp."

I put the sword away. "Look, I've got a lot of Lows in my household. You took three of them, and I'm pissed. I don't want to share this one with you. I want you to let him go and tell me what the fuck happened to my three. And stop taking Lows that have my household mark, or I'll kill you."

"You can't kill me." She laughed. "You're an imp. Granted, you've got a scary-ass broken sword there, but you're still an imp."

"I killed Haagenti. I killed Ahriman. I just killed a fuck-ton of angels in Aaru. I'm the Iblis. And I'm sure I can take you out without either breaking a sweat, or using my sword."

She eyed me. "You're that crazy bitch that's fucking an angel and thinks she's the ruler of Hel. The one who devours."

"Yeah. That's me. Now let him go, and tell me what you did with my Lows. I want them back. Sinew, Booty, and Lash. They had household marks. They're mine."

Cheros dropped the Low, who scampered off, then she waved at me. "Come on. I really don't feel like standing in the middle of the street arguing with a crazy imp."

I followed her to the edge of town and into a squat stone dwelling. This wasn't the house I'd just been to. Maybe she had a second? Although why someone would need two houses in Dis was beyond me.

I knew the moment I got inside that it wasn't a house, it was a torture chamber. Racks, spikes, whips, paddles with nails embedded in them.

"And you're calling me crazy?" I fingered one of the paddles, noting the buildup of dried blood on the nails.

"Hey, a girl's gotta have her hobbies." She hopped up on one of the stools, her scaled feet dangling just above the cuffs. "There's this Ancient, see? He's one of the ones who just woke up a year or so ago, and I guess he's got similar interests to mine. He's paying me to bring him a bunch of Lows. I don't know why all of a sudden he wants them. Maybe he's bored, or he suddenly has a taste for Lows or something. All I know is he pays me for each one I bring him."

"Birch, right?"

She blinked in surprise. "Well, Birch pays me, but he's not the Ancient who wants the Lows. I don't think Birch wants any Lows. He's kind of a prude."

"And Birch also pays Oor on behalf of this Ancient, right? To make sure the Lows actually get to him?"

She looked sheepish for a second. "I liked a few of them and kept some for myself, so he wasn't getting as many or the ones he wanted."

Weirdo.

"Why not just fire you and let Oor bring him the Lows?"

"Because Oor couldn't catch a Low if his life depended on it. They're quick and clever and he's not. I know how to grab them and bring them in in one piece. Oor keeps me focused on the task at hand."

"So this unnamed Ancient has my Lows? I want them back."

She chuckled. "Well, you're probably not getting them

back. They're gone. Probably dead. Just forget about them, and get some new ones."

My stomach twisted at the thought. I honestly didn't have a huge attachment to Sinew, Booty, or Lash, but the thought that someone casually took what was mine, as well as the insinuation that one Low was easily interchanged with another, bothered me.

I'd find them, alive or dead, and I'd punish whoever harmed them, but in the meantime I needed to ensure that the rest of my household was safe.

"From this point forward, you will not take any Lows that bear my household mark. Do I make myself clear?"

She shrugged. "Yes, but I go where the money is. If my client asks for a specific Low and offers an enticing fee, I'm gonna grab the Low, no matter whose household mark it's got."

Clearly there was only way to counter this, since I wasn't sure I could depend on my sword right now.

"How much is this Ancient paying you?"

"More than you can afford." She sniffed. "I can't quit. If he asks me for a specific Low, I need to deliver, although most of the time he's kind of vague about what he wants. If I don't do what he wants, he'll kill me. It's not just the money, we've got a contract. I'm lucky he didn't kill me when I kept those other Lows. I'm not about to push him by quitting or refusing to get certain Lows for him."

I was beginning to wonder about something. "Why does he care if you keep a few as long as you get him his quota? I mean, he shouldn't care if you divert a Low you really like and just substitute another."

She squirmed on the stool. "There are some that are hard to let go. I kinda get attached to one every now and then. Some of them just call to me and I want them for my own. My whole life I've been playing with Lows, I never found

98

clients that specifically target this one or that. Shit, *I* don't even know their names when I keep them for myself. Most of them all kinda look the same, and clients before never cared if I swapped out one Low for a different one."

"But you said the ones you kept were especially appealing?"

"Yeah. Some have that spark, you know? They fight harder and scream louder and it's so much more satisfying to hurt them. And those ones don't die easy, so I can really do some fun stuff and keep them for longer."

I didn't want to think about what Sinew, Booty, and Lash might be going through right now. And my Lows had claimed that Cheros wasn't all that bad. How horrible were the other demons, when being tortured while you fought and screamed, brought to the point of death before being let go, was 'not that bad'?

"And those were the ones this Ancient client asked for by name?"

"Oh of course. I thought maybe he wouldn't know, but he did. This guy is pretty smart that way."

I had a bad feeling about this. "And he asked for my Lows by name? He specified them?"

"Mostly he just gives me a list of attributes, but a few times he's specified certain Lows. And I take them, whether they have a household mark or not. Not that many are marked, or even part of a household." She shook her head in disbelief. "*You* have Lows that you actually mark as part of your household? As important play toys, right? So none of your other household members break them? Because I didn't steal any Lows out of anyone's dungeon."

"Two of my Lows you took off the street, and one you dragged away from my porch. They're marked. They're part of my household. I marked them. How the fuck did you not notice that I fucking *marked* them." I was starting to get pissed off at her obvious attempts to play dumb. They were marked. How the fuck could she take Lows and not notice they were marked? Idiot.

Her dark eyes bulged. "Why? Why would you bother to mark your Lows? You give them status in your household? Fuck, you must be really hurting to have to turn to Lows to join your household. Won't anyone else join? What happened that no one wants to be in your household?"

I winced, remembering all the demons I'd gotten killed in the elven wars. Life expectancy wasn't all that stellar for my household members. It was still a longer life expectancy than Lows had on the streets or elsewhere, which is probably why they flocked to me, but outside of joining me for a few special projects, the only mid-level demons I had were Dar and Leethu and Terrelle, and now Mestal. They were all on the other side of the gates. At least, I thought Leethu was on the other side of the gates. Where the fuck was she anyway? If she didn't turn up soon, I was going to need to track down this sorcerer who kept summoning her and kill him myself.

"Oh no, I have hundreds of non-Low demons in my household," I lied. "They're all across the gates because members of my household get immunity from the treaty."

"The angels won't kill them?" She tilted her head in thought. "Humans are more fun to play with than Lows. Got any openings in your household?"

"You kill a human, and you lose your immunity," I warned her.

"Oh I don't kill them. I just play." Her stare was downright creepy.

"That's a gray area. It still might get you killed. And I'm not doing a fucking two-hundred-page report to get you out of trouble either."

She tilted her head and clacked her beak. "I'll take my chances. Ten years in your household?"

"Big rules. Number one: You can't mess with my Lows," I warned her. "I don't care who your clients are, but you don't take my Lows. And if you cross the gates and get caught torturing humans, I don't know you."

She nodded. "Sounds good."

"You work for me. That means you help me find Sinew, Booty, and Lash. And if this asshole demon wants you to take any of my Lows, you come to me and tell me. You do not, under any circumstances, give him any demon who is part of my household, Low or not."

She nodded. "Got it. Deal, although as a member of your household, you need to defend me against charges of contract infringement and take on any punishment I might incur."

Household bonds were considered above any contracts such as the one she had to supply Lows to this Ancient. I felt fairly confident I'd win this argument, and I planned on facing down this guy anyway and getting my Lows back.

"Done. What's this Ancient's name who wants the Lows?"

"Tasma."

Huh. I'd never heard of him. Although if he'd been slumbering up until the last year or so, I probably wouldn't have ever heard of him.

"And the Lows he named, were they marked?" I asked.

"Yeah. I thought maybe it was an accident, or someone's sick joke or something, so I ignored it. Birch gave me their names. The first two I took on my own and kept, but he found out and...I got punished and I got Oor as a minder. Those were the ones called Sinew and Booty. I had to turn those two over to him, even though they were kinda broken already. He didn't seem to mind, thankfully. And when I took the one off the porch, the Lash Low, Oor made sure I didn't keep him." She licked her lips. "You've got some nice Lows in your household. Sly and spunky. They scream real nice too."

"No hurting my Lows," I reminded her. "No hurting or kidnapping any of my Lows. That's the deal."

She did something with her beak that looked like a pout. "Fine. I don't know why you bother to keep them in your household if you don't want to play with them, but that's your business not mine."

We exchanged vows with all the appropriate words and formality, then I fixed Cheros with a hard stare. "I want them back. I need you to get all cozy with this Birch who is your contact and find out where Tasma is keeping my Lows. Then I need you to figure out how I can get in there and free my three Lows with minimal damage to myself. Got it?"

She hesitated. "It might take me a bit. I'm supposed to meet with Birch tonight, but once I find out where they are, it might take me a day or two to figure out a way you can get them."

I worried that my three Lows might not have a lot of time. "You've got three days. If you don't have anything for me by then, you'll find yourself in my dungeon for a couple of decades."

The demon squirmed. "Okay, but this would be a whole lot easier if you could just charge in with that weird sword of yours and rescue your Lows that way. Why does it have to be all stealthy-like? Why are you worried about damage to yourself? I thought you were the Iblis."

I tried to look badass. "Because I'm a different kind of Iblis. I'm the sneaky, stealthy Iblis. And charging in is my last resort." I might be the Iblis, but I was still an imp. And even though I could devour, hold a shit-ton of energy, and exist inside a deceased physical form, I wasn't exactly the type to charge into a household of powerful demons and muscle my way through a rescue.

"Then I'll do my best." Cheros rubbed her scaled hands

together. "So...when do I get to cross the gates? Now? Next week?"

"As soon as I get my Lows back," I replied.

"Do you have a place I can crash there, or do I need to do one of those home invasion things, tie the owners up in the basement, and take their house?"

I was so going to regret this. "I have a home with a separate building for my demons to stay in when they're over. Just don't mess with any of my Lows. Or my human household members. Or the angels that come and go, or the werewolves, or the Nephilim. Oh, and there's a dragon. Just an FYI."

She squawked in excitement. "This. Is. Awesome. I've never met a dragon before. Or a werewolf. Or a Nephilim. And of course I've never met an angel, because if I had, I'd be dead. And they won't kill me, right? So I can spit at them and call them names, and they can't hurt me?"

I immediately thought of what Gabriel would do if this demon spat at him. "You might not want to do that. Immunity only extends so far. If you really piss one off, he'll decide the paperwork and the punishment is worth killing you."

"Okay. No spitting and no calling names. Got it."

"And before you're allowed to cross the gates on my dime, I need my Lows back. No Lows, no vacation. Got it?"

She gave me a thumbs up and clacked her beak. "Got it."

CHAPTER 11

*D*oriel's residence was a good walk outside of Dis. It wasn't difficult to spot because it was a forest in the middle of the desert. This dense grouping of trees wasn't anything like the elven forests. Twisted black-barked trees stretched over a hundred feet tall. Barren of any leaves, their branches twisted together, a matted impenetrable mass of twigs and vines that made access impossible. There was no path, no gate, no doorbell. I paced back and forth in front of the forest's edge, calling out and knocking on tree trunks that were strangely warm under my knuckles.

The forest shivered then parted, a narrow path revealed in the moonlight. I seriously considered summoning my sword, but I had an appointment. It seemed rude to enter while holding a weapon. Actually it seemed weak. My take-charge-of-Hel plan relied heavily on waving my sword around to assert my dominance, but in my heart I knew that wouldn't work. Only a pathetic weakling would run around, shoving a powerful sentient weapon in everyone's face as proof of their power. The truly powerful were confident, knowing they had mastery of every situation and didn't need to be clutching a sword like a lifeline to pass through a weird-ass forest and face a powerful Ancient.

I wasn't powerful, but I needed to start pretending I was, so I shoved my hands in my pockets and headed down the path.

The moon only lit the first few feet, and that quickly disappeared as the forest closed in behind me. I walked blind, trusting that the woods would somehow guide me to the house, but well aware that if I wasn't welcome here, I'd spend the rest of my short life stumbling around in a pitch-black maze, or entangled in vines and twigs. The good thing about the darkness was that I couldn't see any remains of those foolish enough to head in here uninvited.

The walk felt like hours, and I was beginning to wonder if Snip had been deceived, if Criam hadn't remembered me and decided this would be a good way to get rid of a troublesome imp. I had enemies. Perhaps one of them had paid Criam to make sure I never came out of this forest.

No. I talked myself away from the edge of panic. Doriel was the type of Ancient who would tell someone to fuck off rather than kill me under contract, and I knew that Criam would never jeopardize his position in the household by using his mistress's forest in an unsanctioned manner. I relaxed and kept putting one foot in front of the other, figuring at the worst I was getting a decent workout. It was like being on a treadmill. For hours. In the dark.

I tripped on something and stumbled, managing to stay on my feet. When I regained my balance and looked up, the trees had parted. The anemic moonlight was practically blinding after hours in the dark, and I squinted, exiting the forest and looking across an expanse of gray lawn to a tiny shed.

The Ancients I'd met in the past were either like Harkel, making the best of their situation and going about life in Hel with a certain fatalistic air, or like Ahriman, twisted and cruel with the need to grind everyone they saw under their fiery heel. Doriel was reputed to be one of the most powerful Ancients in Hel, and instead of flaunting her status with an elaborate display, she disguised her home like something humans would use to store their lawn mower and gardening tools, and hid the whole thing in the safety of a forest.

She hid. And I was guessing it wasn't because she feared anyone, but because she wanted to be left alone. Even before she'd slumbered, she was rarely seen, sending members of her household out to do her bidding. And even they were stealthy and careful to avoid bringing notice to themselves. That was how I'd met Criam. I had no idea what errand he'd been on for his mistress when the troll incident had occurred, but throughout it all he'd never bragged about his household affiliation or arrogantly demanded I serve him.

I walked up the wooden steps, and tapped lightly on the door of the shed before opening it and stepping inside. Of course, the inside was huge, bigger even than my house in Dis. Size aside, the inside of Doriel's home was just as sparse and understated as her household.

I stood just inside the door and waited. Most demons had guards outside. Most demons had the equivalent of a butler inside to quickly open the door and direct visitors to a waiting area with refreshments, or kill them depending on the owner's mood. Most demons had visible staff scurrying around. This was a vast empty foyer, the walls a warm shade of cream with royal blue scrollwork along the crown molding. There wasn't a stick of furniture or artwork in sight. I resisted the urge to shout "hello" and remained silent, my hands clasped before me.

My instincts for once were right. After waiting for a second shy of disrespect, a demon appeared at the end of the foyer and walked toward me.

I recognized Criam right away. He hadn't changed one bit and was still in the gaunt human form he'd worn during the troll incident. Dude looked like a plague victim who'd been cleaned up and stuck in a poorly fitting suit for burial. His sparse blond hair was combed over a bald spot the size of Rhode Island, dipping low and plastered to a pale forehead. He was thin to the point of being skin stretched over bones, his eyes sunken in dark hollows, his lips a narrow, bloodless slash below a long hooked nose. He looked like a good breeze would send him tumbling.

Looks were deceiving. In keeping with his mistress's low-profile habits, Criam exuded no energy signature whatsoever. If I hadn't known better, I would have thought him an animated corpse, a human. That alone had made me realize how incredibly powerful this demon was. I had this skill as well, the ability to lock down my energy signature so tightly that it was virtually undetectable. It was a rare skill in those who weren't Ancients. It was an even rarer skill in demons who were less than a million years old.

"Criam." I inclined my head respectfully. "Thank you for arranging this meeting. You're looking well."

He wasn't from a visual standpoint, but from a demon point of view, he did look well. The awakening of his mistress had put a spark of purpose in those dark eyes and an eager, fevered flush to the waxy, pale skin.

"And you..." Criam tilted his head as he regarded me. "Even more the imp than before, but I detect a latent power similar to that of my mistress."

"Devouring part of an archangel does that," I confessed. "They're telling me I'm an Angel of Chaos now, but I still feel like an imp. Although I'm not sure how an Angel of Chaos is supposed to feel."

A meagre eyebrow twitched, as did the corner of his nearly lipless mouth. "I wouldn't know. You can ask Doriel

107

when you see her. Although she claims that she is no longer an Angel of Chaos, I'm sure she remembers. There's very little my Ancient forgets."

"I appreciate your arranging this," I said again.

He nodded, something close to a smile on his face. "Although we never formalized it, I do believe I owed you a favor. Please come with me and I'll lead you somewhere comfortable with refreshments while you wait. It won't be long. Doriel prides herself on being prompt."

I fell in beside him and we passed through what had been a solid wall seconds ago, into a cozy room with cushioned seating, a huge elven sculpture, and a cheery fire in a stone fireplace.

"How have the centuries been treating you?" I asked Criam, curious as to how life in an Ancient's household went. I was tempted to take notes. "Any more troll issues?"

He grimaced. "Thankfully, no. The last year since Doriel's awakening have been busy for all of us, but particularly for me. I'm sure you're aware of how things in Hel are changing."

"Things everywhere are changing," I told him. "Aaru, Hel, in the human world."

"Well, when the universe gives an imp a sword, change is to be expected." He turned to face me. "When I met you those centuries ago, I had no idea this was what your future held."

"Yeah, me either," I drawled. "You've been around a long time. Got any tips for a young Iblis?"

"Survive?" His lips twitched again. "Although as I recall, that's something you excelled at."

"I'm quite the cockroach," I told him, snatching a roast beak from a marble bowl and popping it into my mouth.

"A cockroach with the Sword of the Iblis." He shook his head. "If I were an angel, I would be praying for the Creator to help us all."

This felt weird. From the moment I'd entered the forest, I

felt like I truly *was* the leader of Hel. And Criam was certainly treating me with the respect due an equal, if not an Ancient. But that was all a sham, a bit of playacting. I was an imp with a sword, and no amount of pretending was going to change that.

"Not that anyone gives a damn about my being the Iblis," I reminded him. Best to get back to familiar footing—me the crazy imp, and him the powerful demon that I just lucked into helping out once a long time ago.

"They *should* give a damn about you being the Iblis if they value their lives," he retorted. "Do you think I have the power to get you an audience for Doriel if she did not wish to meet with you? She is reclusive. She refuses to see most of the Ancients she fought beside long ago. For an imp to gain an audience with her, even on my request, is unheard of." Criam made his way to the door. "Only fools disregard a cockroach of an imp, and the terminally stupid disregard a cockroach of an imp who happens to hold the Sword of the Iblis. Neither Doriel nor I are fools or terminally stupid."

He opened the door, and with a nod of his head, exited, leaving me in this cozy sitting room with the cheerful fire, a bowl of roast beaks, and an elven sculpture of an angel falling from the heavens, her wings ablaze.

CHAPTER 12

I eyed the sculpture, admiring the clean lines and attention to detail that all elven works of art held, then grabbed a handful of beaks and sat in front of the fireplace. I needed a room like this. Ahriman's houses were all decorated like torture chambers and I'd been too busy to do something about that. And my home in the human world had been designed with an open floor plan, not taking into consideration the fact that I'd eventually have angels, demons, humans, and werewolves tromping through it like it was Union Station. There were no private areas like this in which to relax, or have a personal conversation away from the crazy.

I snuggled deep into the comfy chair, sticking a fuzzy pale green pillow behind my head and sighed. Doriel could be as late as she wanted, this was a much-needed break from everything I had to do.

The Iblis. I was the Iblis, and behind my admiration of the décor was the shocking realization that there were demons here, Ancients even, who took me seriously. They might not be lining up to follow me, but Criam's words had given me a much-needed injection of confidence. It was one thing to have Gregory's love and faith in my unusual abilities. It was one thing to have a bunch of adoring Lows lined up to get into my household, to have a gate guardian who relied on me, to have angels, Nephilim, werewolves, and humans who had my back. It was another thing entirely to have a powerful demon from my homeland tell me in so many words that he considered me a force to be respected.

No matter what my achievements, no matter how much admiration I might gain outside Hel, the recognition of the beings I'd grown up around somehow counted more.

I heard the door open and rose from my chair to turn and greet my hostess. Most Ancients would have made a more dramatic entrance, but I was learning that Doriel was far from the typical Ancient.

I liked that since I was far from typical as well.

Doriel was in a human form, her face as pale and poreless as so many of the angels I'd met. Her light golden hair was piled on top of her head, making her appear like a Grecian statue come to life. And under it all, her spirit-self was bruised and bent, with the rot that every Ancient I'd ever met had.

"Iblis." She inclined her head and her wings appeared, scarce tattered golden feathers on a leathery background. One fell as she spread the wings, catching fire and crumbling to ash as it floated to the ground.

"Doriel." I revealed my wings as well, stretching the muscles and noting how my matte black feathers seemed to suck the light from the room.

Her gaze traced the length of my wings, then she crossed the room, dismissing her wings before sitting.

I did the same, feeling like we should have teacups with saucers or something. "Thank you for agreeing to meet with me," I told the Ancient.

Doriel stared at me, a tendril of sulfur smoke curling from her nose. "I don't often grant audiences to demons, but when Criam said you had the Sword of the Iblis, I was curious."

I summoned said sword, just to prove to her it was true. "Do you want to hold it?"

No one ever did, but it seemed like the polite thing to ask.

"No." There was something almost nostalgic in that one word. "There was a time when I'd wanted to do more than hold that sword, but I quickly realized such a role was never one for me to have."

I remembered Criam telling me that Doriel had remained awake until three hundred thousand years ago, and then had slumbered until recently—an awakening that timed closely with my getting this sword from the vampires.

But that wasn't what I needed to discuss right now. I dismissed the sword and leaned forward. "I hear the Ancients are awake—all of them. I also hear that they are establishing their hierarchy, looking for a leader, and preparing to take Aaru."

She nodded. "This is true. We felt something when you became the Iblis, and many of us awoke, but there was another event, something that shook the foundations of Hel. All the Ancients rose, and in our hearts we knew that it was now possible for us to take back our homeland."

It was a speech that should have been in a rousing epic novel. "How come no one else noticed this Hel-wide earthquake big enough to awaken the slumbering Ancients? And why is it now possible to take Aaru, where it wasn't a few years ago?"

It hadn't been the sword. What had happened recently besides me becoming the Iblis that would have the power to negate Gregory's carefully worded banishment? My palms sweated at the obvious answer staring me in the face. I'd banished the angels and locked down Aaru, but what if my not-so-carefully-worded banishment had undone Gregory's? What if by removing the angels, I left a back door open that only the Ancients, the formerly banished Angels of Chaos, could use?

"I was speaking metaphorically when I said the event rocked the foundations of Hel. It felt that way to us Ancients. We sensed a shift in the energy. It was as if a huge rock broke the surface of the still, stagnant waters of a pond."

A disturbance in the Force. Great.

"This shift…we knew it meant we now had the means to return home. I can't explain why, or even how, but I know deep in my spirit-self that Aaru is now open to me, where it was not before."

I wasn't sure whether to believe her or not. Demons lied, and so did the former Angels of Chaos, but her words rang true.

"So you guys had a meeting of Ancients or something to discuss this? Do you all intend to actually make an attempt to take back Aaru?"

She leaned back in her chair and folded her hands gracefully in her lap. "We met only a few days ago. And yes, there are plans to move on Aaru once we determine a leader."

I shook my head. "You've been awake for a year or two, but you just met a few days ago? Why wait so long if you all realized you had the opportunity to take Aaru earlier?"

"You must understand that many of us have slumbered for hundreds of thousands of years, some have been asleep since shortly after our fall. Awakening after such time is disorienting. There were personal things to attend to as well as the need to determine who remained alive and who had died since we were last active. And we do not yet know why after millions of years we now have the ability to regain our homeland. No one wants to foolishly mount an attack on the angels without fully understanding the circumstances. Is there suddenly an artifact available to us that we need to utilize? Is there a specific Ancient who needs to lead us for our attempt to be successful? We can't just push forward with only the awareness in our spirit-selves that it is possible."

They might be Angels of Chaos, but they were still angels, and operating on angel-time. My presence had gotten the Ruling Council off their asses and expediting shit, but it seemed these Ancients were still willing to take years, even centuries, to plan their attack.

It was reassuring, knowing that I had the luxury of time.

"What is the process for picking a leader?" I asked her, hoping that process would be long and convoluted enough to delay their attack even further.

A brief smile flashed across her face. "Many, many meetings where those who wish to be considered extol their virtues and attempt to gain key alliances. I expect a few assassinations to occur that will whittle down the contenders. Right now, six Ancients seem to be the forerunners: Nebibos, Asmodiel, Remiel, Sugunth, Irmasial, and Bechar." She leaned forward in her seat. "I'll admit that I thought *you* might be the one to lead us. You do carry the Sword of the Iblis, after all."

Thought. Past tense. "And you no longer think I'm the leader you're looking for?"

"You're not a leader, you're a disrupter." She let that sink in for a moment. "You're to be respected, to be carefully watched as you indicate what's to come for all of us. Those who disregard you are fools but those who follow you are also fools." She smiled. "None of us may survive what you're bringing about. All we can do is navigate the waters and do our best to endure."

I wasn't sure how I felt about any of that, but I was glad

the Ancients weren't intending on slapping the equivalent of a crown on my head and insisting that I lead the charge to Aaru.

"So who are you thinking is going to come out on top?" I asked. "Out of the six Ancients, who are you putting your money on?"

"I'd bet on Asmodiel. He's ruthless, and is a brilliant strategist. Of course, we still don't understand how we're able to break the banishment and enter the gates of Aaru. If it requires some kind of artifact, then the Ancient who holds the artifact will become the leader."

"It's not the sword," I told her, worried that she was changing her mind about my suitability as their leader. I might lack the skills, but I didn't want her thinking it was the sword that would get them into Aaru.

She nodded. "We know. The sword allows *you* entrance as the Iblis, but would not break the banishment we are under. It's something else that has happened to give us this chance— something or someone."

Hopefully something or someone that it took them centuries to find. "Are you planning on going with the army when they attack Aaru?" There was something resigned and fatalistic about her that made me think she had her doubts about their chance of success. They might be able to get into Aaru, but Doriel didn't seem to be sure they'd be able to win in a conflict against the angels.

"I've not decided yet. I long to go home. I miss Aaru with every fiber of my being. It's physically painful being separated from the host, removed from our source for so long. There are times when I think if I could just step foot in my homeland, shed my corporeal form and be an angel once more, I could die happy. But the thought of fighting again, going through all the pain and horror of the war all over again…that thought holds me back from committing to this plan. The war took a toll on me and I don't think I can go through that a second time. I'd rather live with the pain of never seeing Aaru again than once more take up arms against those I used to call my brothers and sisters, those I once loved."

She looked down at her hands in her lap, then spread her fingers, lifting them upward. "But that's not all. I fear that it's been too long, and that there is no going home for us. We've changed. I'm sure Aaru has changed as well. Better for me to live with my memories than have them overlaid by a brutal and unpleasant reality."

That was heartbreaking. Her speech made me even more convinced to orchestrate a reconciliation between the denizens of Hel and the angels. It might be very long before the angels allowed their old enemies to come home—if *anyone* could go home, that is—but at least I could get the two groups to respect and tolerate each other. And to eventually love each other once more.

"Thank you again for your honesty. Can I count on you to send me notice if things change? If the Ancients decide on a leader, and set a definitive time for their attempt to enter Aaru?"

She smiled, a twinkle of mischief in her eyes. "I may not be the first to know these things. I am a bit of a recluse, after all. Perhaps you'd be better off asking another Ancient, or even a demon to be your eyes and ears in this matter."

So that was a "no". I took a breath and asked her what I had been wanting to ask since I walked through her doors. "Doriel, did you know Samael?"

"Yes, of course. Everyone knew Samael. He was the Iblis, the leader of the Angels of Chaos."

I'm sure everyone knew of him, but I got the feeling that Doriel had a more personal relationship with the former Iblis. "Is he still alive?" I asked.

She shrugged. "I know he was alive for some time after the fall. He disappeared. Some say it was ten thousand years after the war. Some say it was a hundred thousand years after the war. Some say a million."

"How can that happen?" I asked in disbelief. "He was the Iblis, the leader of the army. He was your *leader*. How could you all just lose track of him like that?"

"We were all disoriented and desperate after the fall," she said defensively. "One moment we were in the heat of battle, and the next we were stripped of our grace and forced into corporeal form in a strange place full of trolls and dwarves. None of us knew what was going on for quite a while. By the time we regrouped, Samael was gone. He had been gravely injured, and after the fall he walked away from his household and cut off contact with them. There were reports of sightings, but I myself think he died after the fall. I think the loss of Aaru and separation from his brothers was too much for him to bear."

It's what everyone seemed to think. "What happened to him in the last battle of the war?" I mused, more to myself than her.

She took a deep breath, and twisted her hands together in her lap. "That huge final battle he almost took Michael's wings. I was there, nearby, and Samael had the upper hand. One stroke and he would have killed his brother and taken his spot as the most powerful angel in all of Aaru. We would have won the war and the world would have been a much different place for us as well as the humans."

"But Michael turned it around and got the advantage?" I assumed.

"No. Samael's sword tore through Michael's wings, and the archangel dropped to his knees. But instead of taking the killing stroke, Samael hesitated. He lowered his sword and stepped back." Her eyes met mine. "It gave Michael the split second he needed to recover. He raised his sword and slashed as the other lowered his, and sliced through Samael's unprotected side, nearly cutting him in half. Samael jerked back, and that instinct saved him, otherwise he would have died there in that battle."

No. No, I just couldn't believe that of my beloved, even though her words rang true. I'd seen how he struggled with the sins of anger and pride. I'd seen firsthand how he regretted the things he'd done in anger—things he wished he'd never done. But not this. To have been spared, then to take advantage of his brother's mercy and attempt a killing stroke... I just didn't want to believe that of the angel I loved.

"Samael lay there before his brother," she continued, "but instead of finishing him off, Michael pronounced the banishment, and we all fell."

He'd been angry enough to banish them all, but in spite of his initial impulse, Michael had held off killing his brother. That had to count for something. It was all so tragic. I wasn't sure if I could bring about a reconciliation after such a betrayal, even if the youngest archangel *were* still alive. No wonder my beloved had built the gateways to Hel, left a proverbial light on for his brother. The guilt he carried must be a horrible burden still.

"What was he like?" I asked softly. "What was Samael like before the fall?"

Before my eyes, Doriel softened. "He was beautiful. Samael was the most beautiful of all the angels. He shone with a clear, pure light. He had a power to him that rivaled Michael's, but instead of an oppressive heat, his was sharp and cool. It didn't demand attention or strangle you with its force, it just was. His energy, his power was such that an angel couldn't help but notice, couldn't help but bow before it. Not because of the weight of it, but because of its very lightness.

"He was never mean or cruel, and he always spoke the truth even when he lied. You knew that if there was something difficult to say, he would say it. If other angels were uncomfortable with something, or avoiding it, Samael would bring it into the open. He illuminated all the dark shadows, revealed all that others wished to hide. Angels of Chaos are beings of the darkness, but Samael was our light. He was the bridge between the nighttime and the day. He was our morning star."

A morning star that had been extinguished in the fall from heaven. A light that would never be seen again. I gave my thanks to Doriel and took my leave, feeling a sense of hopelessness greater than what I'd had when I'd arrived.

CHAPTER 13

*T*he long walk out of Doriel's forest gave me time to think about things, including the more positive parts of our conversation. The Ancients weren't anywhere near ready to move on Aaru. Samael's probable death meant those Ancients would most likely spend the next century squabbling over who should lead them. And although my opinion of Gregory was tarnished by Doriel's tale of that last battle, I still only had her point of view. Normally I tried to not dig into those still painful wounds with Gregory, but I needed to know his side of the story before I made up my mind about the truth of what happened during that battle.

In the meantime, I had three of my Lows I needed to retrieve. Cheros better be well on her way to coming through with that one because having all of my Lows crammed into the Patchine house wasn't good.

I'd taken to teleporting from Hel to a spot down the lane from my home, so I could walk past Wyatt's house and survey all that was mine on my approach. It gave me a moment to switch over from the imp who was a nobody in Hel to the Ha-Satan returning to her home. It allowed me to make sure Wyatt was okay and that there wasn't any nasty shit lurking around my house planning an attack. It kept me from popping into my living room at an inopportune moment. Yes, this was my fucking house and I should be able to come and go as I pleased, but lately my house had become a sort of hotel. Nils, Dalmai, and Little Red lived in the stables with the horses. My Lows and guests occupied the new separate dwelling that had cost me a fortune in bribes to get through the county permitting and past the nosy neighbors. Technically only Nyalla and Boomer were living in the house proper, but I'd come home to find Candy, Michelle, half a dozen werewolves, humans with babies, and the random angel hanging out in my house. Popping unannounced into my living room had actually gotten me shot a couple of times, and bashed with a lamp or coffee table a few other times. Best to walk in and announce "I'm home" at the door.

But the surveillance of my estate was the primary reason. If it leaked out that the angels were barred from Aaru and it was my fault, I'd have a list of hit-angels on my back a mile long. Add to that demons I'd pissed off, werewolves I'd pissed off, humans I'd pissed off, and unicorns I'd pissed off, and it was definitely prudent to make a careful perusal of my surroundings before making myself a big target in a lit-up house with shouts of laughter and the crash of something breaking.

Something breaking. Huh. Nyalla's parties usually weren't the kind where people were shrieking loud expletives and encouragements while breaking stuff. Nyalla's parties usually consisted of a bunch of women watching a heart-wrenching romantic drama while wearing yoga pants and sedately drinking white wine from long-stemmed glasses. Occasionally there were toddlers and babies crawling across the floor. Occasionally some of those babies were in the form of wolf puppies or lion cubs, or something weird like gryphons.

I opened the front door. There had been nothing lurking outside, because tonight all the monsters were inside. Two werewolves, a vampire, and a Nephilim were chasing a half wolf/half lion Nephilim toddler around my dining room table while his mother laughed. Nyalla and Ahia were in the middle of what looked like an epic trashy paperback swap, with towers of precariously stacked books on coffee tables and the floor in front of the sofa where the girls sat. Boomer was by the back door chewing on who knows-what. There was a Low doing a jig on my kitchen counter, a Low hanging from the light fixture, a Low crawling through the pass-through between my kitchen and great room. There were Lows playing fetch with Big Red outside by the pool, tiki torches blazing. Lows slid down the banister, rolled across my floor, and were throwing pepperonis against my walls.

They all turned to look at me. A chorus of voices called out greetings, then resumed their activities. I made my way through the crowd to where Ahia and Nyalla sat on the sofa, books covering their laps.

"Not that I don't mind a good party, but why aren't they doing this in the guest house?" I asked.

"They're out of beer in the guest house," Ahia said. "Ooo, you have to read this one, Nyalla. She's a biker chick, and he's an accountant with a really kinky side."

"And there are too many Lows for the guest house. They're setting up cots in the basement and in the spare bedrooms." Nyalla grabbed the book and shoved different ones at the angel. "Guy runs a BDSM club outside Atlanta and she's a corporate CEO and a sexual submissive, or small town runaway bride falls for a Navy SEAL with a secret."

Ahia wrinkled her nose. "Can I have both?"

"As long as I can have the sexy vampire hunter one."

"Deal"

"Hey." I waved to get their attention. "What do you mean there are too many? The guest house can sleep twenty—forty if we stack them like cordwood. Is my whole household here?"

Nyalla blinked up at me. "How many are in your household?"

Fuck if I knew. "Fifty? Seventy?"

"I think there's close to three hundred in the guest house and the field," Ahia commented. "And I'm guessing another thirty or so in here right now."

"Head's up!" Someone shouted. I ducked and saw a bottle of ketchup fly past my head to smash against the fireplace.

"Sorry, Mistress!"

I recognized that voice. "Snip! Get your ass over here. Everyone else, get out. All demons, out. The werewolves, and humans, and Nephilim, and vampire can stay. You can stay too, Ahia."

There were moans and groans and complaints. One of the werewolves came over with a roll of paper towels and a garbage bag and started to clean up the broken ketchup bottle. I herded whining Lows, most of whom I didn't even recognize, out the back door and past a pouting Little Red toward the guest house, which did in fact look to be overflowing with guests.

Heading back into the house, I grabbed Snip by the arm and pulled him into the kitchen where we could be private. I noticed that the bulgy-eyed Low, Gimlet, was still there and trailing along behind us. I wasn't sure whether his presence was due to Snip keeping an eye on him as I'd said, or Gimlet had decided that catching a free ride to party on my dime was an awesome idea.

"What the fuck is going on?" I turned to face the two Lows.

"A party!" Gimlet announced.

"I can see that, but why are there hundreds of Lows here? Party in Hel, at any of my three houses. Don't haul half the population across the gates. Whose brilliant fucking idea was this?"

"Mine!" Snip grinned, clearly pleased at what he considered to be my praise.

In my annoyed state I'd forgotten two important things—Lows can only process one question at a time, and they had no sense whatsoever of sarcasm.

"Why?" I demanded.

"Because they're scared and nowhere is safe in Hel. Some of us aren't sure about Cheros being part of our household now. She swears she won't hurt us, but she looks at us funny. And now that she says she won't take any more of us if we're in your household, *all* the Lows want to be in your household. And just in case she's lying, they all came here because it's too much work for her to cross the gate and drag Lows back to Hel."

Shit. "Snip, I can't admit all these Lows into my household."

"Why not?" Gimlet leaned against the fridge. "Aren't you the Iblis? The ruler of Hel? Technically they're all in your household anyway."

"That's different." I struggled to suddenly explain why it was different and realized that I couldn't. "Snip, you've got to get these Lows back to Hel. I don't have enough room for them here. County zoning is going to kill me. My neighbors are going to kill me. They're already pissed off because of the demon hitmen, the angel hitmen, the elves, the dragon—fuck, these Lows need to go home!"

Gimlet snorted. "The Iblis is afraid of her neighbors and the county zoning people?"

"I'm not afraid of them," I shot back. "I'm busy. I'm too fucking busy to deal with their human shit."

"Busy doing what? It's not like you're running Hel or anything."

I opened my mouth to tell Gimlet about the non-stop Ruling Council meetings, the humans with crappy credit scores, the four-nine-five reports, the monsters coming through the rifts, the elves, the werewolves, the Fallen, the angels locked out of Aaru…

Just let it happen.

The irritation and stress fell from me like shedding a robe, leaving me naked and feeling gloriously free. Why was I fighting against the very chaos I'd set in motion? Let the monsters come, let the rifts happen, let the angels deal with the elves and the werewolves deal with the werewolves and let the rest of it just happen.

"You're the Iblis," Gimlet continued. "You're in charge of Hel and the demons. Isn't that the job? I seriously thought that was the job, not humans and werewolves, and elves, and reports."

Had he read my mind? How the fuck had a Low read my mind?

"There's a lot of meetings she has to go to," Snip defended me. "I mean a *lot* of meetings. Those Ruling Council angels are always having meetings. They're locked in a room for hours and hours with hard chairs and the thermostat stuck on sixty-five and only stale coffee and cheap pastries to eat and drink. It's torture."

"Sometimes there's bacon," I grudgingly admitted. "But that's not the issue here. My house is overflowing with Lows and they need to go back to Hel."

Snip and Gimlet stared at me. I stared back.

DEBRA DUNBAR

"Fine. Temporary. This is a temporary vacation. I'll rescue Sinew, Booty, and Lash, and tell this Tasma guy he needs to knock it the fuck off. Then I'll talk to Cheros and tell her that *all* Lows are off the table."

"Off the table? Can I have them on the floor? Or stretched on a rack? Or submerged in boiling oil?"

The two Lows spun around, then darted to hide behind me. Cheros stood at the entrance to the kitchen, gazing around with a smug look of satisfaction on her face. She was in a human form, but even that looked somewhat lizard-like with rough, scaly greenish skin. I had an urge to offer her a giant bottle of moisturizer and tell her to hit the tanning bed.

"You've got a real nice place here, Iblis," the demon commented. "Hope your guesthouse is just as nice because I'll be staying there tonight. We have to go back to Hel first thing in the morning, because I had a brilliant idea. Can you act like a Low? I need you pretend to be a Low, or this is just not gonna work."

Ugh, I just came from Hel. But that Gimlet dude was right, I needed to get this done or I'd end up with tens of thousands of Lows camped out at my house.

"She's an imp." Gimlet's voice was muffled since he was pressed to my back, trying to hide from the other demon. "It's not like she'd need to pretend a whole lot to be a Low. She's one step away from one as it is."

I was starting to hate Gimlet. "Actually, it *is* a special talent of mine. I can clamp down my energy signature. I've walked right past archangels and had them think that I was a human. That's how good I am."

"Yeah," Snip chimed in. "Only the most powerful demons can pretend like that and get away with it. It's the ultimate lie. Mistress is the best. She's the most powerfulest, devouring, lying demon there ever was, that's why she's the Iblis."

I was the Iblis because the sword decided I was the Iblis. I appreciated Snip being my cheerleader though, even if he was doing it so he wouldn't get in trouble for letting hundreds of Lows in my house and property.

"Good." Cheros grinned. "Then get your Low on, Iblis, because I've got a plan, and if you can pull this off, you should be able to get Sinew, Booty, and Lash back."

"I'm not just getting those three Lows back," I told her. "I'm getting them all back. Every single one of them."

"'Bout' damned time," Gimlet mumbled.

CHAPTER 14

"*C*ockroach, there are hundreds of Lows coming through the Columbia Mall gateway. Hundreds. And every one of them is claiming to be in your household. Beatrix isn't sure what to do with them."

Gregory had appeared in my kitchen not an hour after I'd arrived home. I'd been about to text him and ask him to come over, but had struggled with how to word my message. *I need to ask you about the battle where you nearly killed your brother* didn't seem like a good choice. Neither did *Come over ASAP so I can accuse you of having done something terrible to your brother millions of years ago.* I was glad he'd visited on his own, even if he was scowling at me and being the grumpy, somewhat distant angel he'd been since I'd ejected everyone from Aaru.

"I know, I know." I put on a pot of coffee because that's what I always did when Gregory came over, although lately he never seemed to stay long enough to drink a cup. "I spoke to Beatrix just now and called a few Ubers. If they keep coming, I'll need to charter a bus or something. I've got no fucking idea where I'm going to put them all. The guest house isn't going to hold all these Lows. They're already setting up makeshift tents in the fields and cots in my basement. I wonder if the Holiday Inn Express would give me a discount."

"Why are they all coming here?" Gregory demanded. "Why can't they stay in Hel? When I told you that your household had immunity and could freely cross from Hel, I meant those of your household that were needed to complete your duties as part of the Ruling Council. And don't try to tell me that you need hundreds of Lows here to assist you."

"I don't, but they're panicking right now and trying to join my household in droves. There's an ancient demon named Tasma who is gathering them up. No one knows if he's killing them or just torturing them or what, but he's grabbed a dozen or two in the past week. I'm working on the situation, but all the Lows are too scared to stay in Hel right now."

"So kill Tasma. Or punish him. If he's violated one of your rules in Hel, then you need to take him to task for it. Cockroach, you cannot let these infractions slide. It will only make you look weak in the eyes of your subjects."

How funny that Gregory thought I had subjects.

"It's on my agenda. Tomorrow morning I'm heading back to Hel to take care of this Tasma, then I can start booting these Lows out of my house."

"Why do they even need to come here?" he demanded. "Make these Lows part of your household and mark them, so they'll be safe in Hel, but don't give them a pass to come here en masse. Just mark them as yours and no one will dare take them."

We'd been together years and he still didn't understand how things worked, or didn't work, in Hel. "This Tasma guy had three of my marked Lows taken, one right off my front porch. I've got that to stop, I think, but the Lows are worried my household mark won't be enough if I'm not physically in Hel to protect them. That's why they're coming here."

The angel's eyes widened in astonishment. "Someone disrespected your household mark? And they're still alive?"

"Tasma is an Ancient," I countered. "I can't just waltz in there and dust him with my sword. I have to be sneaky. And maybe bargain or something. Drop a piano on the guy from the window of a tall building. Or, an anvil."

"This is why you have so many problems in Hel, Cockroach. You can't be sneaking around and dropping pianos and anvils, and it shouldn't matter whether this demon is an Ancient or not. He broke the rules. Punish him."

Times like this I wish I was an angel. Well, no I didn't, but it certainly would make things a whole lot simpler. Got a sword? You're the boss! Instant obedience.

"It's easier for you guys," I complained. "Even the rebel angels want to follow rules—they just want to follow different rules or follow them with a greater strictness than you do. Demons don't want to follow rules. And I really don't want to enforce rules either. Hel is kind of an anarchy. Actually, there's no 'kind of'. Hel is an anarchy. We have some basic structure so that everyone knows what will get you ganged up on and eviscerated, and what you can get away with, but each demon takes care of protecting their own and coming down on those who don't respect their household or their stuff."

"Are these Lows yours or not?" Gregory demanded. "Not just the ones with your household mark, but all of them? As denizens of Hel, do they belong to you as the Iblis?"

Fuck. "Yes, they are."

"Times like this I wish I was a demon," he muttered. "Take care of this Tasma Ancient. Either he stops trying to kidnap the Lows, or you kill him. See? Simple. And you didn't need twelve meetings and a six-hundred-page document to get it done either like you would if you were in charge of a choir of angels."

Kill Tasma. Oh how easy...if I were a six-billion-year-old archangel instead of a fairly young imp with a few icky talents and a stupid disobedient sentient sword.

"In the meantime, you have between one and three hundred Lows here, possibly more on the way. What are you planning on doing with them? And I'm not talking about lodging." Gregory scowled at me.

"It's just for a night or two until I take care of Tasma, then they're going back to Hel," I told him.

He raised an eyebrow. And waited. Because he knew as well as I did that it was going to be very difficult to get hundreds of excited vacationing Lows to cut their fun short and go home.

"Fine." I blew out a breath. "I can use them. We might need them to fight the rebel angels if they act up. Or the elves if whatever indoctrination you're doing doesn't stick. Or maybe we can send them out to handle the rifts."

"Lows can't detect rifts, or so you told me. And I can't see a Low demon fighting the monsters that come through them."

"I could use them to help with the non-credit-worthy humans." I was really grasping at straws here, but I did need to find something for these Lows to do or they would destroy my place and probably half the state as well.

"Just make sure they follow the rules."

Right. Like that was going to happen. "I put Snip in charge of them."

He sighed and eyed the coffee. "Fine. I've got to go. I'll see you—"

"Wait!" I reached out and grabbed the sleeve of his polo

shirt before he could gate away. "I need to talk to you. There are…things I need to ask you. And tell you."

He stood there for a moment, then looked down at where my hand was crushing the fabric of his shirt. "Yes?"

He wasn't making this easy for me at all. And worse, there was nowhere private in my house for us to have any sort of conversation. Ahia and Nyalla were still swapping books. The werewolves and Nephilim and that vampire were still in the dining area. A few Lows had snuck back in and were firing up Call of Duty on my Xbox.

"Walk with me." I turned and lead the way out the French doors, past my covered pool and the stables and down through the field to a small copse of trees, the leaves still yellow-green and clinging to their branches even though it was early fall.

"I've yet to discover any significant plot for a large group of demons to descend on the human world." I turned to face him just as the moon came out, filtering through the spaces in the trees and lighting our surroundings to shades of gray. "Although with most of my Lows this side of the gate, my intelligence gathering ability in Hel is a bit compromised. I'll make sure I assign, which means bribe, some unaffiliated demons to keep an eye on it for me, and let you know what I find."

He nodded. "That's acceptable. And?"

"The Ancients in Hel are indeed awake, and there is a plot to move on Aaru, but no definitive date or plan of attack has yet been determined. They are still trying to figure out who their leader is, and that may take some time."

"I told you, Cockroach, that they cannot enter Aaru. They were banished. And on top of that, you also banished them. Doubly banished. Those Ancients can plan all they want, they are not entering the gates of heaven."

"Yeah, well they think differently." I kicked a stone with

my foot. "I spoke with an Ancient by the name of Doriel, and she says that there was an event that happened recently that caused them all to suddenly sense that they now had the means to enter Aaru."

Gregory froze.

"And I didn't banish them," I added. "My banishment was specific to the angels. I'll admit that I don't know the details, or know yet how to reverse it, but I do know it included all of the Angels of Order. Every angel allowed in Aaru was banished, and that seemed to include me as well. I'm assuming it also included Ahia as she's a true angel, but I'm positive it didn't include the Ancients. I've never considered them angels, really, so whatever I did during that battle, in my moment of fear and rage where I thought I'd lost you forever, didn't include them. They are banished by your edict only, and they feel deep within their spirit-selves that they are either now free of that banishment, or that they have the means to free themselves."

"You undid my banishment?"

I winced at the note of fury in his voice, remembering Doriel's story of that last battle. If he could almost kill the brother he'd deeply loved, then his love for me could so easily turn to hate as well.

"I don't know. The timing of this seems to coincide with my banishing of the angels, but Ancients aren't very good at determining when specific events occur."

Gregory was sometimes the same way. I assumed that when a being lived for millions, or billions of years, the margin of error in remembering when an event occurred was often in the centuries, if not millennia.

The angel turned and took a few steps away, running a hand through his copper curls before turning back to face me. "She's lying. She has to be lying."

"She's not lying. At least, not about that." I paused, but he didn't take the bait.

"Who is this leader they seek? You? Do they expect the Iblis to lead the charge into Aaru?" His voice made me feel like skin scraping against asphalt after coming off a bike.

"Well, they'd be disappointed, because I can't get into Aaru." I took a step toward him. "I've tried. Don't you know I've tried? And if I could get in, it would be with *you* by my side, not a bunch of Ancients and their armies of demons."

"You're the Queen of Hel, the Iblis. They are your subjects."

I snorted. "Yeah, tell that to *them*. I'm not a leader, I'm a disrupter. What I want to know is the possibility of this happening. Can these Ancients ascend into Aaru? Is there a way around the banishment beyond this redemption/forgiveness bullshit you spouted off in the Ruling Council meeting?"

He thought carefully. "No. But as you've proven to me over and over in the last two years, I can be wrong. There are things I don't see, that I'm blind to. You are my eyes to those things. So if you see the truth in Doriel's words, if you see the possibility, then I believe you."

I caught my breath. That was the closest he'd come to reaching out to me in a while. Sucked that I was about to smack that tiny olive branch down and crush it under my foot.

"Do you know Doriel?"

He nodded. "She and Samael were close. She was more moderate than many Angels of Chaos. I respected her knowledge and skills."

"Was she truthful?"

Gregory shrugged. "Angels of Chaos lie, but Doriel tended to lie less than most of them."

"She told me a story." I paused, my eyes searching his face

in the dim moonlight. "A story about that last battle in Aaru, the battle where you banished them all and consigned them all to Hel."

He flinched, but said nothing.

"She told me that Samael had prevailed, that he'd nearly taken your wings and in the moment when you were vulnerable and open before him, he stepped back. He refused to deliver that final killing blow."

Gregory drew a ragged breath. "Yes. That is true."

"She said that as your brother backed away, his sword lowered, you took advantage and struck, nearly cutting him in two. She said that the only reason Samael was not killed with that blow was that he turned as your blade swung. You intended to kill the brother that held back in mercy from delivering his own killing blow."

There was a silence so profound that my ears rang with it. The wind didn't stir. Neither birds nor insects made the faintest noise.

"Yes. That is true."

He gave no excuse for his actions. He didn't claim that the mercy that followed somehow lessened the horror of what he'd done. He stood before me, stoic and straight, and admitted what he'd done. That, more than any excuse he could have given, made me forgive him—if it was ever within my right to forgive.

I reached out with my spirit-self to touch him and felt the pain, the derision, the self-hate. I might forgive Gregory, but he would never forgive himself.

"Why?"

His mouth twisted. "Why what? Why did I strike when he didn't? Why did I not finish him off when I had the advantage? Why did I banish every last one of them?"

I kept the contact with his spirit-self. "Yes to all those. Why?"

The angel stepped forward, so close I was almost in his arms. "Arguments had become war, and I'd been filled with rage for so long that in all honesty, his retreat didn't register at first. By the time it filtered through to my consciousness that Samael had spared me, had lowered his sword, it was too late."

I reached out a hand and touched his arm. "But when you realized what he'd done, you stopped."

His laugh was bitter. "Yes. The rage was replaced with a feeling of humiliation. I didn't want anyone to know what I'd done. It was an act completely without honor. I'd struck out at an angel who'd delivered mercy unto me. I'd nearly killed my own brother—an angel that I loved with all my heart. My youngest brother. The only Angel of Chaos among the five of us. And not only had I nearly killed him, but I'd dishonored myself."

He fell silent, and I waited because I knew there was more.

"And in my humiliation, I did far worse than kill him. I banished him. I banished all of them. Anger wasn't my worst sin, it was pride. The legends always stick that sin on Samael, but truthfully it was *my* burden to carry that sin."

"I banished you and the rest of the angels," I told him. "I did the same."

"No, you didn't. You banished us because you loved me and were trying to save me, to save us all. I banished my brother and the others because I was angry and ashamed, and it was my way of avoiding that pain, of blaming them and punishing them for my own sin."

My hand slid down to hold his, my spirit-self soft against his own. "You can make it right. *We* can make it right."

He gripped my hand tight. "I don't think there is anything I, or any of us, can do to make this right."

"Dar and Asta? Rafi and Ahia? You and me? Slowly the

treaty is dissolving, and angels and demons are coming together. I hate that you all are denied access to Aaru, and I don't want these Ancients in there—not now, not while there is still this animosity and desire for vengeance on both sides. Later. Later we'll all share Aaru once more. Well, not me because I think that place sucks big giant donkey balls, but everyone else can share it. Later."

He sighed and I felt him pull back. "You've got a lot to do. Go take care of Hel and your Lows. I'll deal with the angels and the elves and the rifts. Go be the Queen of Hel."

I clung to his hand, refusing to let go. "No. I mean, yeah I need to go to Hel and take care of shit, but the rest of it is us, not just you. You're not in this alone. You've got your brothers. You've got me. Don't walk away here. I need you. I need to know that you forgive me for kicking everyone out of Aaru, that you trust that I'll figure this out and get you back in. I've got a lot of shit going on right now, and you're the only reason I'm doing any of it."

I felt his confusion. "What are you talking about?"

"When we were up in Aaru and I saw you go down under a bunch of rebel angels, when I thought I would lose you forever...nothing mattered anymore. With you gone, I wouldn't want to be the Iblis, or rule Hel, or live here among the humans. With you gone, I wouldn't even want to live. I need you, Micha. None of this shit is worth a damn if I can't have you."

His spirit-self caressed mine. His hand, the one I wasn't crushing in my own, reached out to capture a lock of my hair and rub it between his thumb and forefinger. "Silly Cockroach. I *do* blame you for kicking us all out of Aaru. I blame you for everything. You came into my life and turned everything over, knocked me on my side, rattled my life and destroyed all the brittle, stiff layers that in my pride and anger and sorrow I'd buried myself in. You yanked me from my shelter and left me naked and exposed in the open, not knowing what to expect next. This is all your fault. Every last bit of this is your fault."

I grinned. "Awww. I love you too, big guy."

"I need you, Cockroach. I need you, but you pull the breath from my lungs and leave me a disordered mess. And now that I've felt the terrifying experience of loving you, I would never have it any other way. I could never go back to my life before you. And none of this is worth anything without you, either. I'd carry on, because I feel like I owe it to the humans and the angels to shoulder my responsibility, but without you I would have no joy in my life. Without you, I would rot. I would decay and die."

I launched myself into his arms, felt him crush me against his chest, felt his breath against the top of my head. "What's going to happen? You're omni-something. Tell me when you look at the threads of possibilities that stretch before us, what you see, what you believe will happen."

"*You* will happen, Cockroach. That's all I know. You have increased the number of possibilities a hundredfold, and made them all equally probable. We could regain Aaru. The demons might regain Aaru. Pianos and anvils and locusts could fall from the sky. With you in existence, anything is possible and probable, even the improbable."

"Great," I mumbled against his chest. "Hoping the pianos and anvils and locusts thing doesn't happen, though. That's a weird mix of Looney Tunes and Biblical Plague stuff there. Doesn't sound like fun."

I felt the laugh rumble through him, felt him kiss the top of my head. "Come. What I have to do will wait. Let's go to your bedroom for the night."

"Where I'll sleep in your arms and you'll stay awake and stare at me like some creeper?"

His spirit-self brushed against mine. "Later. First I'd like to do some things that have nothing at all to do with sleeping."

And suddenly everything was right in the world. Whatever happened, happened. It would all fall into place eventually. I had my angel. Compared to that, nothing else mattered.

CHAPTER 15

I expected Gregory to be gone when I woke up, but he was still there, curled up against me, staring at me like a creeper.

"Do you realize how disturbing that is?" I mumbled, secretly pleased.

"What else am I supposed to do for eight hours but watch you snore and drool onto the pillow? Come on. We've both got a lot to do and neither of us is going anywhere without some coffee."

I smiled and snuggled against him. "Sex first? Angel or human style—you pick."

His spirit-self surrounded mine, merging tantalizingly along the edges. "Did we not do quite a lot of that before you fell asleep? Coffee and work first. Sex after you get back from Hel."

I sighed, getting out of bed. There was no sense in show-ering since I had a feeling I was about to get really filthy. And probably bloody. I threw on one of my least-favorite shirts and pair of jeans as a precaution, because they were most likely going to either be sliced up, or destroyed if I had to shift my physical form to something large and fierce. "I might not be back until tomorrow," I warned him. "Even after I deal with Tasma, it might take me a while to find all these Lows. Fuck knows what he's done with them. Or their bodies."

"I'm determining which angels are best suited to assist in monitoring the integrated elves, and assigning them. I'm also interviewing for additional Grigori enforcers." The angel slid out of bed and was magically clothed in his typical navy polo shirt and jeans. "Gabe is helping me write the procedures for the new elven minders, although he's got some dolphin swimming thing he says he has to do first."

I blinked. "Seriously? Don't tell Nyalla. She's been wanting to do one of those dolphin experiences for months now. She'll spend half the next Ruling Council meeting grilling Gabe about the best locations, and what they're really like up-close. We'll never get anything done."

Gregory opened the bedroom door for me. I could already hear muted conversation from downstairs.

"I don't think it's that sort of trip. He's probably scoping them out to receive our gifts if things with the humans don't work out. They were in our top five, you know."

Made sense. There was a fuck-ton of water here and some pretty smart aquatic creatures. We headed down the stairs where two Lows were playing Xbox with the sort of bleary-eyed focus that told me they'd been at it all night. "Why didn't you guys select two? Or all five?" I asked Gregory.

He laughed. "It's difficult enough herding one species to a positive evolution. We angels have our limitations."

Boy, did they ever. I headed into the kitchen wondering if the tenth choir would have fallen by fucking a bunch of dolphins only to see that the coffee had already been made, and Cheros was attempting to waterboard a Low with a cup of it.

"Hey!" I snapped. "No torturing the Lows!"

Rot looked up at me, his face wet, brown drops rolling down his cheeks. "Oh, this is fun, Mistress! Watch me blow coffee bubbles out of my nose."

The Low demonstrated. "Just don't kill him," I told Cheros. Then I poured Gregory and myself a cup each, adding the usual five pounds of sugar and gallon of milk to the angel's. I realized that I didn't need to worry about Cheros killing Rot, because she had stopped trying to drown my Low and was staring at my beloved, shaking so hard that the coffee was slopping over the edges of her cup.

"This is Cheros," I told him. "She's the one who is going to sneak me into Tasma's place. Cheros, this is the Archangel Michael, also known as the angel I'm fucking. Don't piss him off because he's not been in the best of moods for the last three million years or so, and he can smite the shit out of you without breaking a sweat."

Cheros made a squeak noise. Gregory ignored her, taking the outstretched cup of coffee from my hand. His phone beeped and he looked down at it. "There are four sex demons in Hong Kong claiming immunity as part of your household, Cockroach. They say they are unmarked because you granted them an exception so as to not mar their beauty."

"Not mine," I told him cheerfully. "Unless one of them is Leethu because she's unmarked. Or Irix, because he's not technically part of my household but is still given immunity. Wait, *is* it Leethu? I've been looking for her. Ask if one of them is Leethu."

Gregory downed half the coffee, his thumb typing as he balanced the phone on his palm. "No. They are claiming that they are all named Delilah."

I sighed. "What are they doing that they got caught by an angel?"

The angel raised an eyebrow. "What sex demons normally do. Which isn't much different from what a great many humans do in Hong Kong, evidently. We wouldn't have caught them except the human sex workers got angry because they were taking all the customers and complained."

I stopped the coffee cup a few inches from my mouth. "They *complained*? To an angel?"

"They complained to a human, who knew an elf, who said they should tell the angels and gave him the contact information for one of my enforcers." Gregory's mouth turned up in a sardonic smile. "Imagine my enforcer's surprise when her phone was overwhelmed by texts in Cantonese from human prostitutes complaining about the unfair trade practices of four succubi."

That *was* funny. "Can your enforcer mediate?" There were too many demons coming through to toss them all back, and I was reluctant to deliver too harsh of a sentence to four succubi who were only guilty of lying about their household affiliation and fucking too many horny businessmen.

Gregory typed in his phone, then chuckled as he read the message. "She thinks she'll be able to get them all to come to an agreement. Are these four allowed to stay?"

I sipped my coffee and nodded. "They can't leave Hong Kong unless they're returning to Hel, and have them word the mediated agreement as a vow. Let them know if they break their vows, they'll wish this angel killed them because I'll have every one of them servicing my Lows in my Patchine house for the next century."

He nodded, typing, then put the phone away and finished his coffee. "I need to go, Cockroach. And so do you."

His words were warm and affectionate, and so was the reluctant smile that accompanied them. My heart swelled with the whole casual domestic feel of this morning in my kitchen. "Love you," I told him, leaning in to plant a quick kiss on his lips. "I'll text you when I'm back."

He pulled me close and kissed me much more thoroughly, his spirit-self doing all sorts of naughty things to mine. "Love you too."

And then he was gone. I sipped my coffee, looking at his empty cup on the counter with a sappy smile on my face.

"I think I peed myself," Cheros said. "He's fucking terrifying. How do you sleep next to that thing? His power feels like a steamroller, like a burning mountainside crushing me as it melts my skin."

"Yes, it does." I reached out and touched his coffee cup, feeling the residue of his energy on the rim and the handle.

"I like him," Rot said, still blowing coffee bubbles from his nose. "And I think it's sweet how he is with Mistress. Just like those books that Nyalla and the Ahia angel have on the coffee table."

Cheros snorted. "Give me a demon any day over an angel. I'd rather fuck a spiny-dicked Low than let one of those angels close enough to touch me. No fucking way."

"Hey," Rot protested. "There's nothing wrong with fucking a spiny-dicked Low."

"No, there's nothing at all wrong with that," I told him, running my fingers along my angel's discarded cup and remembering the night in his arms. "Nothing at all. To each his or her own. And for me, this one is mine. This angel is mine."

CHAPTER 16

*T*here was no reason to putz around my house any longer, so I finished my coffee and teleported Cheros and myself to Dis. She puked in the street once we arrived, dramatically announcing that from now on she was only going to travel via the gateways, like demons were meant to do.

"My way is faster." I handed her a scrap of cloth from a nearby yard to wipe her mouth. "I can enter Hel via the gateways, but I can't leave here unless I teleport. Basically, my angel had to banish me to save my life. It's a long story."

She looked up at me, took a few deep breaths, then got to her feet. "Fucking angels. You guys can zap yourself around as much as you want. I'm walking. And I'm taking the gates."

I shrugged. "Suit yourself. Now, what's our plan? You said you had a scheme to sneak me into Tasma's place. Is there a secret entrance? Did you bribe someone in his household to let us in? Do we slide down the chimney?"

I couldn't help the last. I'd been thinking of Gimlet's Santa story and wondering if there could be any partial truths to it. Maybe Samael was in the north of Hel, in Eresh? Maybe he was a fat dude? Or maybe he was dead and a bunch of toy-making elves guarded his tomb?

"Nope. Like I said, you need to pretend you're a Low," Cheros said, wiping her mouth and tossing the scrap of fabric to the curb.

"And sneak down the chimney?" I asked. "I want you to get me in to see Tasma without putting him on the defensive. If I need to pretend to be a Low and go down the chimney, then I'll do it." I was starting to get an idea here. If no one in Hel took me seriously, if no one gave a shit about my title or sword, I might as well use it to my advantage.

"No, you pretend to be a Low and we walk in the front door."

How humiliating. But if it got the job done… "Then I sneak around the house, find my Lows, and set them free. Then I set all the Lows free." Then I face down Tasma and hope he didn't kill me.

She laughed. "*Fuck*, you are crazy. You're not going to find your Lows. You're not going to find any Lows. They're dead."

That was the whole idea of my going in there—rescuing Booty, Sinew, and Lash. And the others. Dealing with Tasma was more of an unpleasant necessity, so he didn't continue to take Lows that I had to come back and rescue.

"If they're dead, then where are the bodies?" I asked. "He should have dumped them by now."

She shrugged. "Maybe he ate them."

Eww. And demons thought my devouring was unsavory. "Ate them as in ate their flesh? Because I'm a devouring spirit, and even I don't eat demon bodies."

She rolled her eyes. "He's an Ancient. They're weird. Maybe he likes to eat demon bodies. Maybe he keeps the bodies in his dungeon and lets them rot because he likes that kinda smell. I'm just telling you that there's a good chance they're already dead. And there's a good chance you're going to be dead too if he catches you. I don't care what kind of luck you have or that you killed Haagenti and Ahriman, Tasma is gonna have your body parts mounted above his fireplace mantel if he catches you."

I straightened my shoulders and tried to look Iblis-like. "No, he won't. I'm going to rescue any Lows who are still alive, then I'm going to beat the ever-loving fuck out of this Ancient and make sure he doesn't pull this kind of shit again. Then I'm going to walk out of there, take my Lows, and go home to fuck my angel."

She rolled her eyes. "Oh yeah. If you're such a badass, then why am I sneaking you in disguised as a Low?"

Good point. "It told you: I'm a sneaky kind of badass. Now let's get on with this. I don't have all day here. I'm a powerful demon. I've got shit to do."

"Fine. You ready?" Cheros grabbed the back of my shirt before I even had time to reply, hoisting me slightly off my feet. Damn, the girl was strong.

"Let's get this over with," I told her.

The demon hauled me down the street while I did my best to squeal and fight, keeping my energy signature so tightly contained that I nearly appeared human in my T-shirt and jeans. Well, I would have appeared human aside from the blue fur and little nubby horns I'd assumed when entering Hel. Few turned to look. Lows were plentiful and unimportant in Hel. No one gave a shit about one being hauled away to her death down the middle of the street.

At the edge of town was a narrow stone building, the tower listing an alarming five or so degrees to the left. There was no physical fence or barrier barring entry to the front door, but from the way the air sizzled and popped ten feet from the steps, I could tell the residence didn't need a physical fence.

Cheros pulled an amulet from a weird pocket in her

scaled thigh and dangled it in front of the magical barrier. With a word, she swung the amulet forward. The blue stone turned red and the barrier appeared, a wavy orange semi-translucent substance that looked like see-through lava.

She pocketed the amulet while I eyed the barrier, waiting for somebody to come out and answer her summons. With a shoulder roll, she shifted my weight in her hand, then shoved my head into the magical lava.

I screamed, more in surprise than anything else, and called for my sword. The bitch had set me up, betrayed me. And now I was going to be dead for my stupidity in trusting a demon.

The sword didn't come. The barrier didn't melt my head. I froze as I felt the magic lick through me, searching for something. And suddenly realizing what it was searching for, I held my energy tight, trying my damndest to appear to be the Low I was impersonating. I had no idea what this magical lava thing would do to me if it thought I was an imp—or the Iblis. I was assuming Cheros needed to use the Lows she brought as a kind of key to open the door, so to speak. Would have been nice of her to tell me that before shoving my head into magical lava.

Something seared my fur, then the barrier vanished. I inhaled, happy for Cheros's support as she dragged me across the ground, up the stairs and through a thick doorway.

"Bitch," I muttered under my breath.

She chuckled. "Oh, come on. You're an imp. That was some funny stuff right there. Would have been even funnier if your head had melted off your neck."

No, it wouldn't have.

"And if you would have died…" I felt her shrug. "Kinda woulda sucked for my plans the other side of the gates, but no biggie. I'd rather the barrier nail you then have Tasma kick my ass."

I wouldn't have died. All the times I'd been killed, I'd managed to survive. I was getting pretty good at existing inside a corpse, biding my time until I could recreate my form into something more useful. But beyond that, she was right. If I couldn't pass through a magical barrier, Tasma would have taken one look at me and killed us both. And that time I probably would have died, as in dead-dead.

A pair of webbed feet with long yellow spiraled toenails appeared in front of me. I looked up as far as I could and saw a twig-shaped torso with splintery spikes jutting from the bark-like skin.

"You're early, Cheros," Twig-guy said. "What cha' got this time? Is it one on the list?"

"Nah. Just some piece of shit I found digging in an alley. Couldn't resist, you know?"

He laughed. "Yeah. That's why you're the go-to demon for Lows. Let's see her before I bother the big guy."

She heaved me forward. My chin cracked on the hard floor, and my teeth snapped together biting into my tongue. I let the blood dribble out of my mouth, just for added effect.

The webbed foot with nasty toenails sunk into my side and rolled me over. I stared up into a face that looked like the Creature from the Black Lagoon had received some back-room plastic surgery. The long narrow nose twitched, nostrils flaring.

"Oh, the stench. And those adorable little ineffective horns." He clasped his finlike hands together. "Tasma will love her. I can barely feel her energy signature, she's so puny. It's a wonder she survived to adulthood."

I glared at him, then spit some blood and saliva onto his foot.

He laughed, the sound wet and reedy. "Adorable and

spunky. Does she taste good?"

"I haven't bitten her yet. You know what happened last time. Tasma doesn't like me to sample his purchases."

"Well, she looks in pretty good shape for a Low. He'll be pleased." Twig-guy nudged me again with his nasty toes.

"Then hurry up and call him so I can get paid and get out of there," Cheros complained. "I don't have all day to hang around this dump, and she's pretty tempting. If he doesn't show up soon, I'm going to take her home and keep her for my own."

That got Twig-guy moving. He sped from the room. I bled on the floor. Cheros shifted from foot to foot, her arms folded across her chest as she looked at the furnishings with bored eyes.

This Tasma dude took forever. I took a short nap on the floor in the time it took him to stroll into the room.

"Oh! How lovely. You've outdone yourself this time, Cheros."

I blinked my eyes open to stare at a pair of loafer-clad feet. Above them were legs clad in what seemed to be argyle socks and knife-pleated tan pants. My eyes traveled upward to see a demon in human form wearing a red sweater cardigan. He looked just like Mr. Rogers aside from the glowing eyes that matched the color of his sweater and the energy that rolled off him like a tumbleweed of sharp knives.

"Isn't she sweet? Sassy as fuck, with barely enough energy to hold her form together. You could do all sorts of things to her and not worry about getting so much as a hangnail. Only drawback is you'd need to be kind of gentle. I've got no idea how she's survived this long. I mean, if she so much as stubbed her toe, she'd probably bleed to death."

I looked up at the glowing-eyed Mr. Rogers and tried my best to look both sassy and helpless. His eyes narrowed and he tilted his head to the side as he regarded me for a moment.

Then he took a small bag that jingled with the sound of metal from his pocket and handed it to Cheros.

She peeked inside and counted under her breath, because even high-level demons cheat and steal. Then with a grin and a swift kick to my foot she turned to leave. "Have fun, you two."

Fun. Yeah, right. I just hoped this guy didn't want to do anything particularly horrible to me before I had a chance to find and release the other Lows. It would be especially hard to keep up my act as a Low while the dude was torturing me, but if I revealed who I was, I'd never find out where the others were being held, if they were even still alive. If my cover was blown, the only chance I'd have would be to kill this guy and hope his household knew where the others were being kept—and would be willing to give them up.

I doubted they would care enough to cooperate, even with the head of their household dead. Which would leave me to take this building apart one stone at a time, perhaps paying Kirby or Gareth to do a find spell, or maybe bringing Boomer over to try to track the Lows by scent. I'd have to do something. I couldn't abandon them. Not now. They were mine. Mine.

Tasma crouched down, the loafers making a squeak sound as he shifted his weight onto his toes. His face came close to mine and I stiffened, eyeing him warily. Was he going to kiss me? Bite me? Spit in my face?"

The demon smiled, revealing blocky human teeth that did nothing to reassure me. Then he reached out a hand and gently smoothed the fur on the top of my head, clucking as he touched the damaged horn.

"Ah, you poor little thing. You've had a difficult life, haven't you? Hiding. No doubt you've been snatched off the street and beaten, your bones broken and your body violated. You recover slowly from injuries you're too weak to instantly repair, feeling every burn and cut for days or even weeks. You never had a chance. You were born to suffer and die."

Wow, way to rub a Low's nose in it. Even as an imp, I'd suffered much of what he'd said. Yes, I could repair injuries instantly, but imps were not high on the demon hierarchy totem pole. I'd spent my nearly thousand years being bullied, tormented, trying to fight off attackers or, better yet, run away and hide from them. I wasn't as helpless as a Low, yet his words still struck home.

His hand paused on my forehead and I felt the touch of his spirit-self. *Oh, that's how it's gonna be, huh buddy?* It was one thing to let him beat the crap out of me or take physical liberties with my form, but this wasn't going to happen. I gritted my teeth and pushed his spirit-self away, struggling to restrain the urge to devour.

His eyebrows went up. "Feisty indeed. The will is strong, but the flesh and power are weak. Yes, you might just end up being my favorite." His hand closed around my undamaged horn and he hoisted me upward. I felt something cold, and slippery pour through me, cutting off access to my stored energy, and siphoning away the small amount I'd held at hand, ready to defend myself if needed. My legs shook, barely able to support my weight. Damn this brought back memories. No one had done this since when I'd first met Gregory. I hadn't even realized the Ancients still retained this skill.

"Just in case." He smiled again, the grin downright creepy with his glowing eyes and that disturbing so-very-human form. "Come. You want to meet your new friends, don't you? No fighting, though. All of you must be kind and supportive of each other. Use your words to solve disagreements, not your claws."

I staggered down the hall beside him, the hand on my horn more steadying than restraining. Light flashed as we passed through a series of doorways, making me realize that there was far more to this house than just its physical structure. There was no way to leave figurative breadcrumbs, or memorize our path. If I found the Lows and freed them, I'd have a struggle trying to get them out of this building and back into the streets of Dis.

We stopped in front of a smudged, dirty sand-colored wall. With a shimmer, an opening appeared and I saw half a dozen demons inside a room, every last one of them staring at us with wide, confused eyes as they sat on the floor surrounded by human-style children's toys.

"Oh, Puck. Have you broken Mr. Choo-choo again?" Tasma scolded gently, but the demon holding a gnawed wooden toy shivered.

"Wasn't I supposed to chew it? I thought…I'm sorry, I'm sorry," the Low squealed, trying to shove the toy out of sight behind his back.

Tasma pushed me forward into the room. I felt an icy chill as I crossed the threshold, but my strength and access to my energy returned once his hand was off my horn.

"You know what happens to Lows that don't respect their toys," Tasma warned. "I'll send some bones down at dinner time. You can chew on those, but good Lows do not damage their toys. And you all are good Lows, are you not?"

There was a panicked chorus of affirmative responses, cries assuring the powerful demon that they were, in fact, good.

Good. Demons were not "good" even Lows. What was wrong with this Tasma guy? Was this some sort of horrible torture, that he was forcing these demons to act against their nature? And what was the punishment for misbehavior?

The wall sealed once more, Tasma vanishing on the other side and leaving me in a room full of nervous Lows and children's toys.

"What does he do if you rip the limbs off a Barbie?" I asked. "A time-out? No cake after dinner?"

"We don't know," Puck whispered with a frightened glance at the wall behind me. "Those demons are taken away and we never see them again."

"Even the good ones are taken away," an eight-legged purple Low confided. "And we never see them again either. Best thing is to not be bad, but not be too good. And to hide behind the others and hope he doesn't notice you."

"How many has he taken away?" I looked around the room. Six—no eight—Lows were here, yet a dozen or two had been taken. I could hope all I wanted, but in my gut I knew that four to sixteen demons weren't trying to not-break the toys in another room somewhere, or in a solitary time-out without their cookies.

"There were eleven bad ones," the purple demon told me. "Six got into a big fight and four died before he intervened and took the other two away with the dead. One tried to climb up and escape out a window and fell to his death. Two others choked on some little, jagged plastic things and died. Five good ones got taken away. Or maybe it was eight? It's kind of hard to keep track of everyone."

I looked around at the walls of the windowless room.

"The window is gone," she told me. "He removed it. And we don't have the toys with the little plastic parts anymore either."

This guy was so fucking weird. I'd been in the human world enough that I could see the eerie similarities between this setup and a daycare center run by a psychotic nutjob.

"He was very upset about the dead Lows," a fat yellow blob of a Low told me. "Called them his poor lost ones. We all got punished when they died."

Bastard. I envisioned him whipping the Lows, burning them as he blamed them for the loss of the others.

"It was horrible," the purple one said with a shudder. "The lecture went on and on until I was ready to kill myself. Only I couldn't kill myself because he'd taken away all the toys with the little parts."

"Even bunny-boo doesn't have eyes anymore," a gray Low with huge pointed ears complained, holding up a tattered stuffed animal whose woolly fur had been licked off in patches. "He told me they were a choking hazard."

Puck elbowed me and I leaned down. "We're going crazy. Swivle won't let go of that fake rabbit. Don't try to take it away or he'll cry and Mister Tasma will come. We'll all have to sit for a weird story about how sharing is what good demons do, and threats about what might happen if we take things from each other. We're supposed to say please and thank-you, and eat all of the vegetables at dinner. And no fighting. Fighting gets you taken away."

I had to get them out of here. Those that weren't killed were slowly going insane. Maybe fighting and being hauled away as "bad" would be a blessing, if they were all going to end up like Swivle, clutching the stuffed rabbit and obsessively licking the side of its face.

Were the others alive or dead? If I rescued these ones, would I be leaving behind nine to twelve demons to suffer? Because I wouldn't get another chance at this. Could I live with myself if I only brought eight to safety and left the others behind? I'd claimed them. It would forever eat at me to think that I'd allowed another demon to take what was mine and destroy it.

Although those were the least of my worries. How the fuck was I going to get these Lows out of here? We were deep in the bowels of somewhere, several magical passageways from the physical part of Tasma's home. Were these walls truly walls? Could I just blast my way through them, and how many other ones stood between us and the outside?

I was surrounded by Lows. I couldn't imagine that Tasma would have expended the cost and effort to put big-time security in place to hold a bunch of demons that simple bars and barriers would contain. I mean, these Lows were so puny that they choked to death on Legos and died falling from a window that couldn't have been more than eight feet off the ground.

"Mistress?" A voice I recognized parted the crowd of Lows and I saw Booty with his slick oily fur and his beady little eyes. "Mistress! Oh, has he captured you as well? I would not wish this place on anyone, but I am still so glad to see you."

The Low ran toward me, and I thought for a second he would rake his claws down my side, biting my arm in his usual affectionate greeting. Instead he halted, claws upraised. Then they retracted and he wrapped his greasy arms around me, placing his bony head against my chest as he hugged me.

"Hug! Hug!" Swivle raced toward me, the stuffed rabbit dangling from one paw. He too wrapped his arms around me, setting off a chain reaction. My startled eyes met Puck's as half a dozen Lows gave me a gentle group-hug, a few stroking my back or patting my shoulder with soft words of "there, there".

"They're going insane," Puck told me. "We're supposed to hug, and be gentle with our hands. And kissing needs to be kept to the cheek or forehead with no tongue. Otherwise, he'll know we've been bad."

But these Lows hugging me weren't doing this out of a sense of self-preservation anymore. They weren't acting. Booty had hesitated, but he was one step from this being his default greeting, from losing whatever was demon about him as these others had. How long had it taken Tasma to break them? How long had it taken for him to turn a group of demon Lows into a band of well-behaved, scared toddlers?

CHAPTER 17

*T*asma brought dinner himself, then stood outside the doorway and smiled benevolently as we ate hot dogs that had been cut into tiny little pieces, tater tots, and a healthy serving of soft carrots and peas. We had milk to drink. The entire time, the demon encouraged us repeatedly to clean our plates, while instructing us on proper usage of the utensils as well as constant entreaties to wipe our hands and mouths on the supplied paper napkins and not our own arms, or legs, or the arms and legs of our neighbors.

That weirdo stood there the entire time with that creepy smile on his face, eyes glowing as he watched us. Then when all the plates and utensils were collected, he still stood there. The other Lows froze. I felt their unease and wonder what they expected to happen next. I doubted it was cake and ice cream from the fear I felt rolling off them.

"You." Tasma pointed. "You with the stuffed rabbit. What is your name?"

Swivle stuffed the bunny's ear in his mouth and sucked on it, mumbling. The rest of the Lows shifted away from him, like the waters parting.

Tasma's smile widened. "There is no need to be afraid, little one. I will teach you to be strong and brave. What is your name?"

The question this time carried enough compulsion to send a shudder through the rest of the room. The rabbit ear popped out of Swivle's mouth, bedraggled and soggy with spit.

"Swivle." His voice was hushed. Then I felt the power from Tasma shift, and the Low got to his feet, walking as if transfixed over to the doorway. The others sighed, obviously relieved that they were not the ones being selected this time. Tasma beckoned, that creepy smile still on his face.

"Let him go." I stood, and now the Lows edged away from me. I saw the purple one try to hide behind a toy fire truck.

"It's a good little Low who is concerned about her friends," Tasma told me. "And I admire both your courage, and that you're using your words. Our friend Swivle will not be hurt. He wants to come with me, don't you?"

"Yes." The word was hard and jagged, as if it had been forced from the Low's lips. He began to shake, and with a whimper, stuck the rabbit's ear back into his mouth.

I took a step forward, then another, feeling as if I were walking against a hurricane gale. The other Lows watched me in horror.

"Don't be bad," Puck told me. "Sit down and let him go."

And be grateful it wasn't me, was the subtext.

"I don't know where you're keeping the other Lows, but you need to let them go. And you need to let these ones go as well."

I finally managed to stand before Tasma, who was regarding me with mild surprise, still smiling.

"They're safe here with me. Out there, they are preyed upon and killed. Out there, no one loves them or takes care of them. Here with me they are safe."

"Here with you they are prisoners. You kidnapped them, and are keeping them locked up in here, punishing them when they don't do what you want. How is that any better than what they face out in Hel where at least they have their freedom?"

"You will soon learn that it's better here, that we are all friends and there is nothing to be afraid of as long as you are good. Right? Aren't you all happy?" He waved his hands outward as if he were a conductor.

There was a chorus of "yes" and "oh so happy" and "we're good". Swivle took another step toward the threshold, and while Tasma was distracted by his unwilling sycophants, I snatched the Low up in my arms. The stuffed bunny felt cold as the sodden fur touched my shoulder, but the Low didn't struggle.

"Put him down," Tasma commanded, his smile twisting into something less benign. "He's my chosen one for the evening. And you are being a very bad Low."

I put him down all right. I tossed him behind me into the other Lows then stepped forward, summoning my sword.

The Lows all screamed "no", and ducked for cover as, miraculously, my sword appeared—a sword and not as a banana or a pool noodle. Tasma eyed me in surprise. I didn't give him a chance to react as I thrust the sword through the doorway. The shock of it disrupting the magic tore through me, twisting my bones and burning the fur from my skin. I gritted my teeth and kept the sword in place, repairing my damage as quickly as it occurred.

"Why, what do we have here? The bad one has a weapon." Tasma made a tsk noise. "We are not allowed weapons here in the playroom."

I really didn't give a shit what was allowed or not, but I noticed he made no move to try to take it from my hand. With a slashing motion, I felt the magic give way and the entire wall in front of me vanished. There was nothing between me and Tasma but my sword.

"Run," I shouted to the Lows, hoping that they'd heed my words and manage to somehow find a way out of this place while I was battling this demon. There were ten Lows behind me. I saw roughly six of them tear past, each of them clutching a favorite toy. Tasma waved his hands, imploring them all to come back, to be safe before they hurt themselves. Then with the smile gone from his face, he turned to face me.

"You have been very, very bad." The khaki pants and sweater vanished, as did the human form. With a flash of light, Tasma became a giant scorpion with the head of a bull and arms of a really hairy human. Each hand ended in six sharp blades. With a snort, he dipped his head and charged.

I dodged to the left, swinging my sword and hitting Tasma in the ass with the flat of the blade. He spun around, but I didn't wait to engage. There was a giant opening in front of me, so I took it, and hauled ass down the weird maze of narrow hallways, hearing the demon bellow in rage behind me.

The bellow and scuttle of scorpion feet wasn't the only thing I heard. Footsteps. And squeals of outraged Lows. Four of those fucking little bastards, the ones who hadn't run, clearly were suffering from some sort of Stockholm syndrome. I wondered for a quick second if my vow to free all the kidnapped Lows included these guys, or if I could in good conscience leave them behind.

I needed to buy the other Lows time to get out of here, so when I realized I was recognizing a few hallways and might possibly know a way out, I took the opposite turn. And each time, I slowed to give my pursuers a moment to gain on me before taking off again. After I felt like I'd run a fucking marathon and given those Lows enough time to figure out how to escape, I turned to face my attackers and drew my sword once more.

It wasn't a sword. It was a whip—a rather short whip. I wasn't thrilled with this quirk of my weapon, but appreciated the irony of confronting a scorpion/bull with a mini bullwhip.

He charged as fast as his eight legs could go, head down, knives flashing, tail stabbing. And behind him were four Lows, like a bunch of pissed-off goblins, frothing at the mouth and ready to beat the crap out of anything left after Tasma was done with me.

Dodging horns and knives, I managed to lay a few well-placed stripes along Tasma's back. The carapace glowed red and split, smoking with a horrible odor, and I realized that having a whip instead of a sword was wicked cool. I ducked under the jabbing stinger and flicked another three lines along the demon's underbelly, rolling to avoid the stomping points on his eight legs. Rolling to my feet on his left, I hit him twice more with the whip, timing another duck-and-roll movement for when he spun and tried to poke me again with the stinger.

He drew the tail back. I tensed, ready to evade. That's when I got hit upside the head with an Optimus Prime. The Transformer threw me enough off balance that the stinger ripped through my shirt and carved a line down the side of my arm.

Everything went numb in that limb. My whip fell to the ground. I grabbed for it with my left hand and was pelted by hundreds of teddy bears, Legos, and Barbie Dolls while I scrambled for my weapon.

"Bad! Bad!" the Lows chanted.

"She *is* bad!" Tasma roared.

I snatched my whip and rolled as his knives slammed into the floor where I'd just been. More Legos bounced off my body. I tried to hit Tasma's underbelly while simultaneously attempting to evade eight legs, and a tail that was now jabbing blindly underneath the demon. Rolling to avoid the stinger, I miscalculated and felt a leg stab through my stomach, impaling me firmly to the ground.

"Bad!" the Lows screamed, still throwing toys at me. I struggled to free myself and saw Booty out of the corner of my eye pick something up and make his way through the crowd toward me. He'd come back. Why had he come back? He should be out of here and halfway to my home by this point.

"Bad, bad," he chanted in time with the rest of them. Then he raised a brightly painted wooden chair and swung. Instead of me, the chair hit Tasma. His leg bent backward and he screamed, pulling the pointed end from both the floor and me in his haste to get away from Booty.

I rolled, healing my gut wound and once more summoning my sword to my hand. It was still a whip. Tasma's tail with its barb swung toward me and I decided to try something different. Ducking, I looped my whip around the Ancient's tail and went for a ride.

He realized I was on his tail, and began to thrash around, smashing me into the walls and the floors as I scrambled to get on top of the tail. Gripping the scales and struggling to keep from being dislodged, I pulled myself up and inadvertently touched the stinger.

Everything went numb from wrist to shoulder and I nearly fell off his tail. My whip dropped to the ground and vanished. I held on frantically with one arm looped around the tail and tried to swing my leg up over the top, all the while being beat into the walls and floor, toy projectiles still whizzing past my head. I slipped and fell, hitting the floor hard. The stinger came down toward my middle and I rolled.

I didn't roll fast enough. The stinger jabbed me in the

chest and everything in my body seized. My lungs stopped. My heart stopped. My muscles froze. I stared out from eyes that wouldn't move. I'd been in a dead body enough that I was starting to be able to animate it somewhat—not enough to walk around like a zombie, but enough to seriously freak the people at the morgue out. This was tricky, because whatever Tasma had in his stinger had this body locked down tight. My spirit-self was in no danger. Once he removed the fucking stinger from me, I could recreate my body, but he didn't know that and I'd rather do the zombie thing because it tended to surprise demons, and angels, as well as humans.

Tasma was no idiot. He held the stinger in place long enough to ensure that I was truly dead. If I'd been a demon, a run of the mill imp, I *would* have been dead. Existing inside a non-living form was something very few angels knew how to do. None of the demons I knew could do it, and I wasn't even sure these Ancients had the skill.

He finally yanked the stinger out of my chest. I heard the Lows cheer, saw Booty's face peering down at me with concern before the little guy was yanked away.

"And now I need to do something about this other bad boy, the one who hit me with a chair," Tasma announced. "Bad boys must be punished."

I heard Booty squeal in alarm, heard the other Lows begin their chant of "bad, bad" once more. As quietly as possible, I purged myself of the poison, and sat up, rising from the dead.

"I'm the only one who punishes the bad," I announced. "And right now, the only bad demon I see in this room is you, Tasma."

I reached out to grab his spirit-self, and found him unguarded and open. With a yank, I began to spool him into me, just enough to let him know what I was about to do, but not enough to truly devour him.

He shouted and tried to pull away, but I held fast, tackling his physical form just to make sure he didn't get out of range. The Ancient squirmed frantically, stabbing at me with pincers and that fucking stinger. With my free hand I reached out and grabbed it, using my energy to snap it off his tail.

"Yield?" I snarled at him. "Do you fucking yield?"

"To a Low?" His eyes narrowed. "An imp! You're not a Low. You deceived me, you nasty imp. You bad, bad, imp."

"Bad, bad," one of the Lows whispered, but they all held back, their eyes wide with fear.

"Yield," I snarled, spooling a bit more of his spirit-self into me, just to show him I was really fucking serious.

"I will not yield to an imp," he announced.

Oh well. Guess I'd just kill him then. It had been a while since I'd devoured anyone. Gregory didn't like me to do it as he was always worried I'd lose control and eat all of creation, like a demon black hole. But Gregory wasn't here, and what he didn't know wouldn't hurt him. Or me. Or anyone besides this Ancient that I was about to absorb as if he were a spilled glass of wine and I was a really super-absorbent paper towel.

"Don't kill him," the Lows squealed. The one closest to me began to cry.

Damn it all. Suddenly they were all crying. Swivle was clutching his rabbit, sobbing at me not to kill Mister Tasma, to be a good demon and eat my carrots and not kill Mister Tasma.

What the fuck was I going to do now? I could kill Tasma and free however many Lows he'd managed to mind-fuck into being his little minions only to find these minions determined to kill me and avenge Tasma. Slaughtering all the Lows with the Ancient didn't seem like a great choice either. There were some demons who would give that kind of slaughter a resounding thumbs-up, but would the street cred be worth the future distrust on the part of the Low members of my household? Or the amount of gore I'd have to deal with?

They were crying. Begging me not to kill Tasma, to be a good demon.

Fuck. Fuck. I couldn't bear the thought of the look in Snip's eyes once he heard about this. Or Nyalla's. The girl was bound to find out, and my heart hurt at the thought of how upset she'd be with me.

And who was I kidding? Gregory would find out that I devoured this Ancient, and he'd be furious. Or worse, disappointed. Fuck. Fuck!

"Yield," I told him, hoping that he'd take this chance I was giving him. Then inspiration hit me. "Please."

Something flickered in the Ancient's eyes. He glanced over at the sobbing Lows, at Swivle who had half the stuffed rabbit in his mouth at this point. Then he looked back at me.

"Since you asked so politely, yes I will yield."

I eased his spirit-self back into his body and climbed off him, dropping the severed stinger on the floor. This was big. I'd killed high-level demons before, I'd even killed an Ancient, but I'd never had one yield to me. We had very few rules in Hel, but this was one of them. We'd fought. I'd prevailed. He'd basically given himself and his household to me instead of accepting death. Now it was my turn to make sure this worked, because he was still a powerful Ancient. If I pushed this too far, he'd challenge me to the demon equivalent of a duel to the death, and I really didn't want to have to go through this again. I'd won this time, but now that Tasma knew my tricks, he wouldn't be so easy to beat.

Not that this had been easy. And not that he assumed he knew all my tricks. The key would be to come to an agreement where it wasn't so humiliating he'd decide that combat was the better choice.

I shed the demon Low form and assumed my human one, somehow managing to keep the tattered remains of my clothing in place. Then I revealed my wings, shredding the back of my shirt. And because overkill is always an acceptable practice in Hel, I summoned my sword, which thankfully this time appeared as a mighty, sentient sword.

"You will no longer take any Lows by force," I told Tasma. "Neither you, nor your household members, nor anyone you hire are to take Lows by force. The only Lows you can have and keep are those who voluntarily come to you and stay with you. Any Lows who choose to remain with you have the same privileges as the other demons in your household. They can leave at any time and break their household bonds. You are to provide for them, ensure their physical, mental, and emotional well-being, and they are to serve you with their lives if need be."

Tasma looked up at me in surprise. "They can stay? My little friends can stay?"

"Only if they want to," I reminded him. "I find out you're forcing them, or blackmailing them, or that you're grabbing them off the street again, then I will kill you. Lows are demons, and they are to have the same rights as any other demon, including blood-price if you kill one, accidently or not. Got it?"

He wrinkled his nose. "What kind of blood-price would a Low have?"

"More than you can afford." In reality the blood-price wouldn't be much of a deterrent, but I'd have to make sure there was more than a financial penalty attached.

"I am the Iblis," I announced, raising my sword and spreading my wings as far as they could in this narrow room. "I am the ruler of Hel, and while I don't intend on putting in place a bunch of boring rules and shit like that, you need to obey me and do as I say. You have the independence of your household, but you owe fealty to me, and if called upon, you will provide the services I request."

I heard a whispered "bad". A rubber duck bounced off my head. Which didn't exactly lend power to my statement.

Tasma set his jaw and eyed my sword. I could feel him hovering on the edge of rebellion. An imp. I knew he was thinking that it would be humiliating to bow down before an imp. To give him that extra little push, I pulled my wings in tight, then snapped them out again. My wings. My beautiful matte-black feathered wings. I knocked a few Lows over in the process, but I still knew what impact those appendages had when it came to the demons in Hel—even the Ancients. For added measure, I brought all my considerable stores of energy to the surface, blurring my form and causing my corporeal self to glow with a squint-worthy light.

"I recognize you as the Iblis and promise my fealty and service." Tasma's eyes watered, but they stayed locked on mine. "But can we keep this quiet? If you call on me, then everyone is going to know, but in the meantime, maybe we can keep this arrangement just between you and me."

And a dozen or so Lows. They might be brainwashed, but they were still Lows. I gave it four hours and it would be all over Dis. Which would be a good thing. The more powerful demons and Ancients that were known to be allied with me, the easier time I'd have of this sort of thing in the future. Maybe.

"I have no plans on bragging about the arrangement to anyone," I told him. "I do need to speak with Lash, Sinew, and Booty, though. They have the option to return to my household with me, or to remain with you, but I want to hear their decision directly from them. And every Low and other demon in your household must know of your fealty to me. I don't care what kind of public secrecy you impose on that, but they need to respect me as the Iblis."

He nodded. "I vow on all the souls I Own that it will be so, Iblis."

I stepped back, slipping a bit in my own blood as I allowed him to rise. Then I dismissed the sword because I no longer needed it, and dismissed my wings, because they were a pain in the ass to have out in confined spaces, and pulled my energy back down inside so I didn't blind everyone with the light.

Another rubber duck hit me in the shoulder. "Hey," I shouted. "Respect, guys. That means no throwing toys at me."

I heard a giggle and a "sorry", then the Lows fell silent as Tasma turned to them and waved his arms to gather them close. They scurried forward then sat in a semicircle facing him, their legs crossed, their gaze rapt. It kinda made me want to puke.

"Little Ones, you have heard the agreement I have made with the Iblis. What is your decision? Will you stay under my care and protection, obeying me and being good, or will you go forth into the wilds of Dis where other demons will prey upon you, where you may starve, freeze at night, suffer heat stroke during the day, have no one to fix your injuries for you when you cannot?"

I rolled my eyes. When he put it that way, I wasn't sure any Low would refuse to stay. And as weirded out as they made me feel, these Lows did have it good comparatively. Hel was a hostile place for a powerless demon, and as creepy as Tasma was, he was caring for them in his own freakish way.

Every Low except Booty shouted that they wanted to stay. Tasma then called the others to him, and I saw more than three dozen Lows pack into the tiny room, squishing up against each other and me in an effort to give Tasma a respectful distance. I saw Sinew and Lash, and their eyes widened as they recognized me, but they said nothing, and made no move to come to my side. Tasma again made his speech and went to each Low in turn for him or her to state their intentions. When he came to Sinew and Lash, the two demons hesitated.

"Tasma has recognized me as the Iblis, and owes fealty to me," I told them. "You are still members of my household, but you have the right to leave and affiliate yourself with another at any time."

Sinew scratched his head and dandruff fell like a brief snow shower to the ground. "I don't know, Mistress. He's got some good food here and regular meals. I like the toys, especially the Play Doh. And I get to sleep in a bed shaped like a race car."

"And we won't die fighting angels or elves or other demons," Lash chimed in.

More skin flakes fell from Sinew's renewed scratching. "Yeah, but I kinda like fighting stuff with the Iblis. It makes me feel brave and smart and important." He pursed his lips in thought. "And the parties are fun at the Iblis's house. And there's the chicken wands…"

"Ooo, I do like the chicken wands!" Lash said.

"I think I'm going to go with the Iblis," Sinew proclaimed. Then he shot an anxious look at Tasma. "Does that make me bad? I don't want to be bad."

Ugh. I hoped Sinew wasn't going to constantly be needing reassurance that he was a "good Low" or I was going to have a problem.

"No, you are not bad," Tasma told him gently. "Although I am very sad that you are leaving. I will miss you, little one."

Sinew's eyes filled with tears. His lips trembled. Then he took a deep breath. "I will miss you too, Mister Tasma."

This was turning into a Lifetime movie. "Okay, so Sinew comes with me. How about you, Lash? Hurry it up and decide. I don't have all fucking day, you know."

Lash frowned, his head swiveling back and forth between the pair of us. "I'm going to stay with Mister Tasma."

The other Lows cheered. Tasma smiled warmly. Sinew looked like he was going to cry again. I pushed through the crowd to grab him before he changed his mind. "Come on, buddy. You can vacation on the other side of the gates for a day or two. I'll even let you play with a chicken wand. Little Red likes to eat poultry, and it's fun to watch him chase chickens around the back pasture."

CHAPTER 18

There were more than Lows at my house when I returned with Sinew and Booty. A group of three warmongers and two greed demons were sitting around my dining room table, drinking coffee and helping themselves to a box of pumpkin spice donuts that Nyalla was passing around.

"Please tell me that Snip cleared all the other Lows out of the guest house," I asked her. Six Lows were playing "Plants vs. Zombies" on my XBox, so I sent Booty and Sinew over to join them and grabbed a donut from the box.

"Nope. They're refusing to go back to Hel," Nyalla told me. "Snip tried, but they say they don't want to be drafted into the Ancients' army and they don't trust that Tasma won't still find a way to grab them and torture them, or whatever he's doing to the Lows he kidnaps."

"He's feeding them wholesome, fiber-rich foods and providing them with stimulating enrichment activities and toys," I told her. "I've lost one of my household to the guy already. Some of those Lows in my guest house might want to reconsider."

Her lips twitched into a smile. "So I take it you've resolved that situation in your own imp-like way?"

I bit into the donut. It was still warm. The guy who ran the donut shop down the street must have a thing for Nyalla because she always got the hot, fresh donuts. When I went in, half the ones in my box were stale. I practically broke a tooth on a cruller last week.

"Tasma will no longer be kidnapping Lows off the streets or keeping them captive in his household. A whole bunch of brainwashed Lows are remaining with him, including Lash, who decided three square meals and Legos trumped the occasional roast beak and the rare opportunity to play with a chicken wand."

Nyalla patted me on the shoulder. "Your Lows love you, Sam. Snip and Rutter…those two especially would do anything for you."

My heart warmed to think of my little household. "What do you think about Gimlet?" I asked her. "The new guy who isn't in my household but is hanging out here with Snip. Have you looked into his heart?"

A small frown creased a line between her dark blonde eyebrows. "I can tell he's smart, and he's got a naughty streak, but it's hard to know what's deep down inside him. There are all these layers of hurt and scars that take my breath away. Lows are complex and difficult to read. Honestly, the angels are far easier to see inside than your Lows."

I could understand that. They had more to hide, and a brutal life focused on survival and filled with pain and betrayal. "Do you trust him, though?"

She laughed. "Do I trust any demon? I would be foolish if I did."

"Do you trust me?" Somehow her answer was so very important.

"I trust you to be you, Sam." She smiled to soften the

words. "And I know that when it comes to me, you will do all in your power to help me, to please me. I know that your love for me is greater than just about anything. I know that if you had to choose between saving my life and saving your own, that you would struggle with that choice."

"I'd choose your life." There would be no hesitation there. Yes, I'd sacrifice myself without a second thought to save Nyalla, because she was a daughter to me, and no matter how short her human life would be, I wanted her to enjoy every moment of it, and have it last as long as possible. Nyalla needed me. She was mine, and it was my responsibility to make sure that she had a long and glorious future ahead of her.

"But back to Gimlet." She shrugged. "No, I don't trust him, but deep down I think there may be something there, a core of good, something that the right spark can ignite. Sometimes, I see this twinkle in his eye, and I know at one point in his life he was just as lovable and loyal as Snip."

"But does his belly shake like a bowl full of jelly when he laughs?" I couldn't help joking, since she'd mentioned the twinkle in the Low's eye.

"Like Santa?" She laughed. "Hardly. But I don't think he's quite Krampus yet, either. Maybe Jack Frost. Now go talk to these demons at your table before they drink all of your coffee. They've been here for hours and they're getting restless. The greed demons have already stolen several DVDs."

I grabbed another donut and pulled up a chair at my table. These warmongers and the two greed demons I recognized as the ones who'd joined in when I'd assembled a small group to help Gregory fight the rebels in Aaru.

"Iblis,". Hammer nodded to me. "We owe you a debt of gratitude for including us in the fighting with the angels. Our status was considerably enhanced by that battle, even if we did lose."

"We didn't lose," I argued. "We just…uh, fell out of heaven in the middle of things. It was a terrible accident. I'll make it up to you all sometime, I promise."

"I hope so," Inferno growled. "I was right in the act of slicing one guy in two, when *poof*, I'm bouncing off rocks and breaking nearly every bone in my body."

"Stop whining," Hammer snarled. "You got to keep that awesome, magical, dwarven-made sword. And if you'd fixed your bones and gotten your ass off the ground, you could have scavenged all sorts of injured angels. I've got three sets of wings on the wall from that. There's a tactical advantage to be had in every situation, if you're smart and think fast."

Inferno pushed his chair back and stood, leaning over the table. "I *am* smart. I just fell in an area with no injured angels laying around. You got lucky, Hammer. Doesn't make you a better demon."

I sensed that my dining room was about to see the next violent conflict. "Guys. Knock it off. You didn't sit here for hours drinking coffee and eating donuts just to fight over who got the most wings out of that battle."

Inferno sat back down. "No. We came to warn you."

"About the Ancients?" I asked. "Harkel beat you to it."

I enjoyed a moment of silence, all six of them impressed that I was on familiar enough terms with the revered warmonger that he'd warn me about anything.

"They want us to join them," Hammer told me. "We're the only demons besides you and the Lows who've been to Aaru in millions of years. They're confident that they can get in and that they've got the strength to stay there, but they don't know how things stand with the angels. It's been too long since they were banished, and most of them have been asleep for a lot of that time. They don't know much about the humans, and they had no idea there had been another rebellion."

I did a quick mental recap of what ancient history I'd learned and realized that the humans were fairly low on the evolutionary scale at the time of the banishment. Part of the original disagreement that led to the war had been over whether to give the humans the angelic gifts of grace or not. Angels of Order were in favor. Angels of Chaos were most definitely not. It was the spark that ignited eons of philosophical differences and fractured the heavenly host right down the middle.

"The Ancient I spoke with was quite excited that the angels were fighting amongst themselves," Glitter told me. "It weakens them. They'll be unprepared to mount a cohesive defense. The Ancients feel they could basically walk right in and take Aaru without much of a fight at all."

And how true that was. I imagined the shock on their faces as they stormed in, swords raised, and found no one at home, the empty halls echoing with their battle cries. It was funny, but not funny.

"Who is leading them? Last I heard they were still fighting over who should be in charge." I remembered Gregory's words and felt this horrible worry that they would get in. And once in, we'd never be able to get them out. I doubt I could command them not to do it—they'd just laugh at me. I might be gaining some respect and loyalty among the demons in Hel, but the Ancients would be another thing. They were powerful and old, and they'd remember Samael's rule. They'd be the last beings ever to pledge fealty to a young imp, no matter how often I proved my worthiness for the title.

"There's some disagreement about who is in charge," Hammer said with considerable amusement. "Of course, they all think they're the one who is leading the group. They'll fight it out and someone will come on top eventually. They all know that needs to happen if they have any chance of taking Aaru back from the angels."

"So, there's no Samael? The former Iblis hasn't shown up out of nowhere to lead them?" I imagined they'd all be fighting if their original leader, one of the archangels, was at the helm.

"Samael? Shit, he's a legend. He nearly took the archangel Michael's wings in battle," Snake said.

"He nearly got sliced in two in battle," I reminded him. "He lost. He got himself and the rest of the Angels of Chaos banished. Don't go making him out to be some kind of god."

Hammer held up his hands. "Okay, okay. Sheesh. Little touchy about that, Iblis? Maybe you're feeling inadequate in comparison with your predecessor?"

I glared at each of them in turn. After a moment of defiance, they all dropped their eyes and made a show of slurping coffee and munching donuts.

"Right now there seem to be three or four angels vying for the top spot," Snake told me, crumbs falling from his mouth. "Asmodiel, Irmasial, Bechar, and this Remiel dude."

I wondered what had happened to Nebibos and Sugunth.

"Who is the frontrunner? I need to meet with him," I demanded.

"Asmodiel," Hammer said. "He's the one who was trying to recruit us. I can set up a meeting."

I nodded. "Yes. Tell him the Iblis wants to meet with him immediately."

They all squirmed.

"No offense, Iblis, but it might be better if I told him that I was considering joining the army but needed to have some additional information. You can go in as a member of my household. He'd expect a warmonger to bring a squire along."

Part of me rebelled at the thought of sneaking into a

meeting as a squire, but I'd just snuck into Tasma's house as a Low, so this was kind of a step up. It wouldn't do any good to bash my head against his door and demand entrance. I needed to see this Ancient, and if being sneaky got me in, then I was going to do it.

Sneaky Iblis. That was me.

"When do you think we can meet?"

"Tomorrow morning? They're eager to get this all settled and make plans for their attack. We've got experience in Aaru, we've shown that we won't have any problems getting in if they transport us. And having us on his side will strengthen his claims as the leader of Hel." He suddenly caught himself. "I mean leader of the Ancients. Because you're the leader of Hel. At least you'll eventually be leader of Hel once you manage to get everyone to acknowledge you."

This was so fucking embarrassing.

I stood. "Nyalla, is there room in the guest house for these six demons?"

She poked her head out of the kitchen where I was sure she'd been listening. "No, but I kicked the Lows out of the rooms upstairs and had Nils bring in some extra beds. They can sleep there for the night."

"Hammer, you go back to Hel and make the arrangements for us to meet Asmodiel tomorrow morning. I'll meet you at my house in Dis at dawn. The rest of you are welcome to remain here as my guests. We'll order pizza, and I'll boot the Lows off the XBox so you can play 'Call of Duty.'" The warmongers would enjoy that.

"We accept, Iblis," Glitter told me. Then he pulled something out of his pocket. "If we're going to play 'Call of Duty,' I guess I should give this back to you."

I snatched the game out of his hand and sighed. Greed demons. I'd have to take an inventory after they left and figure out what was missing.

After making sure my guests were all fed, and that Sinew was happily playing with Little Red and a chicken wand, I texted Gregory.

There was nothing I wanted more right now than to curl up with him and tell him all about the fight with Tasma—minus the almost devouring part, that is. He'd be so proud that I'd bested the Ancient and brought him to heel as well as retrieved two of my three Lows and set those free who didn't want to be trapped in a demon version of Romper Room.

Instead I gave him the short version and let him know that I was meeting with another Ancient early in the morning. Before he could even reply, I headed back to Hel. It was insane how often I'd been back and forth in the last few days. This was more teleporting than I'd ever done before, and I was starting to get tired. Still, it was better than driving back and forth to the gate in Columbia, and having to walk all over Hel. Being a sort-of angel had its perks.

During the day, Dis was scorching hot and desolate. The only demons out and about were usually household members running errands, demons doing business with Gareth and the other humans who did not encourage nocturnal visits, and the Lows who found the heat of midday preferable to the roving bands of partiers that tended to fill the nighttime hours.

Once the sun set and the moons came out, Dis cooled. Well, sometimes Dis cooled. There were nights that seemed just as hot as noon, nights where a cool breeze blew across the sands, and nights where frost glistened on the rocks and demons shivered with the abrupt swing in temperatures. Tonight was one of those nights. My breath clouded in front of my face. Windows in abandoned buildings were glowing orange with small fires Lows had built to stay warm. No doubt a few of these buildings would be burned to the ground come morning, the Lows charred to ash inside the rubble.

It was never too cold for a party. Bands of demons roamed the streets, shouting and laughing, every last one of them looking for trouble. Some would go hunt sand wyrms, some daring each other to swim naked, some looking to catch humans, or lower-level demons for some entertainment. Others would set out for the mountains, gone for weeks on troll hunting expeditions.

There was a time when all that seemed so much fun. Now the very idea bored me. Life as a demon in Hel felt purposeless, dull, one long aimless slide toward death—either at the end of some foolish risk, or through our own hands unable to bear the ennui any longer, to pretend that any of this was actually still fun. No wonder the Ancients had fallen into sleep. No wonder those who hadn't had mostly gone mad or killed themselves. No wonder they were desperate to get back to Aaru.

Gregory hadn't just banished them, he'd condemned them to a horrible, long-drawn-out death. It had to stop, their sentences commuted, but not by a battle for Aaru. That wasn't the solution.

I made my way through the magical wards I'd had installed outside the huge dwelling that used to belong to Ahriman, and in through the doors. The building was empty, all my Lows having first fled to Patchine, then across the gates to my Earthly home. The vacant feel added to the surreal sense I'd been feeling every time I came back to Hel. I'd struggled to define it to Gregory, but once again that dusty moldering stagnation seeped in through the walls to press against me, to suck out my energy, my will to live. Had Hel gotten worse, or had I really changed that much in the last few years?

I sank down on the demon-hide sofa and thought back

on my childhood—the jockeying for position among my peers, the struggle to survive, the fear I'd had that someone might discover my devouring. But even with all that, I'd had a sense of wonder, a curious joy about the world around me. I'd chased durfts, played with elves, swam in the swamps. I'd carved doodles into Oma's table while she fed me lunch and scolded me. I'd hid behind Mere or Pere when Pasquit was tormenting me, feeling safe in their ability to blunt the powers of any demon and keep me from harm. I remembered all the punishments, the lessons in survival as a little imp in Hel, my first journey across the gates with Dar, the very first human I'd Owned.

I was less than a thousand years old. Where had those feelings gone? Had becoming a sort-of angel, becoming the Iblis, assuming all this stupid responsibility stolen my youth?

It had all changed in a flash, seemingly overnight. But the change wasn't complete. I could feel it waiting just outside, waiting to blow through that dusty feeling of stagnation, that sense of bored desperation, and blow everything the fuck up. The humans were free. The elves were gone. The Ancients were on the move. It was happening here. It was happening in the world of the humans. It had happened in the homeland of the angels.

The angels would say the worst was yet to come, but as I pulled a durft-fur blanket up over me, I decided to disagree. Chaos. Change. This disruption brought uncertainty and pain, but it was oddly exhilarating.

The *best* was yet to come. But the process of getting there wouldn't be easy, and it wouldn't be painless. The best was yet to come, but for that best to arrive, we first needed to get through the apocalypse. We first needed an Armageddon.

CHAPTER 19

J was up at dawn, gnawing on some dried jerky-like bitey fish that I'd found in my cupboard. There wasn't much left in the house to eat. Lows were like a pack of piranhas. I was probably the only demon in Dis that liked bitey fish, so it was no wonder they were still in there. Otherwise I would have been stuck with stale willow crackers or bone meal paste.

I needed a steward. My last one had left in a huff just after Ahriman burned down my house and I'd never replaced him. Snip was kind of my acting steward sat this time, but there were limits to what the Low could do. Besides, I needed him to run errands and basically be my right hand, not do things like make sure there was enough food in the cupboard, that the blood got cleaned off the walls, and that Poo-poo wasn't locked in the third floor closet.

Hammer showed up just as I was cramming the last of the dried bitey fish in my mouth. I'd done a lot of thinking last night, and before we headed out I wanted to make one thing clear.

"I'm not going to sneak in as your squire," I told him. "Let

181

them think what they want, but if they ask, I want you to tell them I'm the Iblis. Tell them I'm the one who lead the demon army into Aaru, the one who got you in the door."

"Technically didn't that angel get us in the door?" Hammer scratched his nose. "I seem to remember an angel showing up at your house and bringing us in."

"That was so we arrived at the correct time and location for the battle. Without me, you never would have gotten into Aaru. Without me, you never would have been able to fight angels and get those wings hanging on your walls. Asmodiel reached out to you because you've made sure everyone in Hel knows about those wings, but he doesn't know the part I played in your acquisition of them."

He shifted from foot to foot. "But you're an imp."

"An imp with a sword. An imp with angel wings. An imp who brought you into her household for that battle. I've kept my part in that quiet until now, but that ends."

"Why?"

"Why what?"

"Why keep quiet? You should have bloody, tattered angel wings on your wall. You should have Ahriman's skull on a pike outside your house. You shouldn't have a household full of Lows and be gone out of Hel nearly every moment of the last forty years."

I winced, because he was right. In his eyes, I was a demon and needed to act like a demon. But I wasn't really like the other demons, not anymore.

"That battle aside, I'm not advocating the wholesale slaughter of angels. I'm building an alliance with them—an alliance that will bring us rights on the other side of the gates as well as the ability to form unions and work together with angels. It's kinda hard to do that when I'm slapping their severed wings on my walls. And that's why I've been outside of Hel so much lately. As for Ahriman, well I dusted him.

And he was in one of those smoke like forms when I killed him, so even if I hadn't turned him into a pile of sand, there wasn't really a head to mount on a pike. I like Lows. They're loyal and smart and useful, and if the rest of you demons don't realize that, then it's your loss. Now, any more questions before you lead me to Asmodiel's house, and introduce me as the motherfucking Iblis?"

Hammer blinked. "Uh. No. We're good."

I followed Hammer down one of the main thoroughfares of Dis, to the cluster of mansions that were all owned by Ancients. Many preferred the outskirts of the city. Others preferred to make their main home in Eresh. But most Ancients liked to have a presence in Dis, and liked to rub their power and status in everyone's faces by occupying one of the ostentatious buildings in this row.

Asmodiel's house was a tall pillar with solid gold walls in a shiny raised pattern. There didn't appear to be any windows, but I figured some of those gold panels could be like the mirrored glass walls in human skyscrapers and give the residents a view of the outside world. Footprint-wise, it wasn't the biggest building in the row, but it was the tallest by several stories. I mentally compared it with Doriel's understated shack in the middle of a woods, and chuckled. I had no doubt that Asmodiel was powerful, but I'd come to realize that the more an Ancient shouted their worth through impressive possessions and displays, the less confidence they had in themselves.

But I wasn't here to make jokes about how Asmodiel's home was obviously compensating for a small dick.

The demons at the door let us in without even questioning my presence, then took us up what felt like a dozen flights of stairs and left us in a huge room with fifteen-foot ceilings and see-through walls. I'll admit that it was impressive and far removed from either Ahriman's, Doriel's, or

Tasma's style of décor. I liked it. And I hoped that I liked the Ancient this home belonged to just as much. It would be so much easier to get things done in Hel if I had a number of Ancients on my side. Doriel was reclusive, and Tasma reluctant to acknowledge our agreement publicly, but if I could at least get Asmodiel to recognize me as a peer, it would go a long way toward building respect among the demons.

When the Ancient entered, I felt my heart drop. Doriel had clung to the physical form angels seemed to prefer among the humans, even though the gloss had clearly rubbed off her halo along with decay of her wings. Ahriman had given in, becoming a smoky husk that was more demon than the angel he'd once been. Tasma had gone off the deep end and alternated between a mixed-up demon form and his frighteningly bland human appearance. Asmodiel was in a category all his own.

The demon made his way to us, his human-like form shimmering and wet as if he'd walked out of a shower fully clothed without grabbing a towel. His eyes glowed like red coals, and his drowned sooty-colored wings were a mix of demon leather, and mildew-covered feathers. He was gray— gray skin, gray clothing, gray hair. Even the water dripping from him was gray.

I'd done a bit of research last night, digging through Ahriman's records and books, and found that Asmodiel had been one of Samael's generals. He'd left an Angel of Order on the other side of the war, or maybe like Uriel, he'd left Asmodiel. The Ancient had vanished soon after the Fall, supposedly either dead or slumbering, only to awaken three thousand years ago to build this structure and gather a household. He was one of the few Ancients to have ventured into the human world across the gates, and his choice of clothing and construction style told me that his visits had either been in this century, or he'd had a member of his household bringing back copies of Architectural Digest.

Hammer bowed. "Asmodiel, I've thought about your offer and I would like to join your household and fight once more in Aaru, if the head of my current household allows me to do so."

The Ancient patted Hammer on the back, leaving a wet handprint. "Splendid. I'm sure the head of your household will have no issues. Who is he? Chaunta? Elantiel?"

"Me." I stuck out my hand and recited my list of names. "I'm the Iblis."

Asmodiel looked at my hand in surprise, as if he'd expected my outstretched digits to be offering a gift. "You're an imp."

"Very perceptive of you. I'm also the Iblis."

"You're that imp that devoured Haagenti, the one who broke her contract with Ahriman."

"Let's just say Ahriman wanted to add a few amendments to the contract that weren't agreeable to me, so I killed him. There was nothing in our breeding contract that forbade me from killing him, so technically I did not break my vow."

Startled glowing red eyes met mine. Wet lips twitched. "I never liked that Ahriman. Smoky bastard. I always reeked of sulfur for days after meeting with him." Asmodiel reached out and took my hand. I gave it a quick pump then let go, resisting the urge to wipe my fingers on my jeans. It was like clasping a slimy long-dead fish.

"I've been aware that all of the Ancients have awoken and that they have reason to believe now may be the time for them to retake Aaru," I told the Ancient. "Hammer has told me that it has finally been decided that you will lead this campaign? And that you would like him to join you as he has had recent experience with me fighting in Aaru?"

Listen to me, sounding just like an angel there. Clearly I'd been picking up a thing or two from the few times I'd not slept through the Ruling Council meetings.

Asmodiel tilted his head. "I would have thought Hammer lied had he not shown me proof of his battles in Aaru. Those wings are from recent kills. They could have easily been taken from angels who were killed while they were in the human world, but Hammer's description of Aaru causes me to believe that he actually has been there."

"Once. I've been there many times." The Ancient wrinkled up his face in disbelief, so I went on the describe the sections of Aaru I had knowledge of—primarily the fourth circle and the heavenly jailhouse where I'd spent a good bit of time naked and restrained for failure to complete reports in a timely fashion.

When I was done, Asmodiel gave a satisfied nod. "I would like Hammer to join my household and my army. I would also like these other three warmongers and two greed demons to join as well. It's important to have demons in the front lines with recent experience, you see."

Yes, I saw. And I understood that there was one name he was leaving out of his wish list of soldiers. Me.

"I'm assuming there's a reason you are not inviting me to this party?" I drawled.

There was an awkward second where the Ancient was clearly searching for an explanation that wouldn't offend. "You're an imp."

"I'm the Iblis." I stared him down then finally took pity on the guy. He'd been fairly respectful so far, and I didn't want to push him to the point where he was forced to throw me out.

"Look," I told him. "I get it. No one wants an icky devouring imp front and center in their army, whether she's got wings and a sword or not. No hard feelings, dude. I'm happy to sit this one out if you're not interested in my mad skills. However, I'm not particularly inclined to allow my household members out of their affiliation just on a whim."

"I can offer restitution," Asmodiel hurriedly assured me. I could tell he was relieved that I hadn't decided to pitch a fit over his slight and cause a scene.

"We'll get to that later. I've got other concerns I'd like to voice at this moment." I put a fatherly hand on Hammer's practically non-existent shoulder. "My boy here isn't the sharpest tool in the shed, pun intended, and I'm worried that in his zeal to add to his wing collection, he's neglected to make sure this whole campaign has even a remote chance of success."

Asmodiel jerked his head back, affronted. "What do you mean? We are Ancient demons, the Angels of Chaos who fought in the war two-and-a-half-million years ago. We are the Fallen, the banished ones."

I waved my hand, the one not on Hammer's shoulder, in a circular motion. "Yeah, yeah, yeah. You guys lost that war. How do I know you'll even be able to get in? What if you just bounce off the perimeter and fall like a bunch of fiery meteors back to Hel?"

"We can get in now. All of the Ancients feel it. We know that the banishment is not as iron-clad as it once was. It's why those of us who still slumbered awakened."

"How?" That was the question I really wanted the answer to. How the fuck were they getting in? What had changed? Was it the banishment I'd done? Was it me gaining the sword? Was it that a group of demons and I had entered Aaru to fight for Gregory?

"We don't know how." Asmodiel waved a dismissive hand. "And it doesn't matter. All that matters is that when we mount our attack, we will be allowed entry."

This was scaring me. I got a feeling he might be right. So far all the Ancients had corroborated this view, this idea that they suddenly could enter Aaru. I wasn't going to be able to dissuade them with doubts about their ability to get in, so I'd need to try something else.

Because these guys couldn't take Aaru. I couldn't let them barge in and steal Gregory's homeland from him when none of the angels were there to fight for it.

"What guarantee do we have that you'll win this one?" I asked.

I swear I heard the Ancient grinding his teeth. "We cannot give such a guarantee. We do, however, have the element of surprise on our side. And we nearly won the last war. It ended in a stalemate. The Angels of Order won on a technicality."

"They still won. And you all were *banished*. That doesn't sound like a stalemate to me." I gave him a hard look. "What are the odds of success?"

I wasn't sure if it was sweat or water dripping off the Ancient's brow. "Normally I would say fifty percent, but your Hammer here has told me that the angels are fighting amongst themselves. Fractured and weakened by their own battles, with a surprise attack, I say our odds are closer to eighty percent."

"Three hundred Ancients and a few hundred more demons against tens of thousands of angels," I scoffed. "You can surprise them all you want, pop out of a fucking cake maybe, and your chances of success aren't going to be eighty percent. You'll prevail at first, maybe take one choir, then you'll be slowly driven back out of Aaru. Again."

Asmodiel's red eyes flared like gasoline on a fire. "Then we will die fighting. We will never allow ourselves to be banished again. If we had known... Never. Never again will we leave Aaru. Heaven will be ours, or we will die there, fighting to regain our homeland."

I felt his agony as if it were my own. "Hel isn't so bad. And there's always the human world. I'm working to make it so that we have the ability to go there. I'm working on getting changes to the treaty—"

"No." The red in his eyes dimmed to orange. "For nearly three million years we have been trapped in corporeal form, unable to live as we were meant to. I've felt my spirit-self rot, my wings twist and lose their once glorious feathers. My light has dimmed. I am empty, having been cut off from the source for so long that I am as one in the last stages of starvation. So many of us have died since the Fall. And I know that I too will die if I cannot live in Aaru as a being of spirit once more."

I felt great sympathy for this Ancient. What had he been like before the war? What sort of angel was he? I'd been happy with my life in Hel. It never occurred to me that the Ancients might consider every moment to be torture.

"You may die in this battle. You may lose. The odds are that you will lose," I told him softly.

"Then I will die in Aaru. Better to die there than live one more day in Hel as this." He gestured to his sodden form.

I took a deep breath, feeling as if I'd been boxed into a corner. "I need to discuss this with Hammer. He'll give you his decision tomorrow. I'll allow him and the others to switch household affiliations if they're still inclined then, but it's temporary for this battle only."

He extended his hand, which I reluctantly shook. Yuck. Then as we turned to leave, I hesitated.

"One more question, Asmodiel." I waited for his nod. "You left an Angel of Order behind in Aaru, one you loved. If you face him in the battle, will you raise your sword against him? Will you kill him?"

The Ancient sucked in a harsh breath. "His name was Perciviel. And no, I will not kill him in this battle because I already killed him—in the last battle before our banishment, two-and-a-half-million years ago."

Damn. Just….damn. There was really no reply to that, so I left, Hammer by my side, because I knew there was nothing I could do to dissuade the Ancient. He was a fallen angel. And he had nothing left to lose.

CHAPTER 20

"This battle won't be like the last one," I warned Hammer. "Don't go. Stay here and let the Ancients fight this one alone."

"I'm a warmonger," he countered. "It's what I do. How can you ask me to pass by a sweet opportunity such as this one? Fighting in the front lines in an army of Ancients—it will be epic."

"An epic failure. This isn't your fight. This is something that doesn't involve demons. It's a battle to bring closure to a war that happened long before any of us were born. Let the Ancients avenge their wrongs. It's not your fight. You don't give a fuck whether they regain Aaru or not. It's not like you want to stay there."

He laughed. "Every fight is my fight. No, I don't want to stay in Aaru. That place is horrible. I feel like it's trying to kill me, like it's trying to corrode the flesh right off of me and let my spirit-self shred to oblivion. I'm positive if I stay there more than a day or two, I'd be dead."

It was something the other Lows and demons who had fought with me there had mentioned. It made me wonder. I'd been terrified the first time I'd been dragged up there to be thrown into a jail naked and restrained, without my physical form or the means to create one. I'd expected to die every second of that punishment, but hadn't. Were the demons feeling that same irrational fear, as beings who'd been born and lived their lives only experiencing corporeal form, in a world where to live as a being of spirit spelled death? Or had our devolution drifted us so far from the Angels of Chaos we once were that we *couldn't* live as beings of spirit any longer?

I'd survived, but if Hammer, or Snip, or even Dar were to go to Aaru and shed their form, would they? Or as they feared, would they die?

"Then why go?" I asked. "Why risk your life fighting for a cause you don't give a shit about in a place you hate?"

"Wings, baby." Hammer wiggled his sparse eyebrows. "I got a collection going, if you haven't noticed."

We'd reached my house, and headed in the door when something struck me. I laughed.

"I guarantee you that if you go to battle with the Ancients in this campaign you won't score any more angel wings. None. Zippo. You're coming back empty-handed, if you come back at all."

He scowled. "Are you doubting my abilities? Have you seen the beautiful trophies I have on my wall? I will kill angels, and I will bring back at least three, maybe four, sets of wings."

I rolled my eyes. Clearly there was no changing this guy's mind. I'd totally struck out today.

Hammer left and I went inside, wondering what I should do now. I had to get back to the other side of the gates for Gregory's party, but I didn't want to give up on this. Maybe I couldn't convince Asmodiel or Hammer, but some of the Ancients might be swayed. Doriel was on the fence, and both Harkel and Tasma weren't interested in the battle for Aaru.

But would it matter? Five Ancients marching on Hel versus three hundred Ancients... No, it wouldn't matter. They'd arrive, find it empty, set up house and call all their buddies in Hel to join them. Why bother to make the effort when just one Ancient entering heaven would blow the whole thing? The angels we'd been keeping this from would now know about their banishment, the Ancients would gleefully have their revenge. It would be a complete turn of the wheel of fortune.

Everyone would hate me. Well, not the Ancients and the demons. They'd probably love me, although they might not be thrilled that they didn't get to kick ass and take wings in the easiest battle they'd ever not-fought. The angels would hate me. Thousands would be calling for my death. My household wouldn't be safe. Nyalla wouldn't be safe. I'd need to retreat to Hel with everyone I loved, sneaking out occasionally to see Gregory when I could.

It sucked, but there was nothing I could do to change it. Nothing.

My doorbell shrieked, and in the silence that followed I heard something that sounded like a rock being thrown against my door. I walked over, thinking that maybe Hammer forgot something, or wanted to borrow a chicken wand for the upcoming battle.

It wasn't Hammer. There standing in front of my door, just on the outside of the magical wards, was Lash.

"Change your mind?" It was gratifying to think that I may have won out over oatmeal and Legos.

"No, I'm very happy where I am, Mistress. I'm a good little Low, and Mister Tasma loves me."

That sounded a bit like he was trying to convince himself, but I let it pass. If Lash came back, I'd welcome him. It needed to be his choice, though.

"So is this just a visit? I'm the only one here, so I don't have much in the way of food or drink."

"Mister Tasma would like to see you," Lash told me. "I need to hurry back, because he worries about us when we leave the house. That's why we always stay, because nobody wants to worry Mister Tasma and make him sad. But he needs to see you, and since I know where your houses are and can still get by the gate guardian if I need to, I volunteered." Lash puffed out his chest. "And that makes me an especially good boy."

Blech. I wanted to see Tasma again about as much as I wanted a hole in the head, but I figured if he was sending Lash to track me down, it must be important.

"Lead the way," I instructed, even though I obviously knew how to get to Tasma's house.

I passed through his security system and by two demons and a dwarf who were sifting through a pile of burned wooden blocks. Lash led me to a room just off the front hall with lots of pink furry pillows and a bunch of tiaras next to a bowl of potpourri on an end table. The Low left me alone to go summon his Master and I plopped down among the furry pillows, sticking a tiara on my head just for the fun of it.

I knew something was wrong when Tasma didn't mention my appropriation of the tiara. He straightened his sweater and lowered himself gracefully into a chair.

"We have a problem," he began.

"Did all your Lows wake up from whatever drug you were feeding them and run off? Are they on a hunger strike from healthy vegetables and high fiber, whole wheat bread? Are they refusing to go to bed on time?"

He scowled. "No. There is an angel in Hel."

"No shit, Sherlock. It's me. Wings and all, baby."

"Not you, a real angel. An Angel of Order."

For a hot second I wondered if there had been an emergency, a tragedy horrible enough for Gregory to break his vow and the treaty and venture into Hel. Was it Nyalla? One of his siblings? Did the elves break loose from Elf Island and take over the planet?

Nah.

I laughed. "Is it Pristal? Sometimes he does these feathered wings as a joke. He flies around and scares the fuck out of everyone."

"No, a *real* angel. It seems one of them wound up in Hel, and fell into the hands of an Ancient. I'm assuming he was Fallen, that the angelic host banished him to Hel, although they must have known it would be a death sentence for an Angel of Order to show up here. He would have been killed if an Ancient hadn't scooped him up and decided to keep him for his own."

Shit. Shit, fuck, damn. There *was* an angel, one I'd thrown through the gates to Hel myself.

But it didn't matter. He was dead. Either dead or some tortured slave in the hands of an Ancient. Bencul had tried to kill people I loved. He'd entranced a human woman, impregnated her, and had every intention of taking her Nephilim away from her to hide away in safety once the baby was born. He'd used Harper as a brood mare, and would have happily killed her once she'd had the baby.

The angels had their ways of punishing one of their own, well so did I. Maybe I'd eventually break Bencul out of this Ancient's dungeon. Or maybe not.

"How did you find out about this?" I demanded. I'd thrown Bencul into Hel last year sometime as far as I could remember. Why was this just now coming to light?

"The Ancient that has him asked a favor of me."

Could the dude possibly be any more vague? "And...? You saw the angel strung up in a dungeon while you were visiting? The Ancient trotted him out to show off?" Crap.

Another idea occurred to me. "Or the Ancient's angel has something to do with the favor he's asked of you?"

"The latter." Tasma shook his head. "The favor I am performing is of the utmost secrecy, so I cannot reveal it to you, but I never vowed I would keep the presence of this angel in Hel a secret. And as the Iblis, you need to be aware of his presence."

"Okay. Thanks for the heads-up. I'm now aware. But why is it important that I know some Ancient has an angel to torture?" I asked.

"It affects this Ancient's status, that's why. We Ancients were angels once, and we've had millions of years to nurse our grudge and let our thoughts of revenge fester. The majority of us want to take Aaru back, to kick the angels out. We want the archangels turned into four piles of sand. And although taking back Aaru is not something I want any longer, every single one of us would love to have a whole choir full of angels in our dungeons to torment. One of them got his wish. For some reason, he's been hiding the fact that he has an angel as his own private prisoner, but it's about to come to light, and when that happens, the other Ancients will rush to follow that one's lead. The squabbles over who is in charge will be over. Asmodiel will step aside, and this Ancient will take charge. And he plans to make an attack on Aaru within the next few days."

Fuck. Double Fuck. This was all moving too fast, and was just as unstoppable as a runaway train.

"Who is this leader?" I demanded. "Who is the Ancient that scooped up Bencul and stuck him in his dungeon?"

Please don't say Samael. Please don't say Samael. I didn't know what was worse, Gregory's brother being dead and lost to him forever, or his brother torturing an angel and preparing to lead an army to Aaru. Would it happen all over again, the war, the fighting between brothers, the anger and eventual banishment? Would this time someone die?

I'd rather Samael be dead than have my beloved go through that again, to dredge up all that hate and pain. I'd hoped for some wonderful reconciliation, but if I couldn't have that, then I wanted Samael to be long dead.

Tasma shot me a smug look. "The Ancient's name is Remiel."

I nearly fell over with relief. "Who the fuck is Remiel? Never heard of him."

No wait, I had heard of him. He was one of the top six potential leaders of this army of Ancients, and he'd made the cut to top four. But beyond that, I knew nothing about him.

"He was the angel in charge of purging sin and purifying angels who had strayed from the path."

I blinked at the demon, trying to figure out what the fuck he was talking about.

"Basically, a prison warden," he clarified. "Angels have very strict rules and when one of them broke the rules, Remiel would rehabilitate them. We don't really have rules here in Hel aside from a few basic ones, and rule-breakers generally forfeit their lives unless the injured party has something more creative in mind than just killing them."

I thought of the whole "naked and restrained" punishment I'd been sentenced to for my tardy four-nine-five reports and shuddered. "So Remiel was the creative type."

"And I'm sure he still is. When he was in Aaru, he was less about punishment and more about putting an angel on the right path, getting them to repent and correct their ways and be upstanding members of the angelic host and all that shit."

"But now he's Fallen; he's an Ancient."

Tasma nodded. "He's been banished, and all of us Ancients…well, after millions of years, we're not quite right anymore, myself included. I'm glad he's been asleep for most of our time in Hel, because he's not an Ancient I'd like to encounter on a daily, or even yearly, basis."

I thought about Ahriman and caught my breath. There were a few exceptions—a few Ancients who had somehow managed to keep their sanity. Harkel was one. Ahriman wasn't. Tasma most definitely wasn't. And it sounded like this Remiel wasn't either.

I didn't want to encounter him either, but I needed to. Somehow, I had to convince him to hold off indefinitely on this invasion. I hadn't made any headway with Asmodiel, but when I'd spoken to him this morning, I'd thought I was out of options.

"I need to see Remiel. Can you use your connection with him to get me an appointment?" I asked Tasma. "Anytime tomorrow morning or after will work for me."

I had a sliver of a chance. I might not be able to stop the runaway train, but if I was very very lucky, maybe I could send it off the tracks.

CHAPTER 21

J was never so grateful for Nyalla and my friends as I was tonight. I came home from Hel to find they'd completely organized Gregory's born-day party, including decorations. The downside to not being in charge of it all was that there did not appear to be any strippers or blackjack tables. And instead of tequila, there were a dozen bottles of some wine that Jaq had brought, and a huge selection of beers provided by Wyatt and some of the other guests.

My house was packed, and this time there were no Lows. Ahia and Raphael were prepping deli trays in the kitchen. Amber and Irix were hanging the last few streamers. Snip and Harper were organizing gifts. Asta and Dar were putting out paper plates and plasticware. I walked over to the table and eyed the variety of foodstuff that covered nearly every square inch. Bean dip. Crab dip. Little sausages rolled in crescents. Sliders. Hot wings. Chips and tortillas. And...ewww.

"What the fuck is that? What. The. Fuck." I pointed at the revolting contents of a fancy Spode bone china bowl on the table. Who would do this? Would could possibly think a kale and beet salad would be an appropriate dish to bring to my beloved's born-day party?

Nyalla snickered then slapped a hand over her mouth. Before I could congratulate her on what had to be a prank another voice spoke up.

"It's a healthy food for the humans. We should be providing them with a nutritious food that won't lead them into sinful sensory pleasures or gluttony."

Gabe. I had no idea who invited him to my party. I'd been shocked when he teleported into my living room, a neatly wrapped gift in his hand. He hadn't been holding this revolting kale-crap when he'd arrived, so I assumed its appearance was an impulse on his part, no doubt to counteract the pizza, egg rolls, barbeque, and vast quantities of beer. Oh, and chicken wings.

"Bean dip is healthy," Amber chimed in. "And red velvet cake. It's got eggs in it and flour."

She had a gleam in her eye as she exchanged a devilish glance with Nyalla. What were those girls up to?

"Cake is full of sugar." Gabe glared at the beautiful confection as if it were devil's food and not red velvet. "Nyalla will eat the kale and beet salad, won't you?"

Nyalla's smile vanished. "Uh, actually I had some beets and kale for breakfast this morning. I'm good, thanks."

Gabe turned his scowl on my girl. "That is a lie."

I'm sure it was, but whatever. "My house, my rules. Nyalla gets to eat whatever she wants. All the humans get to eat whatever they want. I guarantee you that salad is going in the trash."

"A significant part of your responsibilities lies in improving human vibration patterns and their FICO scores. Healthy eating is a vital part of positive evolution."

I rolled my eyes. "Not in my book. You want to take over

that part of my responsibilities? If you think you can do better, then you be in charge of that."

"I don't want your job, I want you to do it."

The door opened and Candy and Michelle walked through, each carrying a present. Candy eyed the food table as she passed by, nodding in approval. "Oh, kale and beet salad! I love that."

For fuck's sake. I snarled and stalked off to the kitchen, unable to tolerate Gabe's smug expression. Wyatt was there helping Nils fill a huge jug with mojitos. Wyatt looked hot as always, relaxed and laughing at something Nils said. Nils didn't look as hot. In fact, he looked like someone had driven over him with the tractor, backed up, then driven over him again.

"What happened to you?" I asked, screwing the lid on the mojito jar and grabbing some mugs from the cupboard.

He glanced out the pass-through into the dining room. "Ran into a door."

"Repeatedly? At Mach 6?" Nils might be a Fallen, but he still had an angel's ability to heal. For him to look this way, the cause of his injuries had to have been insanely violent and probably recent.

"I said something stupid," he muttered. "I won't do it again."

I had no idea what he was talking about. "Yes, doors tend to take it personally when you say stupid things."

There was an uproar from my dining area including a series of squeals that meant the girls were excited about something. I peeked through the window and saw Nyalla with Austin in her arms. The Nephilim was playing with her bracelet—a pretty chain with green and blue sea glass that seemed to be her favorite piece of jewelry lately. Ahia reached out for the child, bribing him with a potato chip as Raphael watched, a sappy expression on his face.

Babies. Blech. My house was full of fucking babies. Well, two babies, but that was two more than I wanted here. Austin tended to be furry more often than not, and wasn't exactly housebroken. Karrae sometimes crawled, sometimes toddled, with considerable wiggle room in her human form's age and abilities. I'd had a whole lot less contact with the young angel, but the last time she was here, she alphabetized my DVD collection, lining them up so uniformly on the shelf that I could have sworn she used a ruler. After she and Dar left, I found all the porn movies in the kitchen trash.

Austin, wooed by the prospect of a potato chip, went to Ahia and gleefully shoved the snack into his mouth, sprinkling crumbs all over the floor. I heard a squawk of outrage and looked down to see Karrae at Gabe's feet, incinerating each crumb with a chubby, indignant finger. Nyalla thankfully picked her up before she could set my floor on fire, smiling at Gabriel as she rose with the angel in her arms.

Huh. Why was Gabe staring at Nyalla like that? Or was it Karrae he was looking at with a weird sort of intensity? First the kale and now this bizarre behavior. I swear if he didn't knock it off I was going to get an elf-net and stick him in the basement until the party was over.

Which might be a good idea. He was a fucking stick in the mud. Kale. And beets. What the fuck? But I had no time to wrestle Gabe to the floor, net him, and lock him in the basement. I had a party to organize. Gregory would be here any minute, and there were still two trays of hot wings in the oven.

There was a knock on the door. Right on time, and just as I'd instructed. I left the wings and ran out of the kitchen, hushing the crowd and flinging the door open.

"Surprise!" everyone shouted.

Gregory looked around the room, a somewhat perplexed smile on his face. "How is this a surprise? You told me there would be a party in my honor and that I had to attend and arrive by the front door. And I knew everyone was here. Even if I couldn't sense all the energy signatures, I could hear them clear down the driveway."

Infuriating angel. I hoped this wasn't how the rest of the party was going to go. "Act surprised," I hissed. "You're supposed to act surprised."

"I do a lot of things for you, Cockroach, but I won't lie. Well, I won't lie very often." He strode into to the room, then stopped abruptly. "So what am I supposed to do now?"

Nyalla laughed. "Now we eat food and enjoy each other's company. In a bit you'll blow the candles out and we'll all eat some cake. Here." She handed him a box with a curlicue bow and stood on tip-toe to kiss him on the cheek. "Happy Birth-day. And may you have six billion more."

He opened the box and pulled out a tiny pair of castanets with brightly colored flowers and the word "Aruba" painted on the sides. The angel laughed, holding them up for others to admire. Others pushed gifts into his hands, and he graciously thanked each giver for everything from a backup navy polo shirt, a hat rack with pitchforks as hooks, a box of gourmet chocolates, and a waterproof case for his iPhone. We all ate, guests milling about my great room and table with overfilled paper plates in hand. Everyone had a tiny helping of kale and beet salad, even Nyalla who was looking down at it in despair.

"You need to eat that," Gabe urged her. I scowled, ready to intervene. Nyalla didn't *need* to do anything that angel said. "That dolphin wouldn't have been able to push you aside if you were stronger."

Dolphin? What? Why would Nyalla have gone with Gabe to his porpoise-and-dolphin meeting?

"Oh, so kale is the new spinach?" Nyalla teased. "I'm going to get bulging arms and an anchor tattoo if I eat this? Seriously, Gabe, I could eat a whole bag of this stuff and I'm not going to be able to wrestle a three-hundred-pound bottlenose dolphin."

She looked up at the archangel. Their eyes met. Then with a smile and an exaggerated sigh, she ate a forkful of the salad. My breath lodged in my chest, the world narrowing to a pinpoint as I stared at the two of them. That bastard. That fucking bastard. Suddenly it all made sense—his vote at the Ruling Council meeting, his uncharacteristic insistence that the angels begin associating with humans, the damned dolphins. And this wasn't some chaste, pure, platonic shit either—not from the way they looked at each other, the intimacy in their shared smile, the fact that Nyalla ate that nasty salad.

I launched myself across the table, knocking a bowl of chips and a tray of hot wings to the floor. Then I grabbed Gabriel and punched him in the face as hard as I could. There was a crunch, and blood spurted from his nose as his head rocked to the side.

"You're fucking my girl," I shouted at him. "You hypocritical bastard. You lying, false, deceitful son of a bitch." It wasn't just that Gabe was doing the very things he'd looked down his nose at others for doing, it was the fact that he was doing them with *my* Nyalla.

"I'm not having unemotional, crass, penetrative intercourse with anyone," Gabe sneered, instantly healing his nose and picking up a napkin to blot the blood from his face.

"Oh? Then oral? Heavy petting? Because I know you're not doing angel sex with a human," I snapped back.

"His vibration patterns have been somewhat low the past six months," Gregory commented as he spooned crab dip onto a plate. "And I caught him sipping a glass of wine a few weeks back."

Asshole. He could have mentioned it to me. Maybe I

could have gotten Nyalla away from him before it was too late. And I wasn't believing for one minute that they weren't screwing like monkeys. Gabe might claim to want abstinence, but there was no way Nyalla would ever go for that in a relationship.

"I'm not discussing personal matters involving intimacies in a public setting, or with *you* at all." The bloodied napkin vanished in a puff of smoke from his hand. "Nyalla and I have a close emotional bond that transcends the flesh."

"Making love." Nyalla smiled serenely. "Because even close emotional bonds that transcend the flesh need to be communicated in a physical fashion when one of the parties involved is a human."

How had I not noticed this? She was even beginning to sound like him in how she worded her arguments.

"Are you 'making love' with my Nyalla?" I demanded as all the guests gathered around us to watch. "Are you?"

Gabriel's lip curled and he looked down his nose at me. "Nyalla is a grown human woman. She is not 'yours', and what she and I do together is none of your business."

"Like fuck it's not." I went to punch him again, but he grabbed my fist with one hand, redirecting my blow to the side as he smashed his plate of food in my face.

Coleslaw dribbled down my chin. I head-butted him, then jumped to knock him to the floor with me on top. We rolled, throwing punches, kicking and biting. Okay, it was mostly me kicking and biting. Somehow we ended under the table and I reached for a weapon, only to find a plastic fork in my hand. I tried to jab the angel in the neck with it, but the stupid thing snapped in two.

Gabe batted the broken fork away, then pushed me forward, slamming the top of my head into one of the table legs. The table shuddered, and the kale and beet salad fell to the floor, the bowl shattering.

"Fuck you and fuck your salad," I shouted, grabbing a handful of slimy red beets and shoving them into his nose.

"They're healthy," he shouted in return, bending my wrist so far I heard the bone snap.

I caught my breath in pain, then as I paused to heal the injury, Gabe threw me forward, out from under the table and against the front door.

As I rolled to my feet, I saw Gregory and Nyalla off to the side, watching us with interest.

"My money is on the Cockroach," the angel said, taking a bite of crab dip.

"I don't know," Nyalla replied. "Gabe is trickier than you might think."

My own girl was betting against me. That's what this dickhead had done. He'd brought a shitty food offering to my party, he'd been hypocritically banging a human, and he made my girl fall in love with him.

I'd never seen her so happy. She practically glowed. I remembered that look they'd exchanged, and the affection, the tenderness, the love in Gabriel's eyes. He'd taken her to swim with dolphins. He'd obviously bought her that sea glass bracelet she so treasured. He'd swallowed his pride and voted for her on the Ruling Council because he couldn't bear to hurt her feelings. He was modifying and changing every idea and position he'd held rigidly for billions of years because Nyalla's arguments wormed their way into his heart.

"You hurt her and you are dead," I told the angel.

He blew beets out of his nose on a napkin. "I would never hurt her. Never. I have vowed to protect her with my life."

I narrowed my eyes. "How about that bottlenose dolphin that pushed her."

Nyalla laughed. "It was just playing, Sam. Gabe gave them all a stern lecture, and after that they were very gentle with me." Her eyes grew serious. "I love him."

I knew she didn't mean the dolphin. "Fine. I meant what I said, though. First time he makes you cry, I'm taking his wings off with a rusty pen knife."

"If the entertainment is over, can we have cake now?" Rafi drawled. "I've been eyeing that red velvet cake since Amber set it on the table."

It broke the tension. Gabe and I exchanged a few glares, then I lit candles on the cake and told Gregory that he was to make a wish and blow them out.

There were no more fights. We ate cake. Candy and Michelle cleaned up the beet salad mess. And as our guests began to gather up their leftovers and leave, I went to find Gregory. I had a special gift for him—one I wanted to present in private.

I found him back by the French doors that led to my patio and covered pool. There was my angel, cross-legged on the floor with two young children climbing all over him. One was Austin, Harper's Nephilim son. He was sometimes a wolf, sometimes a hawk, sometimes a mongoose, but right at this moment he was a human toddler, his thumb in his mouth as he patted Gregory's knee and babbled about something or another.

Karrae didn't look pleased, Asta and Dar's little girl had her golden wings out, batting them angrily as she hovered behind the other baby like a cross between a hummingbird and a pissed off infant Valkyrie. She scowled, reached out a fat hand to grip a fistful of Austin's dark hair, and yanked. The older child let out a scream, then sent a surge of electricity into Karrae. Now they were both screaming and crying, making me want to drown them in the toilet or drive over them a few times with my SUV.

Austin recovered quickly, returning to his babbling and his patting of Gregory's knee, where Karrae had thrown herself on the ground and was on the edge of a dramatic tantrum. Her, I still wanted to drown.

"Well, that's what you get for pulling his hair," Gregory told her. With a motion of his hand the baby was in his arms, still flailing and screaming. I got the impression this display was more about her expressing her outrage than any real pain she'd suffered at the other child's hands.

Gregory seemed to be listening to the baby. I've got no idea what she was telling him since all I could hear was crying.

"Karrae, if I don't want Austin patting my leg, I'll be the one to tell him. It's not your job to ensure everyone stays ten feet from me. Now stop your crying. It's not seemly for a powerful angel to be throwing a tantrum like this."

Her tears halted as if he'd turned a faucet handle. Golden eyes looked up at him, and she raised her hand to touch his mouth. He kissed her palm and set her down, running a firm comforting hand over the back of her wings. "Go and play. Your little cockroach of an aunt has been waiting very patiently to talk to me."

No, I hadn't. I'd been holding off entering because I didn't want to have to deal with screaming children. Or children at all.

"Someday I want to create," Gregory announced before I'd taken two steps into the room.

"Congratulations. And who will be forming this child with you?"

He smiled up at me, then with speed that took my breath away he had me down on his lap. I'll say one thing, the guy knew how to frame a persuasive argument.

"There is only one being who I'd ever consider creating with, and that's you, my Cockroach."

I squirmed. It wasn't just that I really didn't feel any urge to form a child. There were issues when demons, or angels, got their personal energy, their spirit-selves, too close to mine. I devoured. And becoming an Angel of Chaos hadn't seemed to do much to blunt that rather reprehensible impulse.

I'd killed the demon who had been sent to tutor me in how to sire and form, devouring his spirit-self right out of his body. My dwarven foster parents had covered up the incident to protect me, as devouring spirits aren't exactly in high demand in demon society and no one wanted to be labeled as one of *those* demons. I'd been avoiding breeding contracts for all of my nearly thousand-year existence. The closest I'd come had been Ahriman. I would have been happy to devour him, but he'd been powerful enough to keep me from killing him during that time I'd exchanged genetic material.

The memory made me shudder. He'd tortured me. He'd forcibly taken me. I was grateful that he hadn't let any offspring he'd formed with me live because I didn't want to chance coming into contact with one of them and having to relive that whole nightmare like I was reliving it now.

Liar. I often wondered about the child I'd sired with him. What had it been like? In the seconds it had it taken him to discover I'd not contributed the devouring ability he wanted had he considered letting it live? What sort of demon would it have been?

"I'll devour you. And the one time…" I couldn't discuss this with him. I'd never been able to share with him the details of what I'd gone through with Ahriman. I took a deep breath. "The one time…wasn't good. I sired with Ahriman. He killed it as soon as he'd formed it."

Gregory placed a kiss on my head and ran a firm hand along my back, soothing me as he'd done to Karrae.

"I'm sorry, beloved. I hate that he did that to you, that you were forced to do things you didn't want to do with that monster."

His touch was helping, the slow rhythm of his hand on my back, the feel of his spirit-self against mine. "I'm not sure I can ever do that again."

"Then we won't."

That was it. No hesitation. No begging or pleading with me to change my mind. No sorrow or longing glances toward the two children that played near us.

"Maybe. Maybe someday. Right now I don't want to." I struggled to find the words to explain how I felt. "I don't want anything we do to remind me of what I went through with Ahriman. I can have angel sex with you and not have flashbacks of what he did to me. No one else can touch my spirit-self like that without me remembering what the Ancient did, but when you touch me, join with me, all I feel or think of is you. So maybe one day I'll be able to do a breeding incident with you and not fear I'll be reliving what happened before."

His hand was warm as it continued to stroke my back. "It won't be like that with me. I won't be taking from you, I'll be giving to you. You'll be the one doing the forming."

And it would be him—an angel so powerful, so in love with me that his touch sent memories of Ahriman fleeing. But there was still the hurdle of my devouring.

"I'll take too much," I warned him. "I'll try to devour you. Remember when you attempted to bind me and I stole a bunch of your spirit-self and you couldn't get it back? Yeah. Think ten times or more because I'm not very good at self-control when it comes to personal energy."

"No?" He brushed himself up against me and I melted against him, feeling the ecstasy of his spirit-self merging with mine. "I don't feel you trying to tear me apart or devour me right now. I've shared myself with you hundreds of times. In

Aaru, we've completely merged and you haven't attempted to harm me."

As if to prove his point, he pushed more of his spirit-self into my own. I caught my breath and closed my eyes, reveling in the feel of him. I couldn't continue to argue when we were like this. I couldn't continue to even think.

"Please," I begged. It came out so hushed and breathy that it was barely a sound.

"In front of the children?"

Like I gave a flying fuck what the children saw or sensed. "Yes. Now."

He pulled away and a low whine escaped me. Tease.

He chuckled, then merged with me. Every thought in my head scrambled and I fell apart, rushing into one translucent white light with him. As always, he held back to keep our bodies intact, to ensure our spirit-selves didn't unravel in this world where we needed to maintain a hint of corporeal form or die. And when he pulled away this time, I realized he was right. I'd never devour him. The urge I'd always had whenever anyone got their spirit-self within grabbing distance of mine wasn't there when we were joining.

"See? There's no devouring anyone. You won't kill me, or take anything that I haven't given you." He kissed the top of my head again. "I'm willing to wait millions of years for you to decide if you want to create or not. I accept the fact that you aren't ready at this time, and that you might never be ready. I want to create, but only with you, and only if you truly want the same. If not, then there will be many, many young angels in the future for me to shower my affections upon."

I looked over at Austin and Karrae. The two were ignoring us and fighting over a set of plastic army men. Maybe someday...

"I got you a gift." I turned on the angel's lap to better see him, then opened my hand to show him a figurine I'd crafted from a melted beer bottle. It was an angel with outspread wings, its hands raised to the sky. He took it, tracing the tiny feathers, the folds in the angel's robe, the little nubs of fingers at the end of each hand.

"I still have the horse you gave me. Remember? When we were up in Pennsylvania at that cabin, chasing down Althean and you were trying to convince me there was beauty in destruction?"

I smiled. "Every act of creation is an act of destruction."

His fingers gently touched the tips of the wings on the glass sculpture. "And you, my Cockroach, are particularly skilled at making beauty from the rubble of that destruction."

I hoped with all of my heart that something beautiful could come from the mess I'd made of heaven and Hel. That, like a phoenix, something wonderful would rise from the ashes of the destruction I was so very good at causing.

Gregory rose, gently setting me down as he got to his feet. The glass angel vanished, no doubt safely tucked away with the horse I'd given him long ago. Hand-in-hand, we walked back to the end of our party, knowing that tomorrow would bring challenges that both of us would need to face— me in particular. But that was tomorrow. Today would be about cake and presents, and getting used to the fact that the archangel I detested was now sort of a son-in-law, and that we were all one happy, dysfunctional family—humans and angels and demons and Nephilim and werewolves and all. Even that vampire girl.

Today was for joy. Tomorrow I would face the chaos.

CHAPTER 22

J arrived in Hel the next morning to find that Tasma had no problem at all getting me an audience with Remiel—which set my alarm bells off. The guy was an Ancient—a powerful Ancient at that. He'd have no reason to prioritize a meeting with me, or pay me any attention whatsoever, even if he had some business going on with Tasma.

Also concerning was the fact that Tasma was not accompanying me to this meeting. Instead I arrived alone, carefully avoiding the poisoned spikes on his gate and not quite avoiding a huge panther-thing that bit me on the way to the front door.

Once inside, nothing else made any attempts to assault me. I declined the seat his butler dude offered me claiming to be interested in the artwork. A couple of other demons brought in the usual trays of food and a pitcher of some beverage, then the three left me to wait for my host.

Unlike Ahriman's homes, this place had décor that might be at home in a luxurious European castle. Yes, there were a few heads and other body parts mounted in display on the wall, but the ornately carved and gilded wooden chairs and gold embroidered cushions looked very Louis the XIV.

The door opened and I turned to see a demon come toward me. Not Remiel, by the energy signature, although this demon was old enough to be an Ancient, and certainly had held power at one time, although from the looks of him, he'd been put through the wringer and fallen quite far from whatever status he'd normally held.

The demon snarled and stopped just inside the door, his hands flexing then curling into fists. It was then I realized that I recognized this being—both his battered energy signature and his equally battered physical form. This was no demon, this was an angel. Or at one time, it had been an angel.

"Bencul," I said hesitantly, not sure how to greet him. How does one greet an angel that you basically hog-tied and tossed through the gateway into Hel?

"Bitch," he snarled.

Bitch wasn't one of my names, but under the circumstances, I'd accept it. He wasn't attacking me, so I didn't summon my sword or do anything but the same as he was doing, which was stand and stare, with every muscle tensed and ready.

As the shock of his beat-to-crap appearance faded, I noticed a bit more about the angel. He'd been marked. He was part of Remiel's household. And the Ancient hadn't just tagged Bencul as a member, he was tagged as a partner. Not as a consort with authority such as I was supposed to have in the contract with Ahriman, but a partner. It was a cross between how a demon would have marked a very precious toy, and a low-level consort.

Whatever it was, it made my stomach clench. Bencul was basically a slave, but a very favored one. Woe to anyone who gave this angel so much as a hangnail. Which made me glad I hadn't pulled out my sword or done anything threatening. It didn't explain, though, why Bencul hadn't attacked *me*. He clearly wanted to. And I wouldn't really be able to defend myself without incurring Remiel's wrath.

The air shimmered to Bencul's left, and the angel dropped to his knees, his head bent. A large bipedal form appeared, red-skinned with two huge horns curling above his bovine head. Smoke puffed from his nostrils as he reached out a hand and curled Bencul's hair into a tight fist.

"I'm so pleased you've asked to see me, imp-who-holds-the-Iblis-sword. Bencul here has told me that you are the reason he is here in Hel. You are the one I owe for being able to acquire something I value far above any of my other treasures."

"Um...you're welcome?" None of this was going as I'd planned, and I had no idea how to deal with the fact that Bencul had become an Ancient's fuck-toy. He kind of deserved it after what he'd done to Harper, but the dynamic before me was stirring up all sorts of memories of being in Ahriman's dungeon at his mercy. Did I feel sorry for the angel? I wasn't sure if I could find a way to get him out of this, even if I wanted to. And I wasn't sure I wanted to, given what a douche he'd been to the human woman who he'd impregnated with his Nephilim.

It wasn't like I could send him back to Aaru. And I certainly didn't want him in the human world either. Maybe this was the best punishment for him—making him suffer the same sort of relationship that he'd pushed upon Harper.

"Stand." Remiel released the angel's hair and as Bencul stood, the Ancient's hand drifted lower to stroke down Bencul's side to his hip. "It's been so long since I've been with an Angel of Order. Millions of years. I'd nearly forgotten the ecstasy of joining."

The Ancient shimmered, and Bencul lifted his head, his

eyes heavy-lidded, drunk with a feeling that I knew very well. He might be pretty close to a slave. He might have suffered at Remiel's hands. But there was an attraction there that wasn't one-sided. Bencul was just as addicted to Remiel as the Ancient was to him.

And I was two seconds from being a voyeur. Ick.

"Okaaaay. I really had no idea Bencul was still alive, let alone that you'd entered into a…whatever with him. Cool. No biggie. But that's not why I'm here."

Remiel halted his affections with a sigh and turned to me. Bencul shot me a hate-filled glance, then dropped back down to his knees beside the Ancient.

"Then why are you here? Do you have more angels you're planning on bringing to Hel? I know several other Ancients who would gladly pay you to have one of their own."

I was so not going to become the pimp of Hel. Infernal Mates was a different matter entirely. That was a dating service, not snatching angels off the streets and throwing them through the gates into what was basically slavery.

"Actually, I'm here because I heard from several sources that you're gathering forces to make an attempt on Aaru. I met with Asmodiel, because at the time he was the leader of this campaign, but now I hear you are?"

Remiel smiled benignly—well as benignly as a huge red bull-headed demon could. "Yes, I am. And I plan to advance on Aaru within the next day or two. Why wait? Strike while the iron is hot, I've always said."

I'd expected him to deny it or hem and haw. This bland acknowledgement had thrown me just as much off balance as seeing Bencul had.

"But you can't get into Aaru," I said. No one had so far given me anything as to the why they could now enter Aaru —nothing beyond a vague feeling that it was possible. Perhaps Remiel knew more. "You're banished. Only the Iblis, that's me, and my household members can enter. And none of those who I bring into Aaru can be Ancients. There's some wiggle room for demons, but not for those who were originally banished after the war."

Remiel walked over and took a handful of beaks, popping one into his mouth and tossing another one over to Bencul, who remained on his knees. The angel paid no attention to the roasted beak that bounced across the floor and came to rest a few inches from his leg.

"But there has always been an opportunity for reinstatement, for a reversal of the banishment." The Ancient turned to Bencul. "You may eat that, darling."

The angel reached out and picked up the beak, crunching it a few times before swallowing. "Thank you, beloved."

The scary thing was that he meant it. Bencul was battered, but he wore his wounds as proudly as any demon would. His reply to Remiel wasn't defeated, or defiant, or anything besides adoring. The term of endearment he used practically caused the air to vibrate with the force of emotion. Bencul hated me, he hated being in Hel, and he clearly disliked some aspects of his status, but it was clear he was infatuated with Remiel.

"Yeah, I believe to become un-banished, you would need to repent and gain forgiveness," I said. "Now I might be wrong, but you don't seem like the repentant type, Remiel. And I'm positive that none of the archangels have been in Hel to offer you forgiveness."

"See, that's where you're wrong. It doesn't take an archangel to offer forgiveness, it takes an angel. Surprised? I know I was. I doubt any of those flying rats heading the Ruling Council realized that there was a little slip up in section forty-two, sub-section eight, item one-sixty-five of the treaty. It pays to read these things carefully. And it pays to be patient. I was patient. And I *have* been granted forgiveness by an angel. I'm now, how did you put it, un-banished."

I glanced at Bencul, wondering how he could so betray his own kind. "I'm sure there is something in the treaty about forgiveness granted under duress. It's not going to work, Remiel."

He walked back over and stroked Bencul's head. "But it will and it has. I did not coerce Bencul to grant me forgiveness. There was no threat, no bribe. Was there, Bencul?"

The angel looked up at Remiel. "I freely gave you my forgiveness, beloved. As well as my heart, my form, and every bit of my spirit-self. And you have done the same with me. Your repentance has been accepted, and I have forgiven you for all. The doors of Aaru will open to you."

Bencul's words rang true. He really loved this Ancient, and I got the idea that Remiel returned the affection. This might be a weird, twisted sort of love, but it was earnest. And I understood why Bencul had done this. He was trapped in Hel. The only way he'd ever get back to Aaru was if I took him there, or if he attached himself to an Ancient and broke the banishment. I don't think he'd entered into this arrangement for love, but love is what happened. I was pretty sure he'd been passed around between some rather enthusiastic demons before Remiel "rescued" him, then hatched his plot. Then somehow, he fell in love.

What the fuck was I going to do now? I didn't really like Bencul—and that was putting it mildly. I was worried that those Ancients who'd suddenly sensed their banishment had ended were right, and that Remiel's plot might work, but what could I do to stop it?

It would really suck if this Ancient managed to get him and his army into Aaru, only to find it empty and ready for new occupants to take over. Gregory would never forgive me. It was bad enough when there was a chance the rebels would take Aaru, but the thought that his homeland would be taken over by the exiled and demons, while he and his brothers were still denied entry, would pretty much spell the end of our relationship.

It did strike me as poetic justice, but as much as I liked poetic justice, I loved Gregory. No, I would not let this Ancient take Aaru. If I had to stand in front of him with my sword, if I had to kill him or Bencul, if I had to mobilize an army of Lows against him, I'd do it. The first being to set foot back into heaven would be Gregory and no other. Except maybe me. But if I was first, I wouldn't tell anyone, and would quickly go get Gregory to be the first.

"What if there's some glitch in Aaru and you can't get in?"

His smile was a weird combination of tolerant and condescending. "I'm no longer banished. I've been forgiven. And once I'm in, once I open the door to Aaru, the other Ancients will be able to follow. You've proven that yourself. As the Iblis, you've had entrance to Aaru, but until recently, we always assumed that only you would be able to enter. Imagine our surprise when we hear warmongers and greed demons bragging about how they have been to Aaru and fought with the angels. And they're not lying. Several of them have trophies that are recent. If demons can get into Aaru under your household, then I'll be able to bring Ancients and demons in under my own."

I bit my lip, remembering the Ruling Council meeting, the loophole in the banishment. Yes, Remiel might be able to bring Bencul and a bunch of demons into Aaru, but I didn't think his forgiveness would extend to the other Ancients even if they were in his household.

Which should have reassured me. Instead of an army and a bunch of Ancients in a vacant Aaru, there would be one Ancient and an army of demons. That wasn't reassuring at all.

I prayed that my own banishment was not so flawed. As much as I hated what I'd done to Gregory and his siblings, if it saved Aaru from an invasion of Ancients, I'd be thankful.

If. It was a really big if.

"So, what's your plan here?" I asked Remiel, figuring he wasn't going to tell me his evil plans, but it was worth a shot to ask.

"We have a planning meeting tonight, then we move within the next two days. Our army will teleport just to the edge of Aaru, then storm the place. We'll kill any angel who doesn't leave. Well, except for a few that we take prisoner. It's important to have leverage against any of the host who flee, and we all want a chance to take revenge on specific angels who wronged us in the past."

Crap. This was a fucking nightmare.

"Remiel, I'm begging you to wait on this invasion. You and so many of the others have been asleep for so long. Things have changed in two-and-a-half-million years. Lots of things have changed."

"Yes, I hear that the humans have become...interesting. And that the angels are in the midst of another internal war. It's the perfect time for us to make our move."

"It's not the perfect time. If you just wait, then you might never even have to fight them. I'm the Iblis. I'm serving on the Ruling Council with the archangels. Angels and demons are beginning to come together. The treaty's terms are in debate, and the banishment is being revisited. Aaru is...fractured, and many angels regret what happened during the war and want a reconciliation. There will be a path to reinstatement, if you just hold off."

"We've waited two-and-a-half-million years. Are we to wait another million years? We have the strength, we have the ability to enter Aaru, and we will have the advantage with the host currently divided amongst themselves. It's unreasonable to ask us to continue to wait. If we miss this opportunity, we may not have another."

"It won't be a million years, it will be two or three. Or maybe even this year. I'm not at liberty to give specifics, but everything is turning upside down. Waiting will only improve your chances of seeing your homeland once again, not lessen them."

"It's not just about regaining our homeland, it's about revenge. It's about making angels suffer the way we have for so long. It's about putting an end to the archangels."

"What if you lose? What if the angels win and kill you all or throw you back down into Hel? What if you're all killed? Do you want to be the one that spells the end of the Angels of Chaos?"

I didn't include myself in that Angel-of-Chaos designation, nor did I mention Ahia, or the possibility of a whole new race once angels and demons started creating together. Let him think that failure might spell the end of their entire race.

"No Angels of Chaos," I repeated. "Just demons that weaken each time we interbreed. Wouldn't it be better to wait for the angels to bring you back to Aaru than to risk extermination? Risk the end of us all?"

"No. The angels will never allow us back into Aaru. Even if they did, none of us could live with them after the war, after the banishment. There's a hatred there that will never die. I have reconciled with my Bencul here, and he has forgiven me, but other angels will not. We need to move now. The timing is right. We're powerful at a time that they're not, and now we have a way to access Aaru. And for that, I thank you. If you had not thrown Bencul into Hel, we would never have been able to enter Aaru and take back our homeland. I owe all of this, all of our success to you."

Fuck. This was all my fault. I'd fucked up so badly. How

was I to know that Bencul would survive in Hel? That an Ancient would find him, and that the two would fall into a sick, twisted kind of love that evidently sufficed to break the banishment? I'd always been a lucky imp, but it seemed that everything I did lately went to shit. Now I was handing Aaru to the denizens of Hel on a silver platter. And making it oh-so-easy for them to take over by emptying the entire place of their enemy angels.

"You are welcome to join in, along with your household," he said magnanimously. "As a show of gratitude for my Bencul here, I'll give you a section of Aaru. You don't even need to become part of my household since as the Iblis you can enter Aaru on your own. Between the two of us, we can take back our rightful home and oust any angels who refuse to bend their necks to us."

They'd find Aaru empty—if they could get in, that is. And Remiel's offer didn't give me much hope. Yeah, if I could get in, maybe I could miraculously manage to win out with my army of Lows against his more skilled one, but I'd never get in. I'd tried. The only way I could sneak in was under his household.

I bit my lip and thought. Now wasn't the time to place myself under him, not when I was trying to become the mighty Iblis and exert my influence. But if things looked bad, if it seemed like he was going to take over Aaru, to get inside, then I'd need to do something desperate and throw my lot in with him.

And hope that under his leathery wings, I could sneak into Aaru, and once there, un-banish the rest of the angels. There would be a war just like the war two-and-a-half-million years ago. History repeating itself. I hated the thought, but that would be better than Remiel and the demons residing in Aaru while Gregory gnashed his teeth down among the humans, watching his homeland in the hands of those he considered the enemy while he could do nothing about it.

"I'd like that," I lied. "If I can't convince you to wait, then I'd like to be on our side of the invading force. When do you plan on making your move? Most of my Lows...I mean my household, are on the other side of the gates, so I need to plan accordingly."

"Two days. I want to move fast before any word leaks out. Not that I think it will, but there's always a chance that some demon spills the plans to a gate guardian in exchange for his life. Can you be ready by then? We'll leave from my home here in Dis."

Two days. That didn't give me much time to prepare and plan, but two days was better than two hours. "I'll be ready."

He clapped his hands together and sparks flew across the room. "Splendid! Please let my staff know if you have any questions regarding logistics, what weapons to bring, etc. I look forward to working with you."

With a shimmer of his form, he was gone, and I was in the room alone, with Bencul. The angel rose, and suddenly he was a whole lot more intimidating than the battered angel I'd seen when he first entered the room.

"He thinks of you as an ally, and that is your protection," Bencul told me. "But the moment you betray him, the moment you draw your sword against him, or even speak a word of treason to him, I will kill you. And I will love every moment of it."

I smirked. "Better think twice about that plan, Bencul. I might look like a lucky little imp to you, but I'm the Iblis. I rule Hel, whether Ancients like Remiel know it or not. And I refuse to meet my end at the hand of some weenie-ass angel I tossed into Hel."

I walked past him, confident that he wouldn't lay a hand

on me, and headed down the hallway, very aware of him behind me, his hate-filled eyes staring at me the entire way.

* * *

THE PLANNING MEETING consisted of ten Ancients in a huge conference room that was giving me Ruling Council meeting flashbacks. All it needed was a pot of old coffee and a plate of stale pastries, and the image would have been complete. The main difference was that this meeting only held one angel —Bencul.

He was right by Remiel's side, on display. The other Ancients pointedly ignored him, occasionally sliding an envious side-eye to his master. The few demons in the room made no such attempt at nonchalance. They openly gawked. I'm sure they would have poked the angel if the Ancient he was sitting next to wasn't so damned intimidating.

Remiel was as phallic as could be, bare-chested and red-skinned with his bull head and long, shining, curved horns. He was seated, but I couldn't help but drop my pencil and dive under the table for a peek while pretending to look for it.

Yep. Really big set of genitals and no pants whatsoever. I wasn't surprised.

"I called you all here because I am now leading the army to retake Aaru and our timeline has been considerably expedited."

Oops. The meeting had come to order. Guess I better get out from under the table, and try to look all Iblis-like.

Just as I was scrambling back into my chair, I heard the others murmuring in dissent.

"What about Asmodiel?" One of the Ancients asked. All eyes turned to Asmodiel, who was dripping all over his end of the table.

"I have stepped aside in favor of Remiel." The Ancient inclined his head. "He is the key to entering Aaru. His receiving forgiveness broke the banishment for us all. He clearly should be the one to lead the army and be the first through the gates of heaven."

Wait, what?

"Just because Bencul broke the banishment for Remiel, doesn't mean the rest of you can get in," I protested, shooting the angel a narrowed glance. "He forgave one Ancient, not all of you."

"He did forgive us all," Remiel announced, spreading his hands as if he were some savior handing out loaves and fishes.

"It doesn't work that way," I argued. But did it? Gregory had said there were loopholes. I'd thought those loopholes were what got my little demon army into Aaru, but maybe there were more. Maybe Bencul loving and forgiving one Ancient caused some kind of domino effect.

"It does work that way." Doriel stood, casting me a nod of recognition before turning to Remiel. "I felt the banishment fall. We all felt it fall. We are free to return to Aaru, and all thanks to Remiel."

More like thanks to Bencul. Traitor. I glared at the angel once more.

"I assume each of you has assembled your legions with their commanders?" Remiel asked. Each Ancient replied in the affirmative. "Good. We will meet in front of my house tomorrow morning to make our attack. We will fill the streets of Dis with our armies, clad in ceremonial armor that will strike fear into the hearts of the angels."

I snorted, quickly turning the noise into a cough. There were no angels. And even if there were, I couldn't see Gregory and his brothers fleeing in terror because a bunch of Ancients showed up with fancy-dancy armor. Maybe the armor was really ugly with glitter and sequins. That would be enough to send *me* running.

Remiel went on and on about the plan of attack, unrolling a map and putting little figures on it to indicate positions that the various legions should take. I napped a little, then woke up as the Ancients started to stand. From the murmured conversation, it sounded as if we were breaking for lunch.

Good. I was starved. Hopefully Remiel had more on the buffet spread than bitey fish jerky. I followed the herd of Ancients to where I was sure to find food, only to see something far more interesting. Bencul. Slipping off on his own down a hallway. I doubted the angel was sneaking out for a quick smoke, so I followed him and found him alone in a room, staring out a window to the streets of Dis seven stories below.

For someone who wasn't more than an elevated slave, the angel seemed somewhat smug as he looked down at the world. Asshole. He'd sold out his own angels, and for what? He'd sealed his fate with this one act. There was no going home for him now. Even if he ever got out of Hel, the other Angels of Order would never reinstate a traitor, no matter how much he pleaded repentance. He might be returning to Aaru by granting Remiel forgiveness and breaking the banishment, but he'd never be home.

"You seem pretty satisfied with yourself."

He spun around at my words, and although there was hate in his eyes, there was also glee. "I am. More than you would ever know."

"You're a traitor."

He shrugged. "Am I? I really don't care, you know."

What a complete, unrepentant asshole. "How can you do that? Your friends and family up in Aaru, how can you do this to them? You might truly love Remiel and you might think that the Ancients should be able to return home, but not like this. Not starting a war all over again."

Bencul flinched and I saw a flicker of regret in his eyes. "It's not like any of them came for me. When you tossed me through the gates, did any of them bother to try to rescue me?"

"They can't come to Hel. They're not allowed to under the treaty." I saw how lame an excuse that was, but he *was* an Angel of Order after all. "Would you have broken the treaty and risked being torn apart at the claws of demons to come look for someone that was probably already dead? And outside of one or two angels, none of them knew what happened to you. They probably still don't. It's not that they didn't want to find you, they just didn't know where to look."

That flicker of regret in his eyes lingered a moment longer than before. "One or two angels knew. So basically the Ruling Council knew. They knew that you threw an Angel of Order across the gates, to his death in Hel. Were you even punished for that?" He waved a dismissive hand. "Of course not. They don't care about me, so why should I care about them? There's only one being in this world I *truly* love. One. The rest I would gladly sacrifice for him. The Ancients can have Aaru. At least this way I'll be able to go home."

"That's what this is about, isn't it? You knew you could never escape Hel. This was your way out. You might be Remiel's plaything for the rest of your life, but at least it will be in Aaru and not here."

A muscle in his jaw twitched. "I love Remiel. At first…it was just survival. But he's given me everything I could ever want. Everything."

Everything? An Ancient's most favored play toy? Returning to Aaru as little more than a powerful Ancient's slave? How was that everything? What had broken in

Bencul's head that these things were more important than keeping peace, than not losing even more friends and family to war? Although Bencul had always been broken. That business with Harper had shown me the twisted angel he truly was.

Harper. There was a time when "everything" had been defined very differently for Bencul. I dug my phone out of my pocket and pulled up the photos, showing pictures of Austin to him.

"He's getting big," I told the angel, swiping to the next picture. "Look how clever he is, altering his form to reach those cookies on the table. Harper calls him Austin. Did you have a name picked out for him?"

He stared at the images as if I were showing him pics from my last vacation and not shots of his Nephilim son. "Doesn't matter," he told me, his voice flat and uninterested.

Harper was going to fucking kill me for this one. "You can see him. Stop this madness, and I'll arrange for visitation. I'll get you out of Hel, and somewhere you can see your son."

Bencul shook his head. "She can have him. I don't want him anymore. Everything I want is here in Hel, and soon to be in Aaru."

Damn it. I put the phone away, realizing that if the chance to be with his son didn't budge Bencul, nothing would.

The Ancients were going to take Aaru. Tomorrow. And there was nothing I could do about it. Well, nothing beyond warn Gregory and hope he forgave me for putting this in motion, for allowing this to happen.

CHAPTER 23

"*D*o you think he can get in?" I paced back and forth in my kitchen while Snip and Gimlet watched me. I'd let them know everything—my banishment of the angels, my throwing Bencul through the gate into Hel, my inability to convince the Ancients to hold off on this invasion.

"Think who can get in?" Nyalla bounced into the kitchen in her underwear, the T-shirt she was wearing barely covering her ass. My two Lows immediately swiveled their heads to stare at the hem of the shirt, willing it to somehow rise a few additional inches.

"Remiel. He's an Ancient. And he wants to take over Aaru." I knew I could confide in Nyalla. She was like my daughter. I trusted her one hundred percent.

She eyed Snip and Gimlet.

"They know," I assured her. "I told them everything."

She nodded. "Okay. Then how is this Remiel a problem? You guys are all locked out. And aren't demons banished? Even if you hadn't emptied Aaru and locked the keys inside, he wouldn't be able to get in."

I explained the situation, amused that Snip and Gimlet were still intently focused on Nyalla's shirt hem.

"Bencul. I thought he was dead." Nyalla bit her lip. "Harper isn't going to be happy. She's always been worried that he'll somehow come back and snatch Austin away from her."

I was sure that was really far down on the angel's list. That look on his face when I'd shown him the pictures... I got the idea he really didn't care one bit what happened to his Nephilim son or his mother.

"Bencul is alive, but he's also attached at the hip, and probably other body parts, to an Ancient demon. He's not going anywhere. Except maybe Aaru, and I'm hoping to prevent that."

"I'm still going to warn her. And Jaq." Nyalla pulled a bag of chips out of the cabinet. Snip made a squeal noise as her upstretched arms revealed the lower half of her ass. I whacked the Low on the head with a spatula, and frowned.

"Ideas? Come on guys. Should I just ignore Remiel and hope my banishment keeps him out? Should I fold my household under his, just in case he gets into Aaru so I can try to sneak through under his wing? Should I suicidality insist that he's not leaving Hel and make a stand?"

Nyalla ripped open the bag of chips. "I think you should talk to Gregory."

"That's a great idea," Snip said. "And he can go to Hel and kill this Remiel for you. And Bencul. And the other demon who is taking all the Lows. He could rule Hel. He's a total badass. No one would stand against him."

"Et tu, Snip?"

"Sam, you're just as powerful as Gregory, but in a different way. He's the type that goes in swinging his sword and forces everyone to bend to his will. You're the type where people think they're doing what they want only to have an anvil drop on their head. You don't rule by force, you rule by fate, by sneaky stealthy crazy chicken-wand stuff." Nyalla pointed the bag of chips at me. "Talk to him. Brainstorm ideas. Then do what you do best."

Gimlet snatched the bag from Nyalla. "Let Remiel take Aaru. Nobody else wants that shithole besides the angels and the Ancients."

"Hey, I'm in love with one of those angels, and he wouldn't want Remiel and a bunch of demons trashing his home."

"Talk to him," Nyalla insisted. "I'm not saying you should expect him to solve this problem. You're the Queen of Hel, it's up to you to take care of Remiel and bring him in line. I just think that Gregory's knowledge might help you decide what to do. He's really old, and smart, and powerful. And he loves you." Nyalla reached out to grip my arm. "I know you're worried he'll never forgive you if the Ancients take Aaru, but he knows in his heart that you did what you did out of love for him, and that your love doesn't always manifest the same way that his does."

I pulled my phone out of my pocket. "All right, all right. I'm texting him now."

"And I'm outta here," Gimlet announced, heading toward the door with the bag of chips in his hand. "If archangels are gonna be showing up, then I'm not going to be around to see it. If anyone needs me, I'll be in the guest house."

Everyone took off. I started a pot of coffee, and got out the vodka. I was just pouring milk and sugar into Gregory's cup when the angel arrived. He wrapped his arms around me and pulled me back against him. I held there for a moment, just enjoying the feel of his heat against me, the secure feeling of having him surrounding me, of having his spirit-self against my own.

"Vodka?" He chuckled. "If that's for you, then it's business as usual. If it's for me, then I'm worried."

I sighed and tried to pull away from him to grab the coffee. "It's for me, and maybe for you. I need you to talk me off the ledge here."

"Don't jump." He nuzzled my ear, then reached around me to grab the vodka. "Or if you jump, make sure you have your wings out first."

"Remember that angel I threw into Hel?"

"Yes. You almost got a death sentence for that one. Nyalla and Harper netted him and had him down in Wyatt's basement, as I recall."

"No, that was *your* angel, the Hunter who was trying to kill Harper and the baby. He's still serving me and doing shit jobs in my stables with Nils. No, this was Bencul, the father of Harper's Nephilim. He showed up and tried to take her away and the girls and I restrained him. Then I threw him through the gateway to Hel."

"And Beatrix was elsewhere when this was going on?" He asked. "Because I don't recall receiving a report from her on this."

"Ummm, I'm sure you misplaced it. It's probably in a stack of paperwork somewhere that you haven't got to yet." I didn't exactly want to get my favorite gate guardian in trouble.

"There were rumors of you tossing an angel into Hel, but that was during the time when you had killed a few as well. I get them all mixed up, Cockroach."

"Well, anyway, his name is Bencul. I think he might have been one of Gabe's. He was a giant dick, and needed to be punished. And since the Fallen are mine, and the Nephilim are mine, and I assume that an angel creating a Nephilim is mine, I took it upon myself to punish him."

"So you threw him into Hel?" Gregory unscrewed the vodka and poured a generous helping into his coffee.

"Yeah. I threw him into Hel."

"Where he was promptly killed," Gregory surmised. "I'm assuming this somehow came to Gabriel's notice, and he's once again ready to string you up? You're going to ask me to intervene?"

I squirmed. "No. And no."

"No, you don't want me to intervene?"

"And no, he's not dead." I let that sink in for a moment. "He got roughed up by some demons, but got grabbed and gifted to an Ancient. He's…uh, still with that Ancient."

Gregory took a big gulp of the coffee. "Go on."

"There's this weird relationship that's developed between them. I'm talking twisted here. But weird as it is, it seems to fit into some definition of love. And because the Ancient fell in love with an Angel of Order, he's sort of repented. And because Dickhead Bencul fell in love with the Ancient, he forgave him. And they are convinced that this negates the banishment."

I held my breath and watched Gregory hopefully. If he started laughing and declared that ridiculous, I'd be so relieved. He didn't laugh. Instead he drained his vodka-coffee.

Fuck.

"There's a good chance he's right. I told you about my error. Well, this is exactly the sort of thing I didn't account for."

I stared at the vodka, wishing it were something stronger. Maybe I needed to start mainlining Everclear or something. "I'm sorry. This is my fault. I threw that angel into Hel. It's my fault."

He shook his head. "You delivered a very severe punishment—a fitting punishment from the hand of the Iblis to an angel who wronged those you had sworn to protect. How were you to know one of the banished would fall in love with him and that it would be reciprocated? And the loophole in the banishment is my fault, not yours, Cockroach. This is my fault."

"But they will find Aaru empty! There won't be any resistance. They'll just swarm in and take it, and there will be nothing you all can do," I protested.

He reached out a finger and put it gently against my lips. "My fault as well. I brought you and your demons to Aaru to help me fight. I told you what I was going to do to banish the rebels. You were protecting me, trying to save me. And as angry as I was with you, I know I would have done the same for you."

"You're cut off from the source," I mumbled against his finger. "All of you. You're banished. You told me the sort of pain and eventual death you doomed the Angels of Chaos to with your banishment, well I've done the same to you. I've seen those Ancients. I've seen what two-and-a-half-million years away from Aaru has done to them. I don't want that for you or your siblings. I don't want that for any of you."

He turned me all the way toward him and pulled me into his arms again. "We'll find a way to get us back in. Together, we'll fix this and it won't take us millions of years to do it. And when we do, we'll fight for our rightful place in Aaru. We may need to divide it. We may need to compromise significantly on how we rule and what our vision will be for our homeland, but somehow it will all work out."

"I don't want you to have to fight them again," I told him. "I want Infernal Mates, and for angels to take the sticks out of their asses and learn to embrace something different than themselves. I don't want a war in the heavens because the Ancients won't give up on their desire for vengeance, and the angels won't share."

His spirit-self brushed against mine, sending a jolt of electricity through my spine. "What do you think will happen when the Ancients take Aaru?"

"They'll party. They'll probably trash the place." I thought for a second. "The demons who made up their army will go back to Hel, or try to come here because they'll hate it in Aaru just as much as I do."

"How many Ancients are there in Hel?"

"Not many, and some of them won't bother to go. Tasma isn't going. Harkel won't, and he said he's not the only one. So…a hundred? Three hundred tops making the war-march to Aaru?"

"Three hundred Ancients in Aaru."

I suddenly saw it. After the initial excitement and fuck-you exuberance, it would be a hollow victory. No angels to kill or punish or torture, just a huge big empty space with three hundred insane, bored Ancients who weren't even truly angels anymore. They'd been forced to be in corporeal form for two-and-a-half-million years. After so long, a life as a being of spirit wouldn't be nearly the relief they'd hoped for.

And they'd be so lonely. Yes, Remiel would have Bencul, but the others would have no one, not even their demon household. I wouldn't be surprised if in a few thousand years we managed to retake Aaru only to find they'd all died.

And that wasn't what I wanted either. It was terribly undemonic of me, but I wanted a happy ending. Was it wrong to want a happy ending? Could the apocalypse sweep through with all its painful change, and leave us in a better place? And could that better place be one where there was forgiveness and reconciliation on both sides?

It was the closest thing to a prayer I'd ever said.

"So…" Gregory kissed the top of my head. "Who is this Ancient who has fallen in love with a very bad angel?"

Gregory would know him, of course. He fought against these angels, and I doubt he'd forgotten any of the powerful ones who had opposed him.

"Remiel."

My beloved sucked in a breath, every muscle in his body tensing.

"Not good, huh?" I asked.

"No." He let the breath out with a reluctant laugh. "Not good at all, Cockroach."

"Is it bad that I kind of like him? I mean, he's scary as all fuck, and bat-shit crazy, but under all that he still seems to be brilliant and open-minded for an Ancient. I mean, he did fall in love with Bencul, and as much as their affection makes me want to puke, it's genuine and very deep. That can't be all bad, can it?"

"Remiel was in charge of purgatory. He was the angel who took those who strayed in hand and got them back on track, so to speak. His methods were unbending, and so was he. He is not one to forgive or forget, and he'll never give up the pursuit of vengeance for those he felt wronged him during the war."

"But he forgave Bencul," I argued. "Maybe once he gets into Aaru, he'll forgive the others as well."

"Bencul was rarely a combatant in the war. He was mainly a messenger angel, occasionally organizing small groups of intelligence gathering expeditions. Any fighting he did was small back-alley type skirmishes. Outside of being on the opposite side of the conflict, there wouldn't be anything for Remiel to forgive Bencul for. And I'm sure he punished the angel for being on the other side and was satisfied that Bencul had paid his dues."

The other angels wouldn't be willing to submit to Remiel or the other Ancients' ideas of punishment, especially because I was sure most of those punishments were death.

"I can't let them take Aaru," I told Gregory. "I have to do everything I can to stop them. Remiel thinks my household and I are joining in the attack. Since I'm the Iblis and I'm allowed in Aaru, I won't be required to pledge to his household. Maybe I can get there early, and stand at the entrance and…I don't know re-banish them or something."

"Let it be, Cockroach." Gregory took my face in his hands and looked into my eyes. "Let it be. Isn't that what you advised us to do at the last Ruling Council meeting?"

Don't paddle furiously against the waters, but instead ride them to their conclusion, gently navigating but not fighting a battle that we could not win.

"Yes, I did say that, but I meant here in the human world. I meant that the result would be better if we just worked with what fate threw at us, with what we'd unwittingly started in motion. I still believe that's the right thing to do here. I don't think it's the right thing to do in Aaru."

"It is. The pain of being cut off from our source is very real, as is the chance that I may never see Aaru again. Maybe our children will. Just as my banishment didn't account for the demons, the products of inbreeding among Angels of Chaos, maybe your banishment didn't account for future generations, or demons who aren't in your household. There's always a loophole, and you'll eventually find it. I have faith in your ability to land on your feet, as always, and make this somehow turn out right."

"But if you never see Aaru again?"

He brushed his thumb along my cheekbone. "My heart, I am six billion years old. Perhaps it's time for me to no longer be an archangel. Perhaps it's time for me to begin my decline and make room for a new generation of angels to take our place in Aaru."

No. No fucking way was that ever going to happen. Not on my watch.

"I don't want you to decline," I argued.

He smiled. "I'm sure you will keep me alive and kicking with your crazy antics, Cockroach. Never fear that I will waste away from boredom. Not with you at my side."

"Then what will you do?"

He shrugged. "Stay here with you? Watch the humans, and occasionally intervene because I can no longer just stand to sit and watch. You'll scold and screw things up, and I'll try in vain to fix them. We'll have a wonderful life together. And the children will be the ones to rule Aaru. If we have one of our own, we'll call him Micha, just to keep some consistency."

"Like hell we will." I grinned. "And I still haven't agreed to this creation thing. I don't do babies, especially angel babies."

"Fine. We'll call our firstborn something else. What do you suggest?"

I opened my mouth to propose Samael, then snapped it shut. "We'll discuss that in a few hundred thousand years. Until then, Dar and Asta's baby will have to rule Aaru. Or maybe Rafi and Ahia's."

Let it be. Could I? It stuck in my craw to think that the Ancients would have Aaru instead of Gregory, that he might be banished forever. And in spite of what he said, it *was* my fault.

I needed to get him back in. And in order to do that, I needed to get back in. If I showed up with Remiel and his Ancients, could I sneak in with them? Would the banishment I'd stupidly included myself in be negated?

Or...maybe if I joined Remiel's household, I could get in that way. Was that the loophole I'd been looking for? Either way, I had to try.

CHAPTER 24

"We're going to war," I announced at breakfast the next morning. "Right now. We leave in five minutes, so put those coffees in some go-cups and grab a box of fruit bars and let's go."

My words were not met with the cheers and enthusiasm I'd hoped they'd be. Gimlet, Snip, Rutter, and seven other Lows were clustered around my dining room table, eyeing me solemnly.

Gimlet slurped his coffee. "Fuck that."

He wasn't in my household. The others were, which is probably why they weren't saying a word.

"We're going up to Aaru with the Ancients. We need to be in Hel pretty much immediately or we'll be late to the party. Come on guys, it will be fun."

"Wasn't fun last time we were in Aaru," Snip complained. "I'm itchy there. And there's a whole lot of angels trying to kill me."

No angels this time, but I couldn't let the others know that. Not right now. "We won't be there long. Just get in, and get out."

Rutter frowned. "I thought you said it would be a war. That's not usually a get in and get out sort of thing."

I looked at the clock. "There *is* a war. We're not really doing the war part. We're just going to tag along as a sort of experiment, and to be the voice of reason."

Gimlet snorted. "An imp. Voice of reason. That's almost funny enough to convince me to go with you."

"If there's any fighting to be done, I'll handle it," I promised. "Think of how much street cred this will buy you. I'll even have shirts printed up. 'I've been to Aaru and all I got was this lousy T-shirt.'"

Rutter stood. "I'm in. If there's a T-shirt in the offering, I'm in."

"We need to be impressive if we're going to be going to war with a bunch of Ancients," Snip said. "Can we get the T-shirts before we go? Maybe ones that say 'I'm with the Iblis'?"

"No time for that." I grabbed a stack of Styrofoam cups off the counter and started passing them out.

"He's got a point," Gimlet told me. "We need to make an entrance. You're the Iblis. You need to impress these Ancients. They're supposed to walk in awe of you. You can't just show up strolling through the streets of Dis with a bunch of ill-clad Lows following you."

"I don't have time to have shirts made up. We need to leave now or we'll be late."

No one seemed to be listening. They were all pouring coffee into go-cups and talking excitedly amongst themselves.

"We should all be riding flying unicorns," Rutter announced. Five of the Lows agreed wholeheartedly.

"Or fiery chariots," one of the others suggested.

"Or purple and green dragons with glowing eyes," another proposed.

"I don't have those things. Come on. Let's go." I tried to

herd them unsuccessfully into something resembling a very small, ten-Low army. I was beginning to wish I did have a fiery chariot. Snip was right. I was the Iblis. Teleporting us all into Remiel's front lawn where the gathered Ancients would be treated to the spectacle of my ragtag Lows puking their guts out while holding Styrofoam cups probably wasn't the best strategy.

"Those Ancients will probably have flying unicorns and fiery chariots and amazingly cool armor," Gimlet groused. "We don't even get matching T-shirts and an airbrushed cargo van. You suck as an Iblis, you know."

"Fuck you," I told him. I didn't have an airbrushed cargo van, but I had something fairly close to that. And I was just crazy enough to use it.

"Everyone in the SUV," I told them. "Get your asses in there right now, and buckle up, because we are out of time.

* * *

WE BURST INTO HEL, Suburban and all. The only problem was we weren't on the ground.

The Lows screamed, coffee sloshing all over my leather seats. Gimlet tried to grab the wheel, which didn't do anything since tires turning four hundred feet in the air didn't do much.

"It's all good," I shouted over the screams and his shrill cursing. "This happens sometimes. I've improved quite a lot in my teleportation skills, but occasionally I miss the mark."

If I could just concentrate, I could maybe manage to slow the car down and set us gently on the ground in front of Remiel's place. Gently. I closed my eyes and tried to channel whatever angel mojo I might have going on.

"Brace for impact!"

Gimlet's shriek told me that my efforts were not doing

squat, so I opened my eyes and saw the pavement rising to meet me. Might as well get a good view before the front end of my SUV went through my head.

The Suburban hit, then flipped a few times before coming to rest on something soft and squishy. I unbuckled my seatbelt and hopped out, prepared to thank whoever thoughtfully left a mattress in the street to cushion our landing, only to see that we weren't on top of a mattress.

We were on top of a giant panther-thing. It was the same thing that had been prowling around Remiel's house the other day, the thing that had bit me.

My Lows groaned as they climbed from the SUV. They were covered in coffee, but the seatbelts had done their job. None of them were injured, or dead that I could tell.

"Don't think this is gonna help you look any more Iblis-like," Gimlet said as he hopped out of the SUV. He tilted his head and walked over to the panther-thing, nudging it with his toe a few times before declaring it dead.

"Good riddance. I hate that fucking thing. It tried to eat me last time I was here. I'm pretty sure I got rabies from it."

"This is Remiel's mount, the one he was probably planning to ride triumphantly into Aaru on," Gimlet told me. "He's gonna be pissed."

I walked around the back of the Suburban and yanked on the panther-thing's feet.

"What are you doing?" Snip asked me. He, Gimlet, Rutter, and the other Lows were more interested in the beast I'd landed on than the army of Ancients and demons beginning to descend upon us.

"Checking for ruby slippers. I just dropped the equivalent of a house on a Wicked Panther-thing of the West. If I'm gonna get stuck with a mortal enemy bent on revenge, I hope I could at least get a sweet pair of shoes out of the deal. Bonus if they're magic."

Gimlet shook his head, eyeing me sadly. "Pantheramias don't wear shoes. Although maybe his foot will bring you luck if you chop it off and carry it around."

"That's rabbits' feet." I eyed the paws. "And these are too big to fit in my pocket."

It was too late to be chopping feet off of dead panther-things anyway, because an army was making its way down the main street of Dis. Hundreds of Ancients, and a handful of reluctant demons marched in perfect timing with each other. It was a magnificent sight. All the Ancients wore ornate armor that glowed with magic. Their wings filled the spaces between them—tattered, rotted feathers that were a complement to wasted, skeletal human forms, desiccated demon bodies, and wispy, smoke like frames. It was like a horror movie, like zombies and once-dead monsters had taken up arms and were ready to do battle.

They stopped in front of Remiel's home. I'll give them credit, no one batted an eye at my wrecked Suburban.

The entire lot of them snapped their heels together and stood at attention, waiting. I, on the other hand, fidgeted against the side of my SUV. Gimlet pulled a blanket from the back seat and settled in to take a nap. It was noon. It was Dis. It was a million fucking degrees. Sweat rolled down my skin. I was sure my tires were about to melt. And I had no idea why the fuck Gimlet needed a blanket in this temperature.

Just as I was about to succumb to heat stroke, the door opened and a line of demons came out. They went to the left and right of the door, alternating, until there was a nice organized line on the porch. Then came Remiel, his ratty wings bursting into view once he was through the door. He had on armor and the most ridiculously ostentatious head gear I'd ever seen. I didn't have much time to ogle it because right behind him was Bencul.

The angel still looked like someone had worked him over

in a back alley and denied him medical attention, but he was clean and dressed in a scaled-down version of Remiel's armor, minus the hat. His golden hair glowed, and his wings as he came through the door were snow-white with tips of gold on the feathers. The army collectively caught their breath. I could feel their wonder, their admiration.

It had been a long time since they'd seen an Angel of Order, since they'd seen anyone as golden and pretty, as pristine and relatively unscarred compared to themselves and the demons in Hel. Bencul was a gorgeous, shiny thing, and Remiel was their leader because he'd managed to score such loveliness for his very own and give them a chance to take back Aaru and have their revenge upon the angels who had ousted them.

The Ancient addressed his army, never introducing or acknowledging Bencul. It was weird, like the angel was an appendage, not an individual being. He wasn't a slave. He wasn't an equal. It was as if he were a beloved object to covet, but not to give too much notice to. I would have been pissed if Gregory had treated me that way, but Bencul didn't appear at all upset. His eyes never left Remiel, his gaze worshipful and adoring.

Maybe he *was* a slave. Could someone be a slave to love? Bencul wasn't right from before I'd known him. He'd strayed so far from the path of what it was to be an angel, that it seemed to have affected his mind somehow. Other angels took human lovers and created Nephilim, but from what I knew, the majority of them actually loved their human partners. Bencul hadn't. Something had broken in him, and turned him into this desperate being who had bewitched Harper, who had no identity outside Remiel anymore.

I didn't want to blame it on Remiel's "punishments", because I truly think it was something inside Bencul that had long ago gone wrong.

The speech finally ended. It was a whole lot of rah-rah pep talk about taking their rightful place in Aaru, killing the deceitful angels who had betrayed them, and kicking out or enslaving the rest of them. Basically we were going to teleport into the seventh circle—which Remiel felt was the weakest—then take over. Once the seventh circle had been occupied, certain groups would expand out to push into the other regions. Speed was key. Remiel's goal was to immediately take possession of two to three areas, then hunker down and fight his way into the others, taking as long as needed to oust the angels completely.

I wasn't really paying much attention to the logistics, because I knew what was on the other side.

Done, Remiel marched down the steps, Bencul behind him and the rest of his household falling in, only to stop in front of me, open-mouthed.

"What...what...?" he sputtered, gesturing toward a giant furry paw sticking out from under a tire. Bencul glared at me, then his gaze traveled to the same paw. The angel blanched.

"Yeah, well, you know a panther-thing isn't really the best mode of transportation for the powerful and impressive leader of our forces," I told him. "I mean, no one rides a panther-thing anymore. The angels would just laugh at you. It's not impressive. So outdated. So two million years ago. I brought something better."

He looked at the SUV. "It's a metal box. You're telling me this is what the angels, the archangels, are riding on now? A metal box?"

"Oh yes. It's a Suburban. All the powerful angels have one. You should see Michael driving, err flying around on top of his with his flaming sword and his wings outstretched. The other angels tremble before him. Fuck burning bushes and panther-things. If you're going to make an impression when you conquer Aaru, you need an oversized, gas-guzzling sport-utility vehicle."

He stared at it, then turned to Bencul. "Is this true?"

The angel swallowed a few times. "I have not often been in the presence of the archangels, but I do believe I have heard of Michael using such a conveyance when the occasion called for it."

Holy shit, that was the best lie-not-lie I'd ever heard. I might hate Bencul, but the dude had skills.

"Then I thank you, Iblis, for such a generous gift." Remiel placed a hand on my shoulder. I tried not to flinch. "Do you have any questions of me before we begin?"

Yes. Yes, I did. "What the fuck is that on your head?" I couldn't help but stare at it. It was hard to take the guy seriously with that stupid thing.

I hear a noise from the blanket on the ground beside me. Gimlet was either snoring, or laughing.

Remiel spread his wings, his voice so deep it nearly shook the ground. "It's a helm."

"That is the ugliest helm I've ever seen in my life. What's it supposed to be? Eight antlers? Actually it looks like a dead spider. Like when they're dead and they lay upside down with their legs kinda curled up and pointing in different directions? That's what you've got on your head—a giant, upside-down, dead spider."

"It's a helm. The mighty helm of…"

I had no idea what he told me about the notable qualities of the helm because I was too busy wondering why someone would want to stick a big dead spider on top of their head. I mean, I've put a decapitated head on top of my head before as a joke, but Remiel didn't strike me as the joking type. I was convinced he had no sense of humor whatsoever. Which made it all the more funny that he was wearing a dead spider as a hat. Or helm.

"Awesome," I replied when he was done with his speech. "You'll look majestic in Aaru with your dead spider helm riding on top of the Suburban. Are we ready? Let's do this thing before we all melt to death in the heat. Your army has to be dying standing here in their armor. Let's get going."

Remiel leaped on top of the Suburban and sat right on top of the sunroof glass. Then he waved his hand and with a quickly hidden look of horror, Bencul climbed up to sit to his right.

"Prepare!" Remiel's voice rang out. I touched the side of the Suburban, and prepared to teleport.

There was a blinding light, a deafening crack of thunder, and then we were gone.

CHAPTER 25

I'll admit that I'd never attempted to gate myself into the seventh circle in all my attempts to try to break into Aaru. I'd always appeared in the fourth, which was Gregory's circle. The wild gate in Sharpsburg went there, and all my efforts always placed me there as well. It's where Gregory was. It was his home, it was a part of him, and thus the only section of Aaru that I gave a damn about.

Maybe it was Remiel's un-banishment. Maybe it was me touching the Suburban. Maybe it was that the seventh circle was truly a weak link that I'd never found before, but we got in, me included.

It was beyond weird to be at the very edge of Aaru in corporeal form with a bunch of winged Ancients in armor, and a dude riding on top of a Suburban with a giant dead spider on his head. I felt the typical itchy sensation, as if I wanted to shed my physical form, and looked around, expecting the Ancients to return to their spirit-selves.

None did. We all just floated there in nothingness, looking like an army of undead monsters. I looked at Bencul and saw an odd expression of discomfort on his face. He glanced over at me and for the first time he looked scared. Then he shimmered, shedding his corporeal form. Still, the Ancients remained the same. Not sure what to do, I retained my physical form as well.

The paint on the SUV blistered as it began to decay as all physical things did in Aaru. The army stood poised, ready, their swords raised. Then Remiel frowned.

"Where is everyone? I don't feel anyone."

"Are we so cut off from the source that we can no longer sense our brethren?" one of the Ancients asked. "Are we so far gone that we cannot hear the song of Aaru?"

Remiel scowled. "It must be because we are not fully in Aaru proper. Advance. Quickly before they sense us and prepare. As we completely enter the seventh circle, we will sense the angels and know where they are."

He hopped off the Suburban and led the Ancients forward. They were a wall of armor and tattered wings, surging around the vehicle and pushing me against it. I waited for an opening, hoping to blend in with the crowd and make it completely inside.

It was then I realized that Remiel had forgotten about Bencul. The angel was still on top of the Suburban, looking for an open spot to descend. He was the only angel I could sense, and I could feel his uncertainty. Without instruction from his beloved, he had no idea what he was supposed to be doing.

Finally, he found an opening and hopped down. I squeezed in behind him and we marched forward. Demons and Ancients were entering Aaru. I could feel the press of the edge of heaven, the line that delineated where the seventh circle began.

One of the Ancients held back, touching my arm and leaning over to my ear.

"I can't shed my physical form." It was Doriel.

I looked up into her face. "What do you mean?"

"I can't. I tried and I can't. What if I can't when we're inside? What if I can't ever exist as a being of spirit again?" Her voice rose in fear. "What if all this time cut off from the source has destroyed our ability to live outside a corporeal form?"

If that was the case, they would die. All the Ancients would find their corporeal forms disintegrating until they were no more. And if they could not exist as beings of spirit, they would die with those physical forms.

"Remiel?" I called out. "Remiel, wait. Stop. Emergency. Stop. Stop."

The army halted. The crowd parted and a winged being with a spider on his head came forward.

"An ambush, Iblis? Do you sense something?"

"Yes. Yes, I do." I took a deep breath. "Rid yourself of your corporeal form."

He tilted his head. "I won't be able to until I am completely inside Aaru."

"No, you should be able to now. Look. Bencul has. Do it. Shed your physical form."

He stared at me. "It has been too long. I need to be further inside Aaru before I can resume my spirit-form."

"What if you can't? Remiel, you need to turn back. You and all the Ancients need to go back to Hel. It's been too long. You're no longer able to do this. You're trapped inside your physical form, and if you stay in Aaru, you'll die."

"No. No, that's not possible. You have been here. You have brought demons here."

"The demons I brought stayed in physical form and were only here for a short time. And I'm different. It's not just that I'm the Iblis. I stole part of an archangel's spirit-self, I devoured it and incorporated it into my being. I can exist here as a being of spirit, because I carry part of an archangel within me."

"We were angels once," he announced, pushing back his shoulders. "We are angels still. I still have feathers in my wings. I still retain my power. I still am a being of spirit. We will enter Aaru. And once we are within our homeland, it will all be as it was before."

He spun around and the army once more closed in his wake, moving forward. Each step caused my chest to tighten. It felt like a huge hand pressing down on the top of my head. I felt the barrier, saw Remiel pass through it and realized that it had worked. What remained of the original Angels of Chaos had returned to Aaru. One by one they entered. The banishment of two-and-a-half-million years ago had ended and the Ancients were taking their place once more in the heavens.

I just wasn't sure they would be able to stay.

As the barrier neared, the pressure became almost unbearable. I'd never felt this before when I'd entered Aaru, but I'd never come through this way in the past. I looked around to see if any of the Ancients were feeling the same. They looked worried, uncomfortable, but not as though they had a two-ton weight sitting on the top of their heads. We edged closer to the barrier, and I noticed Bencul. He'd resumed his physical form and was gritting his teeth, shuffling his feet as if every inch forward caused agony.

We reached the barrier at the same time, both of us extending our hands forward. A thousand white-hot needles shot through me, and I froze as the barrier quivered, pulsed, and exploded.

It hurt. It hurt when the explosion hit. It hurt being hurtled across dimensions. It hurt when I bounced onto the not-so-soft sands of Dis, bones snapping, muscles and tendons tearing. It hurt, but I'd felt this before. It was the pain of being torn out of Aaru and thrown to the ground. Last time I'd landed in the company of my own demon army and the entire heavenly host. This time I expected to see a bunch of bewildered Ancients, some demons, and an angel.

I recreated my form, fixing all of my injuries, got up and looked around and saw the demons from my household... and an angel. An angel and a horribly crushed SUV, and a snoring form under a blanket that used to be in the back seat of my Suburban.

Bencul healed himself and stood, a puzzled frown creasing his forehead as he looked around. "What happened? Why am I back in Hel?"

"Because you're banished," I told him.

He stared at me. "I'm not banished. I'm an Angel of Order. The Angels of Chaos were banished after the war, but not us. I never was banished."

"You were banished, you just didn't know about it. Actually, nobody outside of the Ruling Council and a few select others knows about it. It happened a few months back, and since you were in Hel, you didn't notice."

"You are the worst liar ever." He curled his lip at me, then continued to look around. "Did my forgiveness not work? Where are the others? Why aren't they here? Why are the only ones rejected from Aaru you and your household, that stupid vehicle, and me?"

"Your forgiveness worked. They're in Aaru where they'll either stay until their physical forms rot and they die, or until they realize what the fuck is going on and come back here." I waited for it to sink in that he and I, my household, and an SUV were the only things thrown out of Aaru. "You're banished. He's not. Sucks, doesn't it?"

There was a glimmer of fear in his eyes as he realized that I wasn't lying. "No. No, I can't be banished. I'm an Angel of Order. We control Aaru. Aaru is ours."

"Remember how you couldn't feel the presence of any angels in Aaru, even when we pushed past the boundaries?" I waited for him to nod. "Well that's because there weren't any angels there. Aaru is empty. Well, it was empty, until now. All the angels were banished. The only beings in Aaru right now are the Ancients and a handful of demons."

His eyes widened. "Who banished us? Was it Samael? It had to be Samael. He's still alive. He used the sword of the Iblis and banished the angels in revenge for the war—"

There was that moment when he realized what he was saying. No one had seen Samael for millions of years. And I was the one with the sword of the Iblis.

"You...you nasty horrid cockroach. I'm going to rip your wings off one feather at a time," he snarled and lunged toward me. I took off and darted behind the only object nearby—the Suburban. We did a few laps before Bencul dropped to his knees and dug his hands in his hair.

"Why? Why did you banish us? You're part of the Ruling Council. You're an imp. You're not even a thousand years old. What would you care about revenge? You don't want Aaru, you don't even like Aaru." He looked up at me. "Did one of the Ancients pay you to do it? So that they could take Aaru without a fight?"

"Seriously? Until you and Remiel had your thing, they couldn't get in either. Aaru has been empty for the last two months. Nobody could get in. Even I can't get in. Didn't you notice that I fell back to Hel along with you? I banished the angels and myself and my household. It was a complete fluke that by tossing you into Hel, I inadvertently brought about the redemption that allowed the Ancients to take Aaru. They've got it. Uncontested. No one else can get in. No one. The rest of us all are banished, except for demons, and they don't want it. I don't even think they could live there if they did want it. I don't think they can shed their corporeal forms. We're banished. Everyone but the Ancients is banished."

My voice was reaching the upper octaves of panic. I know Gregory was resigned to this scenario, that he had hope that eventually they would be able to return to Aaru, and he had faith that even if they couldn't the next generation of angels could. But the whole thing made me want to crawl under a rock and hide for all eternity.

"Why?" Bencul snarled. "Why would you do this to us? Do you hate us so that you would condemn us to the same torture that the Angels of Chaos suffered? I know you hate me—that's why you threw me into Hel—but why do that to the entire heavenly host?"

I felt tears sting my eyes. "The host was fractured. Rebels were trying to take Aaru and remove the archangels and their supporters. There was a battle, and the rebels were winning, and the Archangel Michael was overwhelmed. They were going to kill him and I didn't know what to do. I tried to banish the rebels, to keep them from killing him, and instead I banished everyone, myself included."

He tilted his head, an odd expression on his face. We were kindred spirits, this horrible angel I'd once hated. He would do anything for his love, for Remiel. Anything. And I would do anything for the angel I loved. I *had* done everything for the angel I loved, including ripping him and his siblings away from their homeland possibly forever.

We weren't so different, Bencul and I.

"If I could let them back into Aaru I would," I told him. "If I could let *you* back into Aaru I would."

"I'm banished." He looked upward, his shoulders slumped. "Never again will I be able to shed this physical form. Never again. What a horrible twist of fate that I am denied heaven even though through me Remiel has regained his grace."

"He can't stay. None of them can," I told him. "They can no longer exist as beings of spirit."

"They can. I'm sure it will just take a little time. They're still angels underneath it all," he said confidently. "They'll live in Aaru as angels were meant to be."

"They won't," I insisted. "And that's a good thing. It means that Remiel will have to come back. He'll return to you."

"He has to come back anyway. It isn't supposed to be this way. We were all supposed to be in Aaru. But now…" His face tightened with fear.

"He'll be back," I told him. And I hoped it was true. Surely Remiel would be back once he realized Bencul wasn't able to join him. Or once he realized he could no longer live as a being of spirit.

"He'll return because he loves me." Bencul didn't sound particularly confident. "He promised we'd be together. He promised me…many things. He'll give up Aaru and return to Hel because we were meant to be together. Nothing can separate us. As much as he loves Aaru, he loves me more. Once he realizes what has happened, he'll be back."

I hoped so. But in the meantime Bencul was in Hel, an Angel of Order. And he was attracting quite a lot of attention with his gold-tipped wings and pretty physical form. The demons in my household who'd fallen with us were eyeing the angel as if he were a particularly juicy steak, and several other demons were gathering from the streets of Dis. He needed to get out of here or I'd find myself having to defend the angel with the pointy end of my sword.

"So, you're going to hang out at Remiel's until he gets back? I'm assuming he's got some household there that can protect you?"

The fear in Bencul's face intensified, and he glanced at the demons surrounding us with poorly hidden panic. "His household went with him to Aaru. I can stay there. There are wards."

Remiel's household wouldn't have harmed Bencul even with the Ancient gone and risked his wrath, but the other demons in Dis wouldn't respect the mark the angel bore. Everyone had seen the armies, knew that the Ancient was gone and that his angel-toy was here without a protector. It would be a temptation that few demons could resist, and wards could only hold for so long.

"You're Fallen. You're part of the fifth choir, and you're mine," I told the angel.

He recoiled. "I'm not yours, and I'm not Fallen. How dare you..." He looked around at the demons and understanding dawned on his face.

"Mine," I announced. "As the Iblis I claim you as part of my household."

The demons stepped back. A few wandered off, muttering curses and promising to slice this angel to bits if they got a chance. I took their threats seriously.

"Until Remiel comes back, you're staying with me," I told Bencul. "I've got a bunch of Lows in my household, but most of them are still on the other side of the gates, so you won't have to put up with their crazy shit. Just don't leave my house. I'm hoping everyone will forget about you if you're not out walking around the streets of Dis."

"I have no intention of walking around the streets of Dis," Bencul snapped. "Just give me a private room with food and drink and decent wards, and I'll be fine. Remiel should be back by morning at the latest, so I won't need to stay for long."

I hoped not, because if a mob of demons decided to attack my house and take the angel, I wasn't sure how long I could hold them off. Although Ahriman's former house was pretty badass when it came to confusing labyrinths of passageways and wards. And worst-case scenario, I could always hide Bencul in the dungeons. There was no way anyone who didn't know that house inside and out would find the entrance, and no way Bencul could find his way out.

But there would be no need for that, because Remiel was coming back for his angel. Definitely coming back.

CHAPTER 26

My warmongers were pissed. My greed demons were pissed. Hammer was especially pissed. If I had to hear one more time about how he wasn't getting any more angel wings and hadn't even been able to stab anyone, I was going to scream.

"There *are* no fucking angels in Aaru," I snapped for the gazillionth time. "Even if you had gotten in, you wouldn't have gotten any wings or stabbed anyone. Well, unless you were stupid enough to attack one of the Ancients."

"I'll never get more wings," Hammer complained. Then he straightened, a shrewd expression in his narrowed eyes as he looked over at Bencul.

"Try it and your flayed body will be decorating *my* walls," I warned him. "I'm not fucking joking either."

"Not while he's here. Not while he's a guest in your house." Hammer smiled. "But Remiel will reclaim him, and once the Ancient gets bored of his angel-toy, that pretty-boy's wings are mine."

I needed to get Bencul out of here. Where the fuck was Remiel? Hadn't he realized his boy-toy was missing?

"I'm going out for a bit," I told Hammer and the others. "That angel's well-being is on your heads. If I find so much as a blister on him, I'm getting out the sword. Understand?"

They grumbled, but made the appropriate vows. Once I was sure that none of my household members were going to take liberties with my guest, I teleported out of there, and into the seventh circle of Aaru. Well, not really the seventh circle because I had banished myself. Instead I materialized in that weird courtyard just outside the limits of Aaru, where I could feel the nastiness of heaven without being thrown back into Hel.

There was no one in the courtyard, so I yelled as loudly as I could, then got out my sword and waved it around, hoping I was making enough of a disturbance in the force that someone inside Aaru could hear me.

No Ancients answered my call, but eventually I saw a few demons making their way toward me.

"Iblis!" I recognized the hippo-gecko demon as one of Remiel's household. "Why are you not inside Aaru? Remiel assumed you had gone to claim the fifth choir, but here you are."

Yes, here I was. "There's an issue and I need to talk to Remiel. But he needs to come out here or come back to Hel to talk to me."

Hippo-gecko scowled. "He's rather preoccupied right now. I'll take a message to him if you'll agree to wait here and transport me back to Hel."

Suddenly all the demons were moving in close to me, every one of them promising me favors if I would agree to transport them back to Hel. I wasn't surprised. I hated Aaru, and none of the demons that had been there for the battle had any interest at all in staying. We liked our corporeal forms. And I suspected these demons might not be able to shed them and live anyway. Staying in Aaru would dramatically shorten their lifespan if they couldn't exist as beings of spirit.

I had nothing against these demons and would have gladly transported them for free, but I'm no fool. There was no sense in refusing an offered favor. "Everyone goes back to Hel, but only when Remiel comes out here and has a chat with me. Five minutes. And technically he doesn't even have to leave Aaru."

Hippo-gecko and a few other demons stomped their way back across the barrier, while the others stood awkwardly around, staring at the great nothingness that was Aaru.

"This place sucks," a third-degree-burn humanoid told me. "How do you stand it here? You've been up here a bunch of times, right?"

"Yeah. It was fucking horrifying at first. I didn't do a report and they stuck me in some kind of prison for a day and a half without my corporeal form and all my energy blocked."

Burn-demon sucked in a breath. "Did you die?"

I rolled my eyes. "Does it look like I died?" I wasn't about to tell him that I'd felt on the edge of death, that I'd screamed and cried and trembled, and that Gregory had, unbeknownst to me, been by my side the whole time, ensuring that no harm came to me. I'd experienced horrible things at the smoky hands of Ahriman, but those moments in Aaru had been the most terrifying of my life.

"But angels really live up here? And like it?"

"I know. I don't understand it either. I hate this place." I did, but Gregory loved it and I wanted him to call this his home once more. I wanted our children, if we ever had any, to call it their home as well. I might never feel comfortable here, but I wanted any offspring I formed to experience life as a being of spirit—a life that had been denied to me and every other demon in Hel.

"I'm never coming here again," another demon told me. "There's a big contingent of demons that is planning a raid on the human world soon. Maybe I'll go with them. There's some kickass demon dude leading the charge. He guarantees we'll get past the gate guardians and said he'll take the heat from any angels who try to stop us."

I caught my breath. Was this what Harkel and Mestal had hinted at? Was this the huge attack on the human realm that the archangels had so feared?

"Who is the demon dude in charge and when does he plan this…excursion? And what do you all plan to do once you get across the gates?" Was this just an organized vacation where the "kickass dude" collected a fee and once everyone was in the human world, they all headed off to do their own thing, or was it an organized attack that I needed to worry about?

"No idea." The demon in mongoose-goose form shrugged. "We're supposed to just wait for the call and be ready."

Okay, that sounded like a scam. Some demon was collecting pre-payments and promising the vacation of a life-time…eventually. He'd call once everything was in place. These demons just needed to pony up and be ready. Fools.

"Cool. Sounds like fun. Maybe I'll join you all."

The barrier to Aaru shimmered and I saw blurred, dark shapes. They materialized as six demons and Remiel. He looked like shit, as if someone had dropped him in a vat of acid and he was slowly melting away.

"Why are you still out here?" he demanded.

"Because I can't get in. Neither can any Angels of Order. That's why you found Aaru empty."

He shook his head. "Why? How?"

"It's a long story." I waved my hand. "Bencul can't get in either. He's trapped in Hel without you. I'm keeping him safe at my place for now, but he wants you to come home."

Something softened in Remiel at the mention of his angel, but when I'd said "home" he stiffened.

"Aaru is my home. I'm not going back to Hel. I'll never go back to Hel."

Fuck. "Bencul can't get into Aaru. Hopefully someday that will change, but right now he's alone in Hel, and although he'd kill me for telling you, he's scared."

Remiel's face crumpled. "I want him here. I want him with me, but I'm not leaving Aaru. Someday I hope he can join me here."

I gaped. "You're leaving him? Abandoning him? Dude, he needs you. You've been banished for two-and-a-half-million years. You can certainly hang out in Hel again for another decade or so until I can figure out how to get the angels back to Aaru."

Suddenly the Ancient was cold and distant. "I'm never going back. He knew that once I got to Aaru, I wouldn't leave ever again. I hope one day he can rejoin me, but my love for my home is greater than my love for that angel."

That angel. My lip curled at his words. Gregory would never do this to me. Rafi would never do this to Ahia. Gabe would never do this to Nyalla, at least he better not or I'd fucking kill him. This wasn't love. This was some twisted emotion easily shoved aside once there was a bump in the road. I hated Bencul, but at this moment, I felt deep sympathy for the angel.

"Well you or one of your household needs to deliver that message, because I'm not," I told the Ancient. "Do you have any protections in place for him? You do realize that right now he's like a juicy bone in a den of starving lions?"

Remiel blinked in surprise. "No, I don't. I just assumed he would be with me up in Aaru. I guess he'll need to find a new protector. Perhaps Tasma would like him."

I really wanted to pull my sword out and cut this guy to

ribbons. The gall of him, handing Bencul over to some other Ancient like a used-up toy he no longer wanted. I wasn't sure what I was going to do with the angel, but I wasn't about to deliver him to Tasma, or anyone else, with a bow on his head.

"Piersel can deliver the message for me." Remiel gestured to Hippo-gecko. "Perhaps he'd like Bencul for his own. Would you, Piersel?"

I drew the demon's gaze with my hard stare. The initial spark of excitement in his eyes faded. "Uh, no. I really don't want the angel, Master. Thank you for thinking of me, though."

Remiel inclined his head and smiled. "Well, I wish him the best. Oh, and when you talk to Bencul, let him know that the thing he's searching for won't be found. I made sure of that before I left. He'll just need to find someone else."

I could tell that Piersel was just as confused by that as I was, but the demon nodded and with a flash of light Remiel vanished back into Aaru proper, leaving me with a small army of demons at the edge of heaven.

CHAPTER 27

Bencul looked stunned as Piersel told him the news that Remiel was not returning, only to become enraged when the demon delivered the casual suggestion that he look him up if he ever was able to get to Aaru.

"In the meantime, he suggests you find another protector." Piersel shot me a quick, anxious look. "Not me. Tasma maybe, or one of the other Ancients."

"I'm not going through all that pain and agony a second time, trying to woo some rotted, devolved corpse of an Angel of Chaos," Bencul snapped. "If Remiel doesn't want me, fine, but he needs to return something to me. He's got something of mine and I want it."

I motioned for Piersel to get it all over with. Might as well rip that Band-Aid right off and deliver the rest of Remiel's message.

"Yeah, he said to tell you that you won't find it, that he made sure to get rid of it before he left. He said you'd just need to find someone else."

"Did he hide it or destroy it?" The angel made as though

he were about to grab Piersel, then thought better of it. "What did Remiel say exactly? Destroyed? Or just hidden?"

My mind immediately thought of all the precious things that Remiel might have given to Bencul, only to hide from him. An elf button to transport him across the gates into the human world? Something to protect him from the attack of others? An artifact that could increase a demon's, or angel's, power?

Piersel shrugged. "He said he got rid of it, that you wouldn't find it. That makes me think that he didn't destroy whatever it is."

Bencul's roar of rage shook the room. I was surprised the walls didn't crumble to dust under his anger. "That worm. That deceitful, lying, oath-breaking worm. That decaying sack of offal."

"Yeah, Remiel's a fucking dick," I agreed. He wasn't the only one who was pissed. What the fuck was I going to do with this angel? I couldn't bring him back over the gates. He knew too much—things I didn't want the general population of angels to know. Plus I didn't want him deciding he wanted his Nephilim son back, or wanting to avenge himself on me or Harper once he got his angel buddies to act as back-up. No, I didn't want to bring him across the gates yet, but I could hardly keep him safe here. Yes, I was the Iblis, but how long before someone decided to try their luck and risk my ire to snatch an angel from my house? I'd need to be here full time to guard him, and I couldn't stay in Hel twenty-four seven with my responsibilities in the human world.

"So, are there any Ancients you think you might be able to tolerate?" I asked the angel. "Or a high-level demon since most of the Ancients seem to have decided to stay in Aaru?"

Bencul glared at me. "What are you, my pimp? Am I going to be given away to a demon as a slave? Am I to trade my physical form to him or her for a promise of safety?"

I winced. "You can stay here, but I can't be here all the time to protect you. I can't guarantee you'll always be safe. It might be better with a demon who intends on remaining in Hel."

"I can take care of myself," the angel snapped. "I'm not a complete weakling. I can take most demons one-on-one. As long as they don't gang up on me, I'll be fine."

"Then you can stay here," I told him. "Just don't leave the house, especially at night. Demons tend to roam in bands, and I don't want to find eight of them have roasted you on a spit for dinner."

"I'm not staying here." The angel walked over and looked out the window to the street below. "I need to leave."

"I can't protect you out there," I warned.

Bencul walked over and put his hand on Piersel's shoulder. "Can you take another message to Remiel? Tell him that I beg of him to tell me where it is. That if he ever had any love for me at all, he'll tell me where it is."

Piersel shrugged the angel off. "I'm not doing shit for you. I hate that place. The only way I'd ever go back there is if Remiel commanded it of me."

Bencul's enraged scream nearly burst my eardrums. "No! I can't lose him. Not now, not after I've given up everything I have, everything for him. I can't lose him." He reached out and grabbed the demon's shoulders. "You go back to Aaru and tell Remiel he needs to return to Hel right now. He can't do this to me. Not after everything I've done for him. He can't do this to me."

The drama was getting a bit thick in here. I pushed Bencul back, stepped between them, then turned to the angel. "I'm sorry, but Remiel has made it clear he's not leaving Aaru. This is a shit situation, but throwing a tantrum isn't going to do any good."

Bencul shimmered, glowing around the edges of his

physical form. "That nasty worm of a banished angel. That piece of cow dung. I hope he dies up there. I hope he dies."

Yes, he probably would. And I felt horrible that Remiel had chosen to die in Aaru rather than live down here with an angel he loved. I put out a hand to give Bencul a consoling pat, and he slapped it away.

"I trusted him. I loved him. He was supposed to take me with him. We were supposed to be in Aaru together. All of us. Together. And now he's abandoned me to this horrible place. He's left me. And I don't know where he is. He'll die. And Remiel won't care one bit because his end of the deal is done. He'll die."

I frowned in confusion. Was Bencul losing his mind? He knew where Remiel was—the Ancient was in Aaru. And yes, he would probably die if he could no longer manage to exist without a corporeal form. But I got the feeling that wasn't all Bencul was upset about. *He'll die. And Remiel won't care one bit because his end of the deal is done.* Remiel had hidden something away from Bencul, something the angel wanted. But that "it" had suddenly become a "he" in the angel's rants.

"What *was* Remiel's end of the deal?" I asked.

Bencul turned to me and I saw a glimmer of fear in his eyes. "None of your business. That was between us."

I mulled that over as he demanded again that Piersel take a message to Remiel, then demanded that the demon tell him what Ancients were here in Hel that he might be able to get one of them to take a message to Remiel.

Bencul loved the Ancient, but there was something he loved more and it wasn't Aaru. Yes, he wanted to go home, but he didn't seem ready to off himself because that looked like it was forever denied to him. He wanted Remiel to come back. And more importantly, he wanted Remiel to tell him where something was.

It all clicked. Like puzzle pieces, everything snapped

together. And that was a freaking miracle because when it came to subtleties I wasn't always the first one in the room to figure things out.

"I'll be back," I told the two who weren't paying any attention to me whatsoever. Then I left. And went straight to Tasma's house.

I beat on the door until someone finally answered it and realized that I wasn't going to go away until I saw Tasma. Then I sat in the room with the fluffy pink pillows and tiaras, waiting. It all made sense. Bencul had said there was one being in the world that he truly loved. One. That he would gladly sacrifice the rest for him. I'd thought he'd been referring to Remiel. I'd thought all along he'd been referring to Remiel. Yes, he loved the Ancient, but there was someone he loved more. Someone he'd needed Remiel to create. Someone whose existence made him no longer care about the Nephilim he'd made with Harper. Someone who Remiel had hidden away because sometimes you don't actually trust the person you love not to stab you in the back at the end of the day.

Tasma walked in the room.

"Where's the baby?" I demanded. "The angel. Where are you keeping the baby angel?"

Her jerked to a halt. "Why would I have a baby? If I were to engage in a breeding incident, I would send the creation to a dwarven care facility with a trust fund, just like every other demon offspring in Hel."

"You have a dwarf here. I saw her last time I was here. Now, there's no reason for you to be hanging out with dwarves unless you need childcare. We're not buddies with them. They don't join our households. They don't come have dinner and party with us. And she didn't exactly look like she was here to consult with you on custom weaponry."

He hesitated. "I'm ashamed to admit that I asked a dwarf

to come and help me bring order and obedience in my household."

"Bullshit. You're an Ancient. You can handle pretty much every demon in Hel. You certainly can handle a bunch of brainwashed Lows who want to do nothing more than eat pureed prunes, play with dolls, and have you pat them on the head. The only thing you can't handle is a newly created demon who is erratic enough to burn your house to the ground the moment you turn your back on him."

Tasma straightened his sweater and looked me in the eye. "I don't have any demon young here. I have no desire to spend every moment teaching them to control their abilities. If I were to breed, I would send that creation to a dwarven home where it belonged."

I took a menacing step forward. "No, you don't have any demon young here, you've got an angel. That's the favor Remiel asked of you, the one you needed to keep super-secret so that the sire didn't find out and take away the only real leverage Remiel had over him. That's why you have a dwarf secreted away in your house—because as difficult as demon young are to handle, angel young are worse. Now where is it? Where's the angel?"

He set his jaw. Before he could outright lie to me, I summoned my sword. The thing came, and for once it came in its full glory. It hummed and glowed. I felt the power coming off the weapon in waves. And in response, something inside me rose to the surface. My wings came from my back in a flash of dark light, I felt myself shimmer, my teeth sharpen to points, my eyes darken. In that moment the imp was gone and I stood before Tasma as an angel, as the Iblis.

He cringed. An Ancient cringed before me.

"You're right. There is an angel baby, and Remiel asked me to keep it for him."

I put the sword away. And my wings. And was thrilled to

realize my teeth and eyes had gone back to normal. "Why you? Why not just stick it in one of a thousand dwarven group homes?"

He looked at me as if I were an idiot. "Because it's an *angel*. And he didn't want his toy getting any ideas about snatching it and running off."

Made sense. "Take me to it," I told Tasma.

He teleported us, and in a flash we were in a small, windowless room that I was pretty sure was a few hundred feet underground at a minimum. In the room was a female dwarf who was stacking blocks. Next to her was what looked like a demon with a lizard's body, a lion's tail, and a bull's head. Young are given their first form by their creator—in this case, Remiel. He'd given his offspring a typical demon form, one that would fit in with just about any other newly created demon in Hel. But in spite of its form, this clearly wasn't a demon.

The baby was fixing the dwarf's tower of blocks so they were perfectly aligned, each block a pleasingly contrasting color from the one below and the one above it. Even if I couldn't tell from the energy coming off the infant, those actions were enough to let me know that this was an Angel of Order.

"Don't worry," Tasma assured me with his usual creepy smile. "It will be dead by tomorrow."

What the fuck? "And why will it be dead by tomorrow?" The angel looked healthy enough. And Bencul was still walking around, so clearly the environment in Hel wasn't toxic for Angels of Order.

"Oh, I need to kill it." Tasma patted the angel on the head, as if he'd just announced he was going to give it a cookie. "Remiel wanted to kill it right away once he realized it was of Order, but that toy of his would have had a fit. It's too dangerous to have this thing in Hel. If the word gets out, my place will be under siege with all the demons who want an angel-toy of their own. Plus, it's creators don't want it."

"Its sire wants it," I sputtered. "You're not killing this angel, so just forget that idea right now."

"Better me than have it torn apart by some demon," he said. "I'm not keeping it in my house. This was temporary, as a favor to Remiel. He said to kill it off after they'd taken Aaru. Clearly they've taken Aaru, so there's no need for me to keep this thing around any longer."

He had a point—well, besides offing this angel, anyway. It was too dangerous for this angel to be in Hel. I couldn't force Tasma to keep it as I was pretty sure there would be an unfortunate 'oops'"" the moment I turned my back. I couldn't trust my Lows to take care of it. And I couldn't give it to Bencul. His own days were probably numbered. There was no way he could take care of a young angel and defend it from the demons. It wouldn't be safe in a foster home as an Angel of Order.

I needed to get this angel out of Hel. Remiel obviously didn't want it. I couldn't trust the Ancients in Aaru to not kill it. Which left the human world. Damn it all to fucking hell, I was going to have to cart this baby back with me.

"I got this," I told Tasma, walking over to the angel. "And you owe me a big fucking favor for taking this thing off your hands. Big. Fucking. Favor."

He smirked. "You're the Iblis. I think I pretty much owe you a favor anytime you ask anyway."

The dwarf stood and handed me the angel. It looked at me and spat some sort of green goo onto my shirt. "You're gonna need to change that form," I told it. "Human. You need to look human."

I reached out with my spirit-self and touched the child, showing him all the complex structures I'd used to put together my own human form, then with a flash of light I was holding an actual baby.

"Ugh, that's disgusting." Tasma put a hand to his mouth and gagged. "Why would you do that to the poor thing? Human infants are revolting. If you're going to kill it, at least let it die looking somewhat attractive."

"I'm not going to kill it." What the fuck was I going to do with it, though? It would be so easy to go back to my house, hand this angel over to Bencul, and shoo him out the door. His offspring, his problem. He could take the baby and go hide in the mountains like he was obviously planning to do.

And starve. Or be killed by trolls, or demons, or whatever else happened to come by and find two helpless angels in the wilderness. Bencul might be able to take care of himself, but he would struggle to keep this little angel safe. I couldn't leave the little guy here. I couldn't take him back to my house. I couldn't just hand him over to Bencul and walk away. This young angel couldn't be in Hel. It wasn't safe for him to be in Hel.

It wasn't safe for him to be in Aaru right now either. Or in the human world.

The human world. There *was* someone I knew who was good at keeping angel young safe in the human world—two someones. It wasn't an ideal solution, but it was the only one I could think of right now that didn't end up with tiny angel wings mounted to some demon's wall.

CHAPTER 28

$\mathcal{I}$ didn't want to just appear on the roof of a Chicago skyscraper holding an infant angel, so I teleported down the street a few blocks, scaring the fuck out of the humans on their way home from work. Then I strode through the streets of Chicago dressed like my clothes had been attacked by a swarm of moths armed with knives, holding a shrieking, naked infant boy. No one called social services, and by the time I got to the building lobby, the angel had decided to stop fighting and check out our interesting surroundings. He was particularly fascinated by his reflection in the glass of the revolving door, and on the mirrored elevator walls. I listened to instrumental soft-rock Eminem while the angel cooed and made kissy-faces at himself.

By the time I reached the roof, Asta and Dar had time to sense my energy signature and prepare themselves. Which probably meant they were putting away the dirty laundry, bongs, sex toys, or whatever else they didn't want me to see.

"Hey," I told Dar as I held the angel toward him with both hands. "Brought you guys a present."

He backed away rapidly until his ass hit one of the air intake boxes. Asta came forward slowly, but made no move to take the angel from my hands. I pushed it toward her. Damn thing was getting heavy.

"It's an Angel of Order," she said.

"No fuck. Here. It's all yours."

"No, it's not." Asta crossed her arms and glared at me. "Whose baby have you stolen?"

"I didn't steal him. I saved his life."

Dar snorted. "Guess he's yours now, Mal. Have fun with that."

Asshole. "Look, you've got a newly created Angel of Order that's all hush-hush. Shouldn't be a big deal to add a second one. Take him. Look how cute he is."

Clearly, I'd found something right to say because Asta practically melted in front of my eyes and reached out for the baby.

"Oh no." Dar pushed her hands away. "No. One is more than we can handle right now. I'll get you a kitten, darling, but you can't have this angel. I didn't create it. I'm not the one that saved its life. He's all yours, Mal."

Asta was the weak link here. I needed to prey on her and ignore Dar. "He's all alone. His creator was an Ancient in Hel, a Fallen. He's gone, abandoning this little guy with instructions that the baby should be killed. And the sire...well he's in Hel too. And Hel is clearly no place for a little, itty-bitty, cute-as-a-button Angel of Order now, is it?"

I almost had her. Almost. Then Asta suddenly frowned. "The sire is in Hel? This isn't a demon, it's an angel, and it's an Angel of Order. That means the sire is an Angel of Order."

"Yeah, it's a long story. Look at how cute he is. Sooooo cute."

"Why is there an Angel of Order in Hel?" The frown

turned into a glare. "It's against the treaty for an Angel of Order to be in Hel. And even if it wasn't, not one of us would go there. Which means…"

"Yeah. My bad. I kinda threw him through the gates of Hel. In my defense, he'd created a Nephilim, and he'd been a real asshole to the human mother too. Technically that made him a Fallen, a part of my choir. So I was within my rights to send him to Hel for punishment."

Silence greeted my little speech. It was clear that Asta didn't agree with me.

"How the fuck did he last more than one day in Hel, let alone live long enough to be making babies with an Ancient?" Dar asked, eyeing the little angel with curiosity.

"The Ancient found him before the demons had a chance to kill him. They fell in love. It was all very romantic in a twisted, weird kind of way. The angel made a deal with the Ancient to create this little guy, but when he turned out to be an Angel of Order, the Ancient wanted him dead. He couldn't exactly kill the baby without pissing off his angel-toy, so he hid it with instructions to kill it later."

"So give the adorable little guy back to his sire." Asta sighed and reached out a finger to stroke the baby's cheek.

"The sire is in Hel. And while he's in my household under my protection right now, it's gonna be hard to keep both him and an infant Angel of Order safe. The baby is vulnerable and in danger there, so I brought it here. To you. To keep. Because he's sooooo cute."

Asta stuffed her hands in her pockets and set her jaw. "When neither the creator nor the sire are alive or able to properly care for and raise a young angel, that task falls to the head of their choir. That's what happened to me. I was orphaned late in the war, so the Ancient Revered Archangel Gabriel took charge of my upbringing. As the choir of the

Fallen is yours, and as you are the Iblis, both this angel's sire and creator are yours. Therefore this angel is your responsibility."

Fuck. Fuck, fuck, fuck. "I can't raise an angel. Look at me. Do I look fit to raise an angel? No, I don't. He's cute. Here. Take him."

Asta gave me one of those hard looks that reminded me she wasn't quite the wuss I'd originally thought. "No. He's your responsibility. Either you raise him, or you free his sire from Hel and give the baby back to him."

"I've got some diapers if you need them." Dar was holding back a laugh. "And a baby sling. Maybe you can set up a playpen in the Ruling Council meetings."

Damn it all to fucking hell. "Fine. I can't risk taking him back to Hel, though. Can you guys watch him for me until I send Bencul over to pick him up?"

Dar scowled. "You're going to ditch us with that thing, aren't you?"

I rolled my eyes. "I swear on all the souls I used to Own that I only need you to watch him for one day. Two max."

The demon sighed and rubbed a hand over his face. "Fine."

Asta squealed, holding her arms out. I happily deposited the baby there and turned to leave.

"What's his name?" the angel asked.

"Fuck if I know." I left before they could ask me any other questions.

I really didn't want to release Bencul from Hel. He was a world-class dick, and I didn't think he'd suffered enough for his crimes. Although maybe he had. I'm sure those demons who initially found him hadn't been gentle, and I was equally sure that Remiel hadn't been gentle.

He'd fallen in love, and his loved one had ditched him,

hidden his offspring, and intended to kill his offspring. Maybe he'd suffered enough. He'd have to have suffered enough, because as much as I didn't want to release Bencul from Hel, I really didn't want to have to raise his baby.

CHAPTER 29

I headed back to Hel, satisfied that for now that baby angel was safe. I wasn't so convinced that releasing Bencul was a great idea, though. Five minutes after he was in the human world, every angel there would know they were banished from Aaru, the Ancients had taken their homeland, and I was to blame for it all. I could try to leverage the baby, get a vow from Bencul that he keep all this secret, but in all honesty I just didn't have the energy for this anymore.

Let it happen. I couldn't hold back the storm any longer. Release Bencul, let him have the child he'd sired, then just deal with the fallout. There was that Ruling Council meeting in two days. I wondered if my horrible news could wait that long or if I'd need to call an emergency meeting.

I was so lost in thought that I nearly ran into an Ancient. Doriel was standing outside my home, waiting as I made my way up the street. I started, wondering what she was doing here, what emergency had caused her to leave Aaru and seek me out.

"I've decided to return to Hel," she said without any greeting or formality. "And I'm not the only one."

"Why? I mean, I hate that place so I'm not surprised, but you guys have waited two-and-a-half-million years to get there. Why return to Hel?"

She spread her tattered wings to the side and I saw another feather fall, catching fire as it drifted to the pavement. "Remember I said that I could not shed my corporeal form? Others are having the same problem. We're worried that we can no longer exist as beings of spirit, that we'd need to continually recreate a disintegrating physical form in order to remain alive in Aaru. And that defeats the reason for living there, in my view. If I can no longer live my life as a being of spirit, then remaining somewhere that constantly reminds me of what I've lost would be a worse torture than returning to Hel."

"How many are staying, and how many are coming back to Hel?" I needed to know this so at the Ruling Council meeting I could tell them if there were three hundred Fallen in Aaru, or five. It shouldn't make a difference to the angels, but I got the feeling it would. It was one thing to have a handful of who you considered squatters in your home as opposed to every living Angel of Chaos ever banished.

Doriel shrugged. "I think about a hundred of us are returning, so roughly two hundred plan to remain in Aaru. I hope that they are eventually able to shed their corporeal form. If they can, even if it takes centuries, then there will be hope for us, too."

"I appreciate your letting me know." I motioned toward my house. "Would you like to come in and have some…uh, dried bitey fish? I'm sorry. I'm not really prepared for guests at this moment, and there's something I need to get to."

She waved her hand. "Oh, no worries. I did want to ask about that angel, though. It seems he was unable to enter

Aaru for some reason. Remiel told me that he was up for grabs?"

Up for grabs. That fucking asshole. "He's not interested in joining another household at the moment. I plan to release him from Hel and set him free."

"Ah, that is too bad. I'd hoped to convince him to come entertain me for a while. I have my faults, but unwarranted rape and torture are not among them. I can promise I'd be kind and fair."

And that would be the perfect solution if Bencul didn't have an infant angel to take care of. "I'll let him know. Maybe in a few centuries he might change his mind, but for now I'm sure he'll want to take care of some things outside of Hel."

Doriel did an odd dip, something between a bow and a curtsy. "Safe travels then, Iblis."

I watched her vanish in a flash of light, then went into my house where I saw Hammer, Snip and Gimlet throwing swords at the wall. Piersel was nowhere to be seen. And neither was Bencul.

"Where's the angel?" I yanked one of the swords from the wall, stood back, and launched it. It bounced off and clattered to the ground.

"Out."

I turned and grabbed Hammer's wrist just as he was about to throw the sword. "What the fuck do you mean 'out'?"

"Out. Said he need to go get something."

"Something from Remiel's house?" I'd told the angel to stay here. Admittedly, I wasn't in a position to demand obedience from him. He could come and go as he pleased. But why would that stupid idiot go to retrieve belongings halfway across Dis when he could have bribed one of my Lows to do it?

"Yeah, that Piersel guy told him some stuff about a favor

Remiel had asked of another Ancient." Gimlet threw a sword at the wall and it sank halfway in, the hilt quivering with momentum. "He said he was going to Tasma's to get it back."

"Fuck." He was going to get the angel baby—the one I'd taken. I wasn't sure what Tasma would do to him if Bencul showed up on his doorstep demanding his progeny. If he showed up at all. Tasma's place was farther away than Remiel's. That was a lot of distance for an angel to walk, with every demon in Dis wanting him for their own.

"I'm going to Tasma's," I announced. "Snip, Gimlet, and Hammer—you guys go out in the streets and find out who saw Bencul. I want to know if anyone saw a demon grab him off the street. If you hear anything, come find me right away."

Then I ran. It would have been faster to teleport, but I wanted to be sure I didn't zap past Bencul while he was trying to fight off a pack of demons. If he was at Tasma's he was safer then he would be in the streets of Dis.

The streets were empty and silent, like a ghost town in an old western movie. I burned the fuck out of myself passing through Tasma's lava barrier without waiting to be let in, and banged on the door.

He wasn't there. Bencul had never made it to Tasma's. And I was positive the demon answering the door wasn't lying because I asked him with my sword burning a hole through his chest.

Where the fuck was he? This wasn't my fault. Yeah, I'd thrown the guy into Hel as a punishment, but it wasn't my problem that he'd been abandoned by his lover and risked his damned foolish life walking unguarded through the streets of Dis to go retrieve an angel baby that I'd already rescued. Fucking idiot.

I made my way back from Tasma's house with less speed, looking for any trace of the angel. If he'd been attacked in the street, there would be blood from his physical form, traces of energy from the fight, traces of his energy. I just needed to go slowly, work the streets in a grid pattern trying to detect any sign that Bencul had been there.

Dis was a huge fucking city. It would take me weeks. He was either dead, or maybe would turn up in a few months when some demon got drunk and bragged about his toy.

"Iblis!"

It was Gimlet, his fat little legs pumping away, his bulgy eyes huge as he ran toward me.

"Iblis, I found him! I found the angel!"

I grabbed the Low, lifting him off the ground. "Where? What happened?"

He panted, catching his breath. "Bereari took him."

Damn it all to fucking Hel. I dropped Gimlet and ran, summoning my sword. I used the weapon to blow through Bereari's wards, cut through three demons who got in my way, and pound my way through the front door. Bencul lay on the floor in a spreading pool of blood. Beside him were three dead demons. Standing over him were three live ones.

"What the fuck gives you the right to grab someone off the streets of Dis?" I snarled.

One demon ran, darting behind me and out the door. The other backed slowly away, looking desperately for a way out that didn't involve getting anywhere near my sword. The other demon laughed. Bereari, I assumed.

"He's an angel. He's not allowed in Hel, and he was walking around all by himself. If I find a treasure discarded in the streets, it belongs to me."

True, aside from a few little details. "He's marked as part of Remiel's household. And he's not a treasure, not a thing for you to lay claim to."

The demon flashed his pointy teeth at me. A sword appeared in his clawed hands, fire licking up along the blade. "Remiel and the other Ancients have gone to Aaru. If he left

QUEEN OF THE DAMNED

this pretty thing behind, then it's logical to assume he no longer wants it. And yes, he is a thing. There is no blood price assigned to an angel."

There wasn't one assigned to Lows before I came along either. This had to stop. Now.

"I'm the Iblis. This angel is under my protection. Step back now, vow that you'll relinquish any claim on him, and I'll let you live."

His response was with the sword. I raised mine and easily deflected the blade. "Last chance."

He swung again and I stepped in, sliding my blade along his until our hilts met. Fear flickered in his eyes as I grabbed his spirit-self and pulled. "Yield."

"I yield," he gasped. "The angel is yours."

Bereari ran, and I knelt down to help Bencul up, alarmed to find that he was far more injured than I'd first thought.

"Heal yourself," I told him, quickly inventorying his wounds. Broken bones, internal bleeding, punctured lung, a nearly severed arm—nothing he shouldn't have been able to heal.

"Can't." His voice was rough and breathy. Suddenly his eyes met mine and he grinned. "Killed three of those insects. Could have probably taken another one down before I died."

"Yes. Good boy. You killed three demons." Why wasn't he able to heal himself?? I triaged his wounds and took care of the critical ones. Then with a muttered apology, I reached into his spirit-self. And gasped.

"Is this...did they do all of this?" He was horribly damaged. No wonder his ability to heal was compromised. It was a surprise the angel was still alive at all with these injuries.

"No. Most of that was from the demons I met when I first got to Hel. Couple of times I didn't think I was going to make it. That last time I wouldn't have made it if Remiel hadn't

283

come along. Then he did some damage of his own. He'd get excited and lose control. Wasn't his fault."

Yes, it was his fault. And not all of the injuries I was finding were old either. These demons had really worked him over. They'd clearly intended on killing him. And I thought they had succeeded.

"I'm going to try to heal you," I told him, wishing Gregory was here. This wasn't really my greatest skill, and I hadn't been an angel for long.

"Think you're too late," he gasped. "These five just wanted to play, but I swore I'd never let anyone do that to me against my will ever again, and when I fought back, when I killed those three, they just wanted me dead."

"Hush," I told him. Then I tried to heal him. Everything I repaired fell apart as soon as I pulled back. This poor angel was held together with wet tissue paper, and this last fight had been too much.

"You stupid fucking idiot," I snapped, tears coming to my eyes. He was hurt. He was more than hurt. And as fast as I healed him, other sections of his spirit-self were falling apart.

"Olapiret. I needed to find him. He's the only thing that matters to me." The angel's face crumbled. "Especially now that Remiel has abandoned me. Olapiret is all that matters."

What a stupid name. It sounded like he needed to be on top of a music box, spinning around in a tutu.

"I was working on it," I told Bencul. "I'd found your angel over at Tasma's and took him to safety across the gates to the human world. I was coming back to get you." Well, not at first, but I was sure he wouldn't catch that minor fib. "Why didn't you stay at my house where it was safe? Couldn't you trust me?"

Even dying, Bencul gave me "that look". Of course he couldn't trust me. I was an imp, the Iblis, an Angel of Chaos.

And I'd been the one who'd thrown him through the gates to Hel.

"It doesn't matter. Nothing matters but that he's safe." The angel gasped, sections of his spirit-being already shredding and fading away. "What does he look like?"

"He's cute." I struggled to find some way of describing the little angel's human form. "Um, he's cute. And he spat at me."

Bencul laughed, then his face twisted in pain. "That's my boy, my little Angel of Order. Promise me. Swear it right here before I die. Swear it."

I didn't need to ask him what he meant. Damn it all. I kind of hated this angel, but I kind of felt sorry for him too. And as much as I didn't want to admit it, I would absolutely take responsibility for the care and upbringing of his offspring. I was the head of Bencul's choir as a Fallen. I was the Iblis and thus the Queen of Hel and Remiel. And these little angels... Gregory was right. They were the new Aaru. Karrae, and this Elephant-pirouette were the beginning of our future—a future I needed to safeguard and nourish. However the fuck an imp was supposed to safeguard and nourish, that is.

"I swear on all the souls I used to Own, I vow it as the Iblis, that I will care for, defend, and raise your offspring. And I'll get help, because I've got no idea what to do with any kind of baby, let alone one that's an Angel of Order."

Then I gathered Bencul in my arms and teleported him out of Hel to the area just outside the seventh circle of Aaru. And there I lay him down and sat with him, holding his hand until his spirit-self unraveled into oblivion and all that was left was a shell, a human form with gold tracings of wings fading away like the remnants of fireworks in the sky.

CHAPTER 30

"*W*hy are we on this plane again?" I pressed a hand to my forehead. I'd gone back to Hel after Bencul had died and hired a steward to get shit organized and running in my various homes. I'd also pressed some demons into the service of my household, laying down rules for how Lows and others were to be treated. They were acting as my deputies when I wasn't in Hel, enforcing shit and being my eyes and ears. Then I'd gone home and kicked all the Lows out of my guest house, assigning them all tasks and putting them to work in Hel. There was a new sheriff in town. It was me. I wasn't happy about it, but as long as I carried the sword of the Iblis, Hel needed to be on the top of my list of priorities.

Gregory leaned his head back and rested his arms on his lap. "Gabe suggested mechanized air travel as a way for us to better understand the 'human condition'. You remember, we voted on it during the Ruling Council meeting? You voted for it?"

Yes, I remembered. Didn't mean I had to like it. There was a time when flying in a metal box full of humans was the highlight of my day. Now I just wanted to get somewhere as quickly as possible. Or, barring that, travel in the lap of luxury with free alcoholic beverages and other goodies.

We weren't in the lap of luxury. We were wedged three-to-a-row in coach next to an old guy with the worst body odor ever. I didn't even get a free pack of peanuts.

"Why isn't Gabe on this flight?" I complained. "Where the fuck is he? I'll bet he's flying first class. I'll bet he's in a private jet or something. Actually, I'll bet he came up with some lame excuse about how he needed to teleport instead of flying on an airplane. How come he's not on this plane? This was his motherfucking idea after all."

The child two rows back screamed. Again. It was one of those ear-piercing, I'm-pissed-off-at-the-world screams. He'd been doing it constantly along with loud garbled furious shrieks nearly every second of this eight-hour flight.

Okay, I was exaggerating, but not by much.

"Gabe is most likely taking a different flight."

I snorted. Yeah, right. He'd pushed this nonsense through a Ruling Council vote and was laughing behind our backs as he teleported to Reykjavik. Actually I didn't think Gabe had the ability to laugh. But I was pretty sure Rafi was laughing. And there was no way in Hel he and Ahia were stuck on an eight-hour flight in economy class with a screaming child.

There was another shriek, this one longer and higher-pitched than the last. I think I felt a trickle of blood from my ear. Shoving my upper half into the aisle, I looked back, shocked to see that the instrument of my torture was near the rear of the plane.

Yeah. The little shit was that loud.

Another scream, then angry loud shrieking. Did he want something? Could the parent responsible for this little monster not understand what he wanted, what would make him shut up? A toy? Candy? A boob-in-the-mouth? Eight ounces of vodka in a sippy cup?

The cheap vodka, because there was no sense in wasting the good stuff on a baby, especially one that screamed for eight hours straight.

Another scream. I snarled, wondering what would happen if I manifested into my first form. That would shut him up. Although a giant dragon with poisonous spikes might not go over too well with the other passengers.

Scream. Shriek. Shriek.

"I'm going to kill that little waste of sperm and egg." I unsnapped my seat belt and went to stand only to have Gregory shove me back into my seat.

"Cockroach, you don't want to know what kind of four-nine-five report you'd need to fill out for killing a human infant."

"I'll bet his FICO score is sub-par," I argued.

"He's an infant. He can't legally enter into contracts and therefore doesn't have a FICO score."

"See? Score of zero. I've killed people with better scores. I mean, I've inadvertently fatally injured people who have proven to be beyond my ability to rehabilitate."

"No."

"What if he accidently fell out of the plane? 'Oops, so sorry. What a horrible tragedy.'"

Gregory reached over and buckled my seat belt, which put his hands right where I liked them to be. I squirmed, capturing one between my thighs and wiggling my eyebrows. "Oh baby. I didn't realize bored, angry children turned you on."

He pulled his hand from my crotch. "Sit. Stay." I loved it when he ordered me around.

Gregory got to his feet and edged past me into the aisle. He was built like a weightlifter and insanely tall, just the sort of guy these tiny airline seats weren't made for. When he squeezed past me, his ass was literally right in my face. So I bit it.

If only he'd been facing the other way, I would have done something quite different with my mouth.

"Stop." His voice was stern and commanding, which sent heat right down between my legs. To contradict the order, his spirit-self reached out in a slow, sensuous caress.

"Not making me want to stop," I told him.

"Later. Right now I'm going to save you from a horrible, horrible report and punishment."

He strode down the aisle, blatantly ignoring the fact that the fasten seatbelts light was on, and stopped in front of the mother with the screaming child.

"Give me your baby."

The woman stared at him. The child stared at him. Then she passed the little bundle of piss and vinegar to my angel. I unsnapped my seatbelt and scooted out into the aisle to watch. Was he going to throttle it? Lock it in the bathroom? Shove it in the overhead bin? I loved this angel who was going to take on that enormous four-nine-five report, just so I wouldn't have to.

The kid reached up, shoved a finger up Gregory's nose, and giggled. I held my breath, waiting for the violent smackdown.

Instead he smiled, singing the kid some stupid tune about love and redemption and forgiveness. The child grew quiet, yanking his fingers out of the angel's nose and patting him on the cheek, the whole time staring into Gregory's dark eyes with rapt attention. It was sickeningly adorable.

And no, I didn't feel my ovaries stirring or whatever the spirit-being equivalent might be. Nope. Not one bit.

"Ma'am, you need to return to your seat and fasten your seatbelt while the captain has the light on."

I turned so I could see the flight attendant slightly behind me, but continue to keep Gregory in my line of vision. He was still softly singing and rocking the kid.

"He's not sitting. He hasn't got his seatbelt on," I complained, pointing at the angel.

"He's keeping that screaming kid quiet. You're not. Sit."

I wanted to argue, but I'd seen that video on YouTube of the airline staff dragging some dude down the aisle and thought better of it. On the ground that might be totally worth it, but not at thirty thousand feet.

"Fine." I sat. I buckled my seatbelt. And I closed my eyes, lulled into a peaceful sleep by an angel's song.

I awoke as we were landing. Gregory had somehow managed to return to his seat as I'd slept, and miraculously that baby was quiet. Sadly, the dude in the window seat still smelled like he hadn't bathed in the last decade.

In spite of my complaints, it seemed we weren't the only ones who had flown commercial. Just outside the security area we ran into Dar and Asta. They were standing there with luggage in hand, as if they were waiting for us. I waved, then my smile faltered as I saw what Asta was holding in her arms.

It was a baby. And it wasn't her baby.

"Here you go." She walked up to me and thrust the baby into my arms. "Here's your angel. It's been two days, actually it's been more than two days, and you made a vow."

I had, and not just to her either. I'd promised Bencul I'd take care of this angel. Ugh. How the fuck was I going to get out of this one?

"And I totally intended to come collect him, but something came up. Something is still up, and I'm hoping you can watch him for just a little bit more."

"No." Dar pulled Asta back a few steps as I tried to hand the baby back to her.

"I'd owe you a favor—"

"No," Dar insisted.

"He's very sweet," Asta said. "Anytime you want a playdate or something, let me know. He and Karrae got along beautifully."

"But not now," Dar told her. "No playdates for a couple of years or so."

Asta pouted. "He's adorable. Sam clearly doesn't want him, and it would be wonderful for Karrae to have a brother—"

"We'll talk about that later." Dar was practically dragging the angel away. "That one isn't ours. We're not keeping it. Nope. Not happening."

I watched them leave, then stared at the angel in my arms. He was kind of cute, and far more quiet than that human infant on the plane. He'd grown some bright gold fuzz on the top of his head since I'd seen him last, and one of his blue eyes had darkened to brown, giving him an appealing, mismatched look.

"What do you have...oh."

I froze at Gregory's voice, realizing that any ideas I'd had of tossing the kid in the recycling bin or leaving him on the luggage carousel were no longer feasible.

"Remember that angel I tossed into Hel? Well he and Remiel created. The angel sire died, and Remiel doesn't want an Angel of Order offspring, so as the head of the Fallen and the Queen of Hel, this little guy is now my responsibility."

Gregory held out his hands like he'd been enchanted. I passed the young angel to him and felt something twist inside me at the look on my beloved's face.

"He's mine," I told him. "Not just as head of the choir, either. I made a vow to his sire that I'd raise him, so he's mine. I didn't fuck up so bad with Nyalla, but she's human and she was eighteen when I bought her out of slavery from the elves. This…I'm not sure how good I'm going to be with this. I'm hoping you'll help me. I'm hoping that he won't just be mine, he'll be ours."

"What's his name?" Gregory asked, rocking the angel gently.

I snorted. "Olapiret. It's a horrible name. I don't even know where Bencul came up with it."

"It means light," Gregory smiled. "It's fitting."

"No, it's not. It sounds like elephants dancing ballet or something, not 'light'." I eyed the infant angel. The airport fluorescents over Gregory's shoulder were shining through the baby's golden fuzz with a luminescence that made him look like he had a halo. "I'm calling him Lux."

It meant light. And sounded a whole lot more cool than elephants-pirouette.

Gregory smiled down at the angel, then turned that smile to me. My heart stopped, then beat like a runaway train as I fell into him. His love washed over me with the touch of his spirit-self.

"Then Lux it is, Cockroach. Our Lux. Ours."

EPILOGUE

They stood before the gateway, thousands of demons in military formation stretching nearly to the city limits. Heat shimmered off the sand, but no one moved as much as a claw. A figure walked through the ranks to stand in front of the gateway. He reached out to touch the narrow strip of light. It expanded, opened, and on the other side was a city with human vehicles driving by, pedestrians on their way to work, and an angel who gasped when he saw what was about to step through the gates from Hel.

The figure turned to the rows of demons. He was beautiful, in a tanned, muscular human form with gladiator-style armor that didn't hide the enormous scar extending from under his right arm down to his left hip. No helm covered his white-blond hair. His crystal-blue eyes flashed as he surveyed his army. Wings spread from his back—huge wings of leather with sparse, glossy black feathers.

"Advance." The baritone voice rolled across the landscape and in response to the command, the demons moved, following the Ancient through the gateway and into the human world.

***

Don't miss Book 10 of the Imp Series. Subscribe to new release alerts at http://debradunbar.com/subscribe-to-release-announcements/

ACKNOWLEDGMENTS

A huge thanks to my copyeditors Kimberly Cannon and Jennifer Cosham whose eagle eyes catch all my typos and keep my comma problem in line, and to Damonza, for cover design.

Most of all, thanks to my children, who have suffered many nights of microwaved chicken nuggets and take-out pizza so that Mommy can follow her dream.

ABOUT THE AUTHOR

Debra lives in a little house in the woods of Maryland with her sons and two slobbery bloodhounds. On a good day, she jogs and horseback rides, hopefully managing to keep the horse between herself and the ground. Her only known super power is 'Identify Roadkill'.

debradunbar.com